the
DISAPPOINTMENT

the DISAPPOINTMENT

a novel

SCOTT BROKER

CATAPULT
NEW YORK

THE DISAPPOINTMENT

This is a work of fiction. All of the characters, organizations, and events portrayed in this novel are either products of the author's imagination or are used fictitiously.

ISBN: 978-1-64622-285-8

The Library of Congress Control Number is available.

Jacket design by Jaya Miceli
Jacket images: curtain © Shutterstock / Curve Curve;
man © Shutterstock / FOTOKITA
Book design by Olenka Burgess

Catapult
New York, NY
books.catapult.co

Printed in the United States of America

10 9 8 7 6 5 4 3 2 1

For summerhouse

the DISAPPOINTMENT

MORE MOTHER

When I find him, my husband is packing his mother's ashes into a carry-on bag, wedging the urn between a pair of old sandals. I watch from the doorway with the phone to my ear, listening to the Portland airport's hold music and picturing a scene from *Parthenon*, the final play I wrote: The protagonist, Rex, stands where I stand, staring at his own grieving husband and finding himself unable to cross the threshold. For two full minutes he totters, alternating his focus between a loose splinter in the doorframe and the crying body on the bed. It is meant to be agonizing. It is meant to be morally opaque. Art, I believed then, and still do, no matter if I've stopped making it, works best at the nexus of contradiction. When Rex eventually leaves, choosing to offer nothing in the way of comfort, the audience should feel equal shares of contempt and relief. I can't say for sure. The play was never produced, read aloud only once in the confines of our living room. What do you call a swan song that never takes flight? A bird dirge. Mine was performed over a wobbly coffee table by a company of middling actors, all drunk. *Très depressing*, my father might have said, had I told him about it. *Oui, papa. Astucieux.*

The scene's overlay extends no further. Randy is not crying, though his grief casts an expression that is somehow worse than that. And I, for my part, do not turn away from him. This does not make me better than the man I have written. I am merely more resolute in what I want for myself. I put the phone on speaker and cross the room. The airport did not say why they were calling, only that it was urgent, and could I please hold? Sure, yes, what's one more bossa nova interlude in a lifetime full of them.

"No mother," I say, now at Randy's side. "Remember?"

He does not react. Really, he doesn't appear to register my presence in the room at all. Randy currently lives in a state of anti-awareness, missing stoplights and kitchen timers, doorbells and horny husbands. It is sad, worrisome, and mildly ironic: the man so regularly hailed by critics as kaleidoscopically attuned to the world has entered a tunnel and stopped. What he sees now is his mother, the ghost of her. All else is vapor at his back.

"Some mother," he eventually replies. The words, inflectionless, hold no shape.

Ms. Rourke's ashes have followed us since Randy retrieved them on an overcast day in April. She's come to the grocery store, to the tennis courts, to a dental appointment where Randy and I needed fillings for the same molar. I finally voiced opposition when it came to this trip—romantic getaways, I appealed, typically exclude moms and dads. I managed to maintain my position all week, but Randy's despair, made electrically manifest across his skin, breaks my resolve. A grievance is nothing in the face of actual grief.

"Some mother," I say. "Fine."

We go to the kitchen, accompanied by the arrhythmic samba playing fuzzily in my hand. The urn is a forgettable vessel, the crematorium's standard-issue cube, painted to look like stoneware but actually plastic. I couldn't bear to touch it for the first week; hovering a hand near, I felt sure it was emitting cold. Soon I learned to treat it as Randy treats it, which is like any other container—largely meaningless beyond its interior. I hold open a Ziploc baggie and he tips his mother toward me. The ashes share the ruinous texture of broken shale or cat litter. They tumble without grace. As in life so in death, I think, instantly seeking penance for this unkindness by tapping the urn's bottom edge to allow more of my deceased mother-in-law to enter. When we've filled the bag a quarter full, I stop.

"Plenty," I say.

Randy nods sadly, just as he walks, talks, eats, and breathes sadly. Sometimes I imagine him as a humidifier of sadness, forever expelling fumes. "No going back," he says.

I nod, though the comment is beyond me. Back in the bedroom, we notice a dusting of ash on his thumb at the same time. He licks the powder without hesitation, then sits on the bed's edge. I hug his head against my stomach. It is another refracted moment from that same failure of a play, the one I hardly got to grieve before Ms. Rourke's flight for the sky, but I push away the association. I am striving toward presence, a condition I seem to have been chasing since birth. Today is always getting washed out by yesterday and tomorrow.

"We're about to have sand under our toes," I say. "Isn't that good?"

I think I see something beseeching in Randy's upcast eyes, something potentially erotic—we are regular beggars for each other, in ordinary times.

"I saw a bridge fall today," he says.

"A bridge? Where?"

A voice clatters onto the line before he can reply. "Mr. Rourke? Is this Mr. Randy Rourke?" The caller sounds as if he's run a great distance to reach us.

Randy leans back and I sit beside him. "Yes," I say.

"We have your bag, sir. Whatever you've been missing is lost no longer!"

"We aren't missing a bag. We leave for Oregon tomorrow."

"Is this not Mr. Randy Rourke?"

"It is Mr. Rourke."

"Mr. Randy Rourke?"

"Mr. Randy Rourke."

"You are missing a bag, Mr. Rourke. Your name is all over it, to say nothing of your telephone number, which is how I am contacting you now. A great pleasure of this job is reuniting possessions with their owners. If you don't retrieve the bag within twenty-four hours, I will be forced to disperse or destroy its contents. There isn't a single part of me that wants to do that."

"Okay, we can pick it up tomorrow."

"I can't wait to see the look on your face, Mr. Rourke.

Ask for Allen in Lost and Found. That's where you'll find me. Look for the man who's busy holding his breath."

The line does not go dead, instead reverting to the previous hold music.

"I wonder what it is," I say, ending the call. "Mistaken identity? Parallel universe?"

Randy does not laugh or smile, grunt or groan. He folds his body forward, setting his elbows on his knees. "The bridge fell here." He doesn't need to point at himself for me to understand him. Then he says, "I need more."

"More what?"

"More mother."

I follow the line of his gaze. Our carpet needs cleaning—better, to be ripped out and replaced with hardwood. Those are concerns for another time. Presently, I am looking at our bare feet and flexing mine. With my toes, I grip the carpet threads and tug at them, something I do long after Randy leaves me for his bag of ash.

WHETHERMAN

Randy awakes, as he does every morning, alive in his former life. With sleepy eyes he squeezes my cheeks. "Look at you," he says. "A beheaded vision."

This must be one of grief's cruelest tricks: shepherding death far enough away to be forgotten, then dropping it back all at once. Randy is most susceptible to these drifts at the border of sleep, a treacherous terrain where alarm clocks become owls and mothers live again.

"Beheaded?" I pull him toward me. "Don't you mean bedheaded?"

His laugh is a beautiful thing. I savor any second in which Randy is who he is—iconoclastic and brash, a man who occupies space magisterially but rarely arrogantly—but always there is the accompanying dread of waiting for his inevitable departure. I see the damage of memory's return every time. Sometimes the knowledge seeps in slowly, a darkening of the pupil from the outside in; other times, a single blink takes him from green to black. In either case, he looks fatally damaged by what he has remembered.

"Right," he says. "Bedheaded. Though you wouldn't look so bad stuck on a spike."

This joke does it, naturally. Randy's right eyelid twitches like a horse hide, then his smile goes. I reach at once for his crotch. A pathetic entreaty, maybe, but one that sometimes works. On those occasions the grief is not gone so much as it is suppressed, wobbling Randy's surface like an undertow. Once or twice, in the wake of his ejaculation, I've felt that his mourning has been passed into me, leaving my body broody for the remainder of the day.

My advance goes nowhere. Randy slumps, pulled inward from somewhere deep inside, then rolls out of bed, heading straight for the open window. For a moment I imagine he is going to jump—a thought that crosses my mind whenever he is near any height, roadway, or body of water.

"There's no wind here," he says. "Do you think there will be a breeze on the coast?"

"I do."

He reaches his arm outside. There is something lavish in the way the morning light finds his body. He is one of the lucky few who has only grown in appeal as he's entered middle age. Streaks of silver run through the black hair he wears swept back ("My Sontags," he brags); stubble shadows his cheeks; and his eyes, once uniformly green, now look as if they've been rolled in pollen. I love it all, envy it all, and try not to make a fuss, although my best features are in a period of rapid decline. Each night my jawline becomes rounder, some merciless god descending to buff away my angles. Each morning my pillow is covered in hair.

"I'd like to feel a breeze on my face," he says. "That's all I'm thinking."

I roll onto my stomach, giving my own obstinate erection some consolatory attention on the mattress. "I'll let the weatherman know."

Randy looks back at me with a near-smile. "The Weatherman, otherwise known as the Whetherman. He chooses whether or not the wind blows. Why has he forsaken New York? Well, why not? We're irredeemable."

These days, tears are always eager to come. The flickering forward of any inane characteristic—his elementary wordplay, his self-satisfaction—can make my eyes itch and my throat tighten. I rub roughly at my cheeks, swallow twice, then say, "Whetherman. I like that."

Randy nods. I can tell from his expression he has already gone somewhere else. The Other Side. The Mother Side. Sometimes words slide together too effortlessly, as if having waited for their chance to transmute.

FOUNTAINHEAD

Of Randy's changed characteristics, travel anxiety is unfortunately not one. We arrive at the airport over two hours early. All through the terminal he frets, glaring back at me as if I were an unruly piece of luggage he's been forced to drag along. His stress is not entirely reasonless—lost passports, misbooked connections. When he and my father first met, they exchanged gripes about my various travel gaffes with relish, excited to have found an empathetic ear. My mother, laughing along, patted my arm pityingly, a signature gesture of hers I'd told Randy to watch for while we cleaned our living room earlier that day. "It's her primary means of affection," I said. "She weaned me after a week because she thought breastfeeding felt vulgar."

"That must be why you're so fixated on my chest."

"Thank you for the free analysis, Dr. Freud."

"Have you considered asking her?"

"For what?"

"Another go at the fountainhead."

I sprayed Windex at him, he smacked my arm, then we were both laughing harder than was warranted.

"You're sick," I said.

"You're missing out."

"On what?"

He must have felt the edge of defensiveness enter my voice, because he stopped himself before responding. My benign estrangement from my parents, if that's what it can be called, has long baffled Randy, whose own experience of estrangement from his father was deeply predicated on volatility. He really did seem to think—and still might, though he's learned to keep it to himself—that connection with my parents was within easy reach, if only I wanted it. Phone calls, letters, nudges, profane or otherwise, to remind them that my life springs from their waters.

"Fresh milk?" he said, a joke to free us both from his implied meaning about the foundational lack in my life. I let him have it, let us both have it, but only after spraying him one more time, the blue cleaner landing on his wrist like a sneeze.

At the gate, Randy finally relaxes, settled into a chair and staring at the jetway door.

"Close call," I say.

He ignores this, then my offer of a protein bar. Nearby, a teenage boy describes his Friday night with a girl named Rina to someone on the phone. "Hottest girl alive," he says, "but down on some freak shit. I got scared, dude. Truly scared." He doesn't quiet even after his family rejoins him. "I don't want to tell you. Let's just say it involves my caboose." I muffle my laugh with a cough. Randy turns toward me, but it's clear he hasn't heard anything.

"I'll tell you later," I say. He continues to look at me, or through me, so I offer something else. "Remember when I booked flights to Georgia instead of Greece?"

Another near-smile. "There were so many cats in Athens, even up on the roofs. I remember their meowing. And how in Santorini the locals wanted them dead."

"They were all missing the tip of an ear."

"And cut off so cleanly. I could never make sense of that. The cleanness. And you got sick on the ferry." The pleasure drops from his face. "That was a low point for me."

"A low point?" I feel shunted from my contentment. What I recall of the ferry ride is Randy's dogged sweetness: tracking down a Dramamine, rubbing the pressure points that alleviate nausea, holding a water bottle to the nape of my neck.

"Of course it was a low point. You're miserable when you're sick. I wanted to read."

"How terrible of me."

Randy nods with agitated satisfaction. I almost tell him I was being sarcastic, obviously, but I can see that now is not a time for him to be handled. Where grief hasn't hollowed Randy out, it has left him unexpectedly sharp, like the lid of a can that cuts you on its way to the bin.

"I'm going to the bathroom," I say, leaving in a huff. Within a few steps my annoyance gives way to hurt, and I wind through travelers hoping to shake it off. The food court provides its share of distractions. A girl unzips her father's suitcase and begins pulling out camouflage underwear, strewing it about with a showman's flair. An old man picks the salt from his soft pretzel and ceremonially delivers the crystals to his tongue. Still, it is not enough for what I need. I feel retaliatory, drab, in need of an EpiPen for my ego. I veer into the bathroom and lock myself in a stall, then take out my phone, open Scruff, and scroll through the grid of men I've come to recently know. They are global and local, shirtless and buff. They send messages that could bore boredom, followed by private albums suffused with life.

Camperfan14 says, *hot man*. Dr.Dragon, who has unlocked his private album, says, *you look like you could take a pounding*. If I were in the sunlit world, I would laugh at a line like this; here, in the bleach-scented latrine, I get hard, opening his album and swiping through dozens of photos and videos of him with other men. I unlock my album for him—how unsteady I look in these photos, doubtful on the matter of my sexiness, the reason I've cropped my face from each—then write: *tell me what you want me to do*. He takes no time to respond, sending a list that includes a healthy dose of acrobatics. My arousal is dizzying, captivated less by the virtual sex than by the blatancy of his desire. I do want a pounding, even a pulverization, except not how Dr.Dragon imagines, not exclusively. It is about being craved so forcefully that I am crushed.

I orgasm before I realize I've been masturbating. The semen has been gracious enough to collect on my fist, what Randy calls a short shot. I allow a drop to fall onto my shirt before wiping myself clean. Though undetectable against the white cotton, it feels like tangible proof, of what I can't say. Freedom. Desirability. Shame. Wiped up with toilet paper, the semen grows pungent. I hold the wad out and imagine the men in the adjacent stalls catching the scent like hounds, becoming enraptured, stroking themselves. Briefly we are a bacchanalian crowd, sitting side by side in our vestibules of lust. Then one of them burps, another farts, and I am flushing my crumpled fantasy down the toilet.

Shame finds me back in the crowd, prickling my neck. I don't meet these online men, only once walking to one of their apartments, where I circled the block four times before returning home. True, I have an occasionally loose gaze. True, I might admire the veins on that man's arms, the hug of that woman's jeans. And true, I have cheated in the past, but never on Randy. Until recently—and one other stretch of months several years ago, a period I'm certain ruined me in the eyes of Ms. Rourke forever—I could hardly envision sleeping with someone else. Considering who I was when I met Randy, this borders on the miraculous. I once zigzagged between partners like a lightning bug, unable to land in any one place for long. With him, my focus narrowed, the scope suddenly set. Evidence, my friends claimed, that I had found a keeper. Proof, I would counter, of his magnificent organ. I was still sheepish in the face of my devotion.

I can see from afar that Randy's frustration has given way to sorrow. It is the place he inevitably falls, and though his face is dour, his foot bounces in time with the Beach Boys, whose voices drift warmly from a Hawaiian-themed restaurant. Something about the buoyant foot levels him, makes him likeable again, loveable again. I hurry back.

"I forgot my swimsuit," he says once I sit.

"I packed it."

He puts his head on my shoulder. "My hero."

Over the intercom, an announcement is made about a guinea pig loose in the terminal. The speaker's urgency reminds me of last night's caller.

"Who?" Randy asks when I mention this to him.

"The guy who called about your bag. Albert?"

Randy sits up straight, a deep crease in his brow. "How do you lose a guinea pig?"

"How do you lose a bag you never lost?"

"I hope they're okay," he says.

"Who?"

"All those cats in Santorini."

When I kiss his hairline, a strand sticks to my lips. I do not blow it away.

HOUSE ARREST

Our last flight together was on a trip to Denver in March. An arts college had invited Randy to give a lecture that he was hurrying to finish on the plane. I had my forehead against the window, the turbulence rattling hard through my jawbone, and didn't realize he was asking me a question until he poked me with his pen. My wrecked career had left me in my own period of anti-awareness, shorter-lived than Randy's by necessity, yet similarly vacant. One day I stood at the open refrigerator and scarfed down its contents until they forced their way back out of me; another, I tripped down the stairs of our apartment building, lucky to only sprain a wrist, though it felt unlucky at the time. I wanted more—a broken leg, a dislocated shoulder. Perhaps as a distraction from my sorrow, as when you apply pressure to pain, or perhaps as a forfeit to my sorrow, as when you envision your own funeral and see it as forgettable.

"What?" I said after he'd poked two more times.

"Suzanne and Lyle. Are you excited to see them?"

I knew our friends would ask about my playwriting, that I'd have to tell them I'd given it up, an admission I'd been making all month. I've put on many faces for these conversations—stoic, self-deprecating, even optimistic about the unknown future—when my presiding feeling has always been fear. In a life built upon a single track, all else is wilderness.

"Not really," I told Randy. "Lyle drinks too much."

"But he makes a good mojito," Randy said, jotting a note on his pad.

He's always been productive on flights. That's what I'm thinking about today, more than the lecture he gave ("Art," he'd declared, "is where we manifest spirit into something tactile, spirit that is otherwise more slippery and strange than an ice slick on your bedroom wall.") or the dinner, memorable for its view of the mountains, and for the way Suzanne and Lyle accepted my quitting without any of the obligatory naysaying others provided, and how this offended me from a new direction entirely. Randy only stares at the seatback, where it appears he plans to fixate for the next five hours. He hasn't been productive anywhere following Ms. Rourke's death—a condition I'm grateful for. To continue my wallowing in an empty apartment while Randy's campaign for most beloved photographer carried forward unhindered might have made me lose the rest of my head.

"Let's play the game," I say, pulling his notepad from

his bag. I flip it open, noting that his last entry was April 2, almost three months ago to the day. *Must shave.* He would have written this before going to see Ms. Rourke die, not that he suspected it then. He'd been told months, a year. Ms. Rourke was certain it would be even longer.

On an empty page, I write *BEACH* at the top and *SONG* at the bottom. We adapted this from the newspaper: starting with the first word, you need to reach the last in twelve tries by forming common phrases, the second word becoming the opening of the subsequent line.

BEACH HOUSE

Randy stares at my starter words for a long time, then takes the pen, filling in the next lines with his tight scrawl.

HOUSE ARREST

"Nice," I say. Randy's eyebrows twitch, and he reaches up as if to stop them.

"Why don't I crack my knuckles anymore?" he asks.

"I don't know," I say. And I don't. I used to be able to read his body better than my own, every jolt and shudder. The current machinations are harder to decipher.

He drops his hand. "Your turn."

I make a muddy move, playing off of sound over meaning.

ARREST STOP

Randy shakes his head. I wait for him to challenge me, rule follower that he is. "I hate rest stops," he says. "They're nowhere places. You can slip right through the cracks."

"We've had fun in rest stops, if memory serves."

He reclaims the pen.

STOP WATCH

The drink cart rumbles past. One flight attendant is

telling the other about his skin-care routine. We enter a patch of turbulence and he raises his voice. "Tepid water! Non-sudsy soap!"

WATCH TOWER

Randy, perhaps anticipating this choice, immediately writes down his next answer.

TOWER GUARD

"Tower guard?" I say. "Don't you mean guard tower?"

"Who watches the tower?"

"Sure."

GUARD RAIL

Randy taps the pen between his front teeth after taking it back. The bottom two are crooked; the top right is a veneer. These are things I still know about him, unalterable facts.

RAIL ROAD

I'm boyishly thrilled filling in the next slot.

ROAD HEAD

"Remember the Rockaways?" I say with a nudge. That day, Randy reached down and fished himself free of his swimsuit after turning onto Cross Bay Boulevard. I could've watched his soft cock sit between his legs for hours, languid as a bull sleeping in a field of poppies, but then he popped my buckle and delivered me to his lap with a hand on my neck.

"Yes," Randy says. "You were so happy."

"We were both happy." My effort to sound playful comes off as stung.

Randy pats the armrest, not realizing it is not connected to me.

HEAD ACHE

He leans back and closes his eyes. "Headache," he says. "I have one."

"We have three lines left. We're not finished."

"I'm finished."

I turn toward the window, where I hold my gaze for the next hour. I'd been able to feel the engine rumbling through Randy's leg, driving across the causeway that day. I'd been able to smell his Dove soap, held in his pubic hair the way shampoo will hold to the head. And while I prefer the animalism of his midday scent, I had been happy. Of course I had.

I find the Rockies less impressive than remembered when we pass over them. Surely it's only a matter of perspective. Anything appears inconsequential from far enough away.

LUCKY DUCK

It is late afternoon when we arrive in Portland. Hunger drags us to a food kiosk, where we spend forty dollars on cafeteria sandwiches and chips. My mood is low, not yet rejuvenated by the calories and still sour from the latter portion of the flight. I'd finally forced myself into *Just Kids*, where Patti Smith and Robert Mapplethorpe pass through their days in the Lower East Side like storybook characters, struggling enough to seem semi-human but most often coming out on top. "She's very childlike," I said to Randy when we began our descent. His eyes had been closed for almost the full flight, though I could tell he was not sleeping. I tried to take some of the disdain from my voice. "Whimsical, I mean."

"Or maybe she's just content."

"Sure. I'd be content if I were her."

"Maybe."

"You don't think so?"

He angled his head toward the aisle, his eyes still shut. "I'm trying to dream."

The book was better when I focused on the backdrop of Smith's life rather than the triumph of it—her descriptions of New York are unique and alive, and I soon found myself homesick for the city I'd only just left. But soon my annoyance at Randy's response muddled everything. I would be content in his shoes or hers. In fact, I would be content with a single one of their shoelaces; it isn't the world for which I am asking. I slid the book into the seatback. I'd read a sweeping fantasy next, a Victorian love affair. If there had to be an artist, let them flop.

Randy looks serene as he eats his chips, his expression wide-eyed and burdenless. It is a look of exploitable innocence—someone for a criminal to con, for a tough wind to carry up and away. But his guilelessness is not that of a child. He looks distracted because he is distracted, attendant to a different world.

We are both licking oil from our fingers when a young woman approaches from behind. "Excuse me?" she says. "Are you Randy Rourke?"

I turn on his behalf. Randy's fanbase extends across demographics, yet each time someone approaches him in public, I think, Of course it's you. So it goes with this woman, a stylish twentysomething with a bleached buzz cut, navy jumpsuit, and wire-frame glasses.

"We've had a long day," I say. "I'm not sure he's up for a chat."

Randy swivels in his stool to face her. She takes this as invitation enough, bringing her phone to his face. "I love your stuff. This has been my background for a year, and before I had one from *Somnolence. Sleeper #44*, I think. The baby in the dryer? I love that photo."

"He never cried," Randy says. "I always want to tell people that. A little baby who didn't cry even once."

The woman swoons at this peek behind the curtains, then begins detailing her plan to get an MFA in sculpture at SAIC. This gleaming optimism makes her the perfect reader for *Just Kids*, I think needlessly, contemptuously. Plus, *Sleeper #43*, the paired photograph in *Somnolence*, is much more compelling. There, a man has squeezed into a washing machine, wrapped around the drum's agitator as the soapy water churns. A pair of sodden jeans is stuck to his shoulder; near his face, a sock floats. I was there for the shoot. The sock is mine.

"Acker," Randy blurts out, interrupting whatever the woman is saying.

"Acker?"

"Kathy Acker. You look just like her. Her mind was a torch."

The woman taps the name into her phone.

"She died on November 30, 1997," he says, pulling from the mental repository of death dates he has mysteriously amassed in his mourning. "My mother died on April 5. I knew it would happen and still didn't believe it. I didn't believe my mother would ever die." His flat tone is at odds with what he's saying, a telemarketer's elegy. "Do you have parents?"

The woman nods hesitantly, as if needing first to remember.

"Lucky duck."

"I'm sorry," she says.

"Don't be sorry." Randy reaches out and grips her hands, which makes her eyes go wide—possibly in fear, possibly in adulation. "You didn't kill her. You didn't kill my mother."

"I didn't," she says. She sounds uncertain, her wide eyes overcast. "I should go. My ride is probably here."

I touch Randy's arm. "Yes. Randy, let's let her go."

He drops her hands and she almost trips backward. "Tell the Midwest bye for me," he says.

She mumbles something inarticulate, then crisscrosses dizzily through the crowd.

"Mom would've hated her hair," Randy says.

"But she would have loved her jumpsuit."

Randy smiles. "Yes," he says. "Exactly."

My embarrassment to have had someone spun around by our alien orbit is replaced by relief that it is just ours again. I scratch the nape of Randy's neck and he leans against me. Then his eyes brighten. "Look, Jack. It's a god in uniform."

"What?"

"A drug-sniffing god in uniform."

At the end of a lead, a German shepherd is sniffing through suitcases. It takes me a moment to realize that Randy is summoning an old joke. There was nothing particularly funny about the bit—each dog was a god and each cat a tac—yet we committed to it for a whole summer. The timing coincided with an unprecedented number of strays in the neighborhood, all mangy and moon-eyed. I wrote a version of this into *Ballast*, my fourth and most successful play. *Let's do it goddy-style*, the protagonist says, playfully bending his boyfriend over. "Like Artaud in a gay bar," *The New York Times* called the production. "Promising."

"A drug-sniffing god in uniform," I say. We have happened into a microclimate, an oasis, a warm spot in a freezing pond. I tilt his face toward me for a kiss, but he resists. We struggle for a moment—Randy pulling down and me pulling up—before he jerks away from me.

"My bag," he says. "Where is my bag?"

"We haven't gone to Lost and Found yet," I say, confused by his alarm.

Like a new parent rooting for their child in the middle of the night, he rummages around with primal intensity, almost knocking me from my stool.

"Randy. We need—"

"Where is she?" Panic electrifies his voice. The entirety of his left deltoid is under my hand, pulled tight as a wire. I scan our surroundings to see what Randy is seeing, or not seeing. His bag—the actual bag—is not here.

Do I become primal, too? As I run after Randy's admirer, who I'm sure has stolen the bag, I go to a place that feels somehow creaturely—heavier breath, sharper senses. Randy lopes after me. His alarm makes him a less focused hunter; while I search, I make sure to corral him, not wanting to lose him to the crowd. Pushing through a group of bedazzled bridesmaids, I am suddenly overcome with my own heroism. I am husband of the year, partner of the century, boyfriend of the millennium. I am high on adrenaline.

But then we fail to find the woman, and our chase becomes a wander, my inspiring protectiveness giving way to dismay at what will become of an ashless Randy. Will he combust, beat his chest, demand we get on the first flight home? His eyes are already bleary with tears when we reach the Lost and Found counter.

"We've lost a bag," I say. "Two, actually."

The attendant shares my face shape, baggy eyelids, and haircut. Our similarities inspire no kinship in me. The opposite, in fact.

"Two bags?" she asks. "Impressive."

"Would you check for them?"

She crosses her arms. Her lavender perfume is cut through with dulled sweat, the sort of smell that seems built across many years. She wears bracelets on each wrist that look like chainless handcuffs, tight to the bone. "What's the operative word?" she asks. "Rhymes with *peas*, *fleas*, and *trees*."

Unclenching my fists takes work. "Please," I say.

"Name?"

"Randy Rourke."

She hums doubtfully. "I'll take a look in back. Best to keep your expectations low and your hopes even lower—hope being the fastest route to disappointment."

"We know you have one of them," I say. "We got a call from Albert yesterday."

"Albert?" She frowns my frown. "I'm not so sure about that."

I put my arm around Randy after she disappears behind a closed door. His shoulders are flexed in a way that feels unhuman, a sun-warmed tarp pulled over wire hangers.

"It's okay," I say. "We'll find it."

"I need her."

I rub his back when he bends forward, hoping to massage him into a softer structure. To take a blanket from a child, to take ashes from Randy—maybe it would be a good, albeit forceful, thrust into independence. His forehead is against the counter when the woman pushes through the door, bag in hand.

"Lucky day for the boys," she says. "Someone just turned this in."

Randy lunges forward, grabbing the bag, unzipping its largest compartment, and sliding his hand inside, at which point he lets out a long moan of relief. He keeps his hand there as he removes his wallet from his pocket and passes the woman his license. His restored calm flows through the baggage claim like a cool wind. "Thank you," he eventually says, zipping the suitcase shut. "My mother is in here."

"And my mother is in Bermuda. I've got a line. Please move along."

"What about the other bag?" I ask.

"There is no other bag."

"But we got a call yesterday. Albert said to ask for him."

"Albert? We've got no Albert in Lost and Found."

"Maybe that wasn't his name."

She scratches the side of her face, then taps her nose. "Allen. We do have an Allen in Lost and Found—or had. He was sacked yesterday."

"What?"

"That's right. Fired. Canned. Something to do with the dark web. I didn't probe, believer that I am in privacy. Anyway, this is the only bag we've got."

I start to push back, then hear someone in line say, "Some people really do think they rule the world."

I beckon Randy away, deciding that if the bag was unknown to us until yesterday, it can remain unknown to us today. He clutches the luggage to his chest, awkwardly cradling its mass until we get to the rental car, at which point he puts it on the backseat, stopping just short of buckling it in.

BLEAK PERIPHERIES

For the first twenty minutes of driving, I am scattered and high-strung, punchy on the gas and hard on the brakes.

"Do you want me to drive?" Randy asks when I almost rear-end an airport shuttle.

"It's been a while. I'll be fine once we're really moving."

This proves true: after merging onto I-5 and joining the southbound commuters, I find my rhythm. "See?" I say. "New York can't kill the California in me."

He gives me a tired smile, deep in the comedown from his own adrenaline rush. "Your fiery baptism," he says. He reaches down to the gearshift and sets his hand on it. "Sometimes I think I never really learned how to drive."

"What do you mean? You're a fine driver."

"I learned how to leave the house. The car was just a way to go."

I take the opportunity to retrieve his hand from the gear-shift, kissing his palm and knuckles before placing it in my lap. He wants me to open the door to the past, I'm sure. I don't want to go there. Not to his parents' divorce, nor to the hourlong drive he took around Columbus as a teenager in order to avoid first their fighting, then the brittle quiet of fatherlessness. These subjects are well-worn, walked to death, boring and upsetting all at once.

"I'm glad it's clear out," I say. "It looks like it rained earlier."

Randy frowns at the patches of steam that hitchhike along the shoulder of the road, then pulls his hand back.

"Look at the trees." I point at the pines as if they weren't towering so obviously above us. "They're like ten of you."

Randy says nothing. We pass a pickup truck with a bed full of loose hay, which flies about freely, shedding its mass in droves. I put on the windshield wipers for the joke of it, but the primary effect is an awful squeak of rubber on dry glass.

"Do you think they realize they're losing so much?" I ask.

"Probably."

"Maybe it's a statement about the degradation of time."

"Probably not."

I squeeze the wheel. The option to apologize, to say I want to hear again about the dissolution of his family, appears on the horizon, then whips right by.

"What's our ETA?"

Randy stares at his phone, taps it twice, then says, "Four."

"Do you remember much of the drive? Is it pretty?"

"I do."

"Tell me more about the beach house."

This request finally causes some yield. Randy's mouth shifts as if he's remembered something delightfully private. He came to Oregon alone two years ago, invited by the owners for an informal retreat while they summered in Hungary.

"The house," Randy says, "is very wrong."

He maintains his unusual expression, so I imagine he is speaking superficially, referring to a decor faux pas or structural mishap. I've never met Sally and Fran, but I have envied Randy's friendship with them for years—a friendship that seems to provide him something others don't. How else to explain his excitement when one of their letters arrives, or the fact that they are the only fans of his he has ever properly responded to?

"Wrong how?" I ask, eager for his possible critique.

"There's a tunnel in the basement."

"A tunnel?"

"And that's not the only thing."

"What else?"

"Christ, Jack. I can't go on describing everything to you all the time."

His voice is abrasive enough to smooth coral, making me flinch.

"I don't want to listen to anything," he says, by which he must mean me, because he proceeds to turn on the radio. The station is tuned to oldies.

As if unplugged, Randy closes his eyes and is asleep—actually asleep—in no time. I drive alone down the 5 before taking the 126 coastward, a winding route through dense trees. And his past still finds me, no matter how hard I try to evade it. He had me sit passenger for the infamous loop of his youth the first time we visited his mother. He seemed self-conscious of the bleakness—flat gray fields were connected to flat gray skies by leafless trees—and I couldn't assuage his worry. It was bleak. It is bleak. I felt there what I feel now: a distinct sense of existential vulnerability, as if at any moment we might be struck by lightning, smote by God, or dropped from the planet, falling upward until blue sky gives way to black. There it was the unending flatness; here, the encroaching forest.

I train my attention on the road. The canopy creates green night on either side of us, swamping the close-set hills in shadow, but daylight survives on the snaking pavement, albeit in meager strips.

ATOMIC DISCHARGE

The landscape eventually levels out in preparation for the coast. Soon we are free of the hills and in a wide valley. A river runs parallel to the road, neat cottages flanking its shore. It is an ode-worthy scene, and when a heron passes by overhead, putting its wings on display, I'm tempted to wake Randy. Yet his sleep is its own idyll. Over the last few months he seems to have found a place of absolute rest, unruffled by any facet of reality. My own dreams are riddled with realism: shopping carts, ringing phones, recurring Randys made of stone. I let him sleep.

By the time we reach the 101, which delivers us directly into Florence, the river has widened and given way to the ocean's influence, its surface choppy and gray. The main strip of town is lined by antique stores and gas stations, fast-food restaurants and roadside motels. Randy mentioned that the population is primarily composed of retirees and vacationers—the source, I decide, of the ambient levels of transience.

A large bridge spans the river ahead, marking Florence's southern limit, and I turn before we reach it, following a sign advertising Old Town. Here is closer to what I'd been envisioning: six blocks of waterfront shops, quaint enough as to appear artificial. It is like a studio set for a seaside town, with flower baskets hanging from every light pole, seagulls decorating the sky, and businesses with names like Traveler's Cove and Beachcomber Pub.

"Wake up, Randy," I say after parking. "We're in Disneyland."

"Disneyland?" He sits up and wipes a dribble of spit from his chin. "Oh." He frowns. "Why did we stop? I thought we were going straight to the house."

"I wanted coffee."

"Coffee?"

"You remember coffee. Brown, hot, bitter?"

He stares beyond me. "You go. I'm too tired."

My sense of defeat is outsized. I'd hoped sleep might deliver him to a happier headspace, that Florence might deliver us, instantly, to a happier life.

"Do you want anything?"

He shakes his head. Something about this—the insolence, maybe—tilts my defeat toward frustration. I slam the door, cross the street, and enter a café. An overhead speaker announces my entry with the sound of a cow mooing.

"Hello, old chap," the barista says. "Fine day for an arms

race." She grins, trying to contain laughter, while a coworker giggles freely behind her.

In a better mood, I might indulge her. The prospect of ad-libbing with a high schooler is a present impossibility. "Just a coffee, please."

"Just a coffee? Are you sure you don't want a Monkey Mocha? Or Mexican Mocha? Or Nutella Mocha? Or the Zinger, Blackjack, or Slider?" With each menu item she grows more impassioned. "Shelby is a latte art professional. She should go to school for it. Leaves and trees and hearts, oh my. Isn't that right, Shelby?"

The coworker, still giggling, nods.

"Maybe next time."

She gives up, taking my money and pointing me toward the end of the counter. I inspect the wall of knickknacks that faces the coffee bar. The items are uninspiring: miniature utensils, shoddily knit finger puppets, jewelry crafted from polished rocks, and an entire rack's worth of bumper stickers. *My Other Car Is a Motorboat. Honk If You Love Big Tuna. Buy Me A Drink If You're Gonna Ride My Tail. Florence, Where People Fly and Dogs Die.*

"Sir?" the second girl, Shelby, says. By her tone, she must have tried to get my attention a few times.

I show her the last bumper sticker. "A bit dark, right?"

"Not really. It's a joke."

"But what's the joke?"

"Is this guy bugging you?" The first girl appears behind Shelby, speaking again in an affected voice. "You know the rules, Frank. You bug the girl, you gotta go."

"Okay, I'll go."

The girl's face slackens. "Do you always give up so easy? The sticker means what it means, in a funny way."

"I see," I say, not seeing. I put it back on the rack, realizing that most of the customers are looking at me. "Thanks again," I say, loudly enough for everyone to hear.

The first barista curtsies. "We're paid to please."

"Should we ask him the question of the day?" Shelby asks. The other nods her on. "Our science teacher told us that two solid objects can pass through each other if their atoms are lined up right. He says it's as close to impossible as you can get without actually being impossible."

"He kept falling against the wall while he was describing it," the first girl says. "He said he could do that for his entire life and never fall through"—she begins hitting her palm against the counter—"or that he might just be lucky enough to see it happen one day."

The situation sounds like a scene from Beckett: a man running into a wall in hopes that its properties might change. Belief is the great deceiver. When it pays off, the story shines; when it doesn't, the failure falls on the person who had the audacity to think they could make something of themselves. Sometimes I take pride in having walked away from my career for this very reason, claiming I saw my wall for what it really is: a bottlenecked, nepotistic, and demoralizing industry. More often I lament that I was never let through the hard plaster.

"You're wondering if I think it's possible?" I ask.

"No," Shelby says. "We've been over that."

The first girl's final slap is her most decisive. "We're wondering what you think it would feel like to pass through something solid."

"For instance," Shelby says, "I think it might be like when you drop in a roller coaster and your stomach comes loose, only the sensation would be in your whole body."

"And I think it would be like the start of a storm. You know when you're outside and can sense there's lightning before you've seen any? Static and creepy. All the hairs on your arms would go stiff."

Mine almost do, possibly prompted by the same impulse that makes me imitate facial expressions when I read them described in novels. Randy once suggested this was my most empathetic response. "Low bar," I'd said. He grinned. "Exactly."

I try to come up with a decent answer, my inclination to satisfy taking over, but am distracted by the uncertain logistics. When would you meet solidity again? And would it be worse for it to happen right away, trapping you within the other object, or never, leaving you free to pass untouched through the world?

"This isn't *Sophie's Choice*," Shelby says.

"Seriously. Everyone else answered right away." The first girl gestures at the seated customers, some of whom nod.

"Maybe water," I say. "Water with pieces of ice in it. You're getting pulled through an icy river at night. That's my theory."

"You and Elaine." Shelby points to an older woman in the corner of the café. I raise my cup in cheers. She doesn't return the gesture.

A bald man in a poncho enters the café.

"Hello, old chap," the first girl says after the cow's moo. "Fine day for a frog race."

I take leave, sensing purgatorial entrapment. The air

outside is fresh and salt-laced. It readies me for whatever state Randy has gotten himself in.

Except Randy isn't in the car. My first thought is that he's lowered the seatback to go back to sleep. My second, upon seeing the empty interior, is that he's fallen through the car and the ground beneath, atomically harmonized for erasure.

SEA LA VIE

I hurry down the street, the phlegm in my throat solidifying into a hard lozenge of worry. Randy hasn't gone out on his own since Ms. Rourke's funeral. Every time I blink I see his monkish face looking back at me, and right behind the face a hundred potential catastrophes. Randy in the water, Randy in the street. How does someone brace for danger when they are busy staring at an invisible elsewhere? I try to swallow and cough instead. The lozenge swells and pulses. Randy bleeding, Randy lost in trees. Last week I tossed him an egg and watched it pass, completely unnoticed, from air to chest to floor. He only looked down when the yolk touched his toes.

My breath, dragged in, sounds like a flag whipping raggedly in the wind. Whatever shares of feral reflex I contain must have gone to the missing bag, for I feel entirely limited to my human capacity: slow, small-lunged, helpless in meaningful methods of pursuit. I look into every business I pass. A gem and mineral store, a kite emporium. I doubt Randy would be drawn into any of these places, but guessing his route is like guessing the route of a sleepwalker, every decision shrouded beneath an inscrutable scrim. The only place to catch my attention is a gallery with a lone painting hung, the subject of which appears to be our apartment building in New York. I halt, confused and briefly seeing this as a lead, its proximity to our life suggesting, by transference, proximity to Randy. But no. The gallery is empty.

A family dressed in Life Is Good merchandise sweeps me up before I can ponder the painting any longer. On their shirts, stick figures boat, ski, and pitch tents under starry skies. We merge into a larger throng of people, all milling with the unique aimlessness of tourists. I try to maneuver through them politely, but the bumbling procession spikes my stress closer to rage; when one of them points to a store mannequin dressed to look like a scuba diver and the rest rush for their cameras, I break through their ranks with some force.

"Excuse you!" one woman calls after me.

"Someone is missing!" I yell back, right before colliding with a wind chime. Saying this aloud sends another surge of concern through me, a surge carrying fresh visions. Randy is not dead or endangered. Randy is in a taxi, or on a boat, or already on a flight back to New York. He is leaving me. *Take me where you're headed*, he says to the driver, a handsome Spaniard with a hoop piercing in his nose. *Imagine giving a decade of your life to someone like that.*

Maybe this vision isn't so fresh, after all. It is with old

stress, and new, that I reach the end of the shops, where a grassy expanse overlooks the marina. Vendors selling fruit and produce block me with offers of peach wedges and berries. I dodge through them, at one point confusing a woman selling corn with Randy, which leads to her angrily brandishing a cob at me.

Exhaustion catches me by the time I reach the gangway. I lean against the railing, listening to the hulls of sailboats as they rub against the dock's rubber bumpers, and try to evaluate my next move. But the exhaustion makes room for sadness, and self-pity, and memories entirely unrelated to the present. In particular I see the moment during the table read of *Parthenon* when my friend Beatrice, who was reading the part of Rex's sister, cringed after a line of dialogue toward the beginning of the second act. This memory has been running a perennial loop in the corner of my mind ever since that night.

Randy's laugh is what reaches me first. And though he is not laughing at me, nor with me, I almost laugh right back, at the ridiculousness of him being on the dock directly below where I stand. He is lying belly down beside a young girl, both of their faces hung over the water.

I rush down the ramp leading to them. "Randy," I say. "Where have you been?"

"I've been here," he says. Neither he nor the girl look at me.

"I thought you were lost."

"Why didn't you call?"

"Call?"

He taps his pocket. "Ring, ring."

"Your phone. Right."

I drop to the damp wooden slats and wait to see what

feeling remains once concern and indignation drain away. Except there is no remaining feeling. I'm a jar wiped clean. The girl turns to me when I venture to ask what they're looking at, just so she can shush me. Then she turns back to the water. Her hair curtains her face, skimming the surface below.

I set my attention on my hand, licking spilled coffee from my knuckles. The cup itself got lost somewhere along the way. This achievable task helps stabilize me. Straight ahead of us floats a sailboat with *Sea la Vie* stenciled on its side. Slapped under the name is a Bush/Cheney campaign sticker, miraculously unweathered in spite of the years.

"Don't move," the girl whispers. "He's coming."

I lean closer to the dock's edge. "Who?" She shushes me again. I see nothing in the water apart from a few strands of kelp emerging from the depths. Like the woods, the river's greenish hue is saturated with darkness, a place where sunlight only reaches a couple of feet. But then a pale face rises from the gloom. At first the face is round and featureless, then its eyes, nose, and mouth come into focus. The whiskers are what finally identify the creature as a seal.

"Told you he'd come," the girl says to Randy. She hovers her hand over the water. "He visits every day. Isn't he cute?"

"Can you pet him?" I ask.

The girl looks at me through a break in her hair. "Why do people need to grab onto things? There are so many adults like you. I bet your fingerprints are all over the ozone layer."

"I hope not." I assumed she was young, a child, but now am not so sure. Her sweater has thumb holes dug near the wrists. Clipped to her belt loop is a carabiner holding a single key.

"Excuse my resolve," she says. "I'm a child of the late Anthropocene, so it's easy to be angry with your generation. My earliest memory is of my father putting out his cigarette in a tide pool. Isn't that perfect? Every time I see an animal I feel the need to apologize. Sorry, seal. Sorry, egret. We know not what we do, except for when we do know and do it anyway."

I try to match her solemnity. The history of my environmentalism amounts to a recycling bin and a compost container in the freezer. It's not that I don't care about the world, but that my concern remains localized to our kitchen. Randy and I are the same in this way, though he was once lauded for his activism when he photographed a derelict pumpjack in Texas. Taken near sunset, the contrasting light makes the rig more of an insect than a machine. There is nothing overtly political in the photo, yet fame often draws in projections of this sort. Randy could photograph an onion and have it taken up by someone's cause.

"Sorry, seal," he says.

The seal continues to stare up, almost motionless. I wonder how it sees us. Friends, foes, idiots. The white fur spanning its body is dappled with Rorschach-like splotches of black. If the girl weren't here, I wouldn't be able to resist reaching my hand in. Perhaps intuiting this thought, the seal sinks away, disappearing into the murk.

"Thank you," Randy says.

"Yes, very cute." My knees ache as I stand. "Time to head out, Randy?"

He accepts my hand when I offer it, then gives his to the girl. Upright, her age remains indistinct. Her face holds the milky blemishlessness of childhood, yet her eyes are run through with fatigued unhappiness. It doesn't take much imagination to forecast wrinkles onto her furrowed brow.

"I'm happy to see you again, Mr. Rourke," she says, clapping him hard on the back. "You look great, all things considered. I'll send a thought heavenward for your mother. You remember what I said?"

"Don't forget my voice."

"Right. Your voice is a gate. Open it."

"I'm Jack, by the way."

She doesn't take my offered hand. "I know who you are. I can always smell the blood of an Englishman." She stomps twice on the dock. "I'm Abigail. Have you found your beanstalk?"

"I don't think so."

"If you do, I recommend running as fast as you can. Giants are much faster than anyone thinks." She turns away, stepping with exaggerated heaviness as she goes. She does not turn back when she shouts, gleefully, "Run, Jack, run!"

Then she heads down one of the branching docks and climbs up on a sailboat. "See you soon, I'm sure," she calls out before disappearing into the cabin.

"Does she live there?" I ask.

"She does."

"With her parents?"

Randy shrugs.

"How do you know each other?"

"We met last time. She was chained to a tree." He smiles. "Do you feel that?"

"What?"

"The breeze. There's a breeze on my face."

QUEL EST TON PLAISIR?

We return to the 101, joining a procession of campers as it lumbers across the bridge. The expanse of dunes leading to the ocean looks like a row of sleeping bodies rubbed smooth by late afternoon light. Their golden balminess, so counter to the dark geographies of the woods and river, help lighten my mood.

"I like how kitschy this place is," I say after we reach the bridge's far side and pass a miniature golf course, firewood supply store, and dune buggy rental in quick succession. The businesses here are more spread out than in town, separated by massive Douglas firs and western hemlocks. I let my eyes trace their trunks from the mossy undergrowth to the sky. "Do you think we should bugger on a buggy? Stroke on a boat? Pee on a tree?"

Randy laughs. His spirits are also noticeably higher. That his levity likely has to do with Abigail does not diminish my enjoyment at the way he holds his hand out of his window while humming a melody. "We could snog on a log," he says. "Or fuck in a truck."

"Sixty-nine and dine."

"Frot on a cot."

We round an arm of a sizeable lake, pausing to note a placidity that seems impossible for its size, before returning to the more pressing matter at hand. Our back-and-forth easily transitions into actual foreplay. Coasting along, we exchange free-verse perversions in our lower timbres, the ones that emerge during dirty talk, and adjust our bulges like strangers cruising on a bus. All of Randy's normal fixtures have me turned on—the forearm dropped against the thigh, the breathy words, the strain of denim—but none so much as his attention. In the rental car, making our turn off the 101 and toward the beach, all of him is looking at me.

It is hard not to speed through the final few streets, and at one point I almost clip a deer with a broken antler, the crown dangling but not yet detached. Once or twice we skid on the sand swept across the road, laughing, and then we are turning at Sally and Fran's polka-dotted mailbox. The long driveway curves through a set of smaller dunes before delivering us to the bluff where the beach house stands.

"This is amazing," I say.

I've barely begun to take in the house's architecture, to say nothing of the ocean beyond, when Randy pulls me toward him. "Amazing can wait," he says before kissing me.

Then we are inside, fumbling through the living room. I like to tease, to have Randy hungry at my heels. We cat-and-mouse past a dark leather couch, a shark-shaped clock, and at least four of Randy's photographs, all accentuated by sleek frames and museum lighting. When Randy grabs my shirt, I hit his hand away; when I slip on the second of the steps leading upstairs, landing hard yet painlessly, I remain on my elbows, surrendered. For a moment all is still, our breathing synchronizing with the clock's tick, then Randy grabs hold of my waistband and pulls my jeans and briefs down in three swift tugs. I say something about showering, the day's travel. He stops me. "I love you," he says, as if love explains away the need for cleanliness. He puts one of his knees between both of mine. "I love you, Jack," he says again, jimmying my legs apart.

I want to reply, to thank him, even. My language is gone, burned up by internal heat. When Randy lets a bead of spit fall onto the base of my tailbone, I groan, a noise I sustain as he presses down on my lower back, arching me. "Spit," he says, his hand beneath my mouth. I do. He joins my saliva to his. My back is beginning to hurt, yet the anticipation of what is to come sublimates the pain. Randy brings the tip of his finger to me, our self-made lubricant allowing his knuckles easy entry. I sink back. Happiness, I am suddenly certain, is only a good fuck away.

"Not yet," Randy says when I grasp for his belt. He withdraws his finger and I push against him, urging him back. This is one of Randy's rituals. After pulling farther away, he looks down for what will be a minute, sometimes two, of no contact. The first time he did this, some eleven years ago, I practically imploded from self-consciousness. I knew he was not looking down on me in judgment, yet trusting he saw me as a subject of beauty took many months. When it did finally click, I looked at myself in mirrors more often, enjoying the novelty of self-confidence. What better gift than to see yourself as someone else sees you and to find the image beautiful.

Soon the waiting becomes torturous. I shimmy my hips, tempting Randy back. He returns, reentering me with one hand and stroking me with the other. It is too much to bear. In no time my body tightens. Randy does not pause at my warning; he finds an even more gratifying harmony. It is the most coherent conversation we have had in months. The finish puts my airport endeavor to shame, spilling across the steps below me.

I must look like a shipwrecked man pulled from the water—collapsed and struggling to breathe. "You're too good," I eventually manage to say.

"I know."

Randy understands the importance of the denouement, continuing in a lower gear as I return to being a fixed object in space again. Once my breathing has stabilized, I roll over to face him. "Monsieur?" I say. "Quel est ton plaisir?"

Randy is flush, smiling, his forehead dewy with sweat.

But then it all goes cold. The red drains from his cheeks, the smile from his lips. "Are you crying?" he asks.

"What?" I touch my face and find wet cheeks. "They're happy tears," I say. The claim sounds doubtful even to me, though I have no idea where they've come from. I quickly undo Randy's belt buckle, ready to bulldoze over whatever is happening inside me. His unzipped fly does not reveal the tented briefs I'd been expecting.

"Happy tears." Randy says these words as if unclear on their pronunciation. "Why?"

"Why?" I squeeze him with my legs. "What do you mean? You make me happy."

"I make you happy?"

"Yes." The word sounds oddly warped. "And I make you happy. Look."

My hand is trembling when I pull down his briefs. I refuse to let myself be taken away from where we just were. I slide lower, knocking my head on the step as I position myself beneath him. It is confusing to look at the core of Randy's body—hairy, lush, a portion of him I cherish for being nonpublic, mine alone—and to feel anything other than arousal, let alone something closer to fear. Still, I pull him over me. But once he is there, I seem to forget what I'm meant to do. Randy is tense and stiff-limbed; I am strained and clumsy-tongued. I feel fresh tears and press my face deeper into his plum-scented heat, trying to hide.

Randy pets the side of my face, coaxing me to let him go. "I need to lie down," he says once I do. He doesn't pull up his briefs or pants before clambering over me. "I need to be flat on my back," he says from the top of the stairs. Then he is gone.

I don't know how long I lie there. I don't know how much time passes with the woodgrain against my back, the scent of semen against my nose, and the sting of failure against my heart. I shift at last when the clock strikes six. To mark each hour, the shark's jaws part, revealing a small fish caught between the teeth.

MINOR ISLANDS

Outside, the house casts a shadow from the porch to the base of the nearest dunes, our car sitting in the center of the bluish rectangle. Its engine ticks in its final phase of cooling, a sound I've loved ever since my mother told me she did. That day, I was watching her solder a necklace's broken clasp at the workbench in the garage. My father arrived before she'd finished, racing inside to check on his crockpot chili. She nodded toward his Buick. "So soothing, right?" I shrugged. In those days, any glimpse of my parents' interior lives disarmed me, and I often responded with exaggerated indifference. I couldn't name it then, how my mother's trivial observation spoke to a sensibility I wasn't aware she contained, one shaped by a life that existed, does exist, and will continue to exist, outside of who I might understand her to be.

Years later, my high school girlfriend and I had driven to Joshua Tree and were sitting on the hood of her car. "I could fall asleep to the sound of a cooling engine," I said, realizing I had felt that way ever since that evening in the garage. If not for my mother's remark, I might have never considered the sound, not properly. It was a revelatory moment, partially induced by the pot we were smoking: if not for my interest in the soldering iron, we would not have had the conversation. A granular loss until you scale outward and see how many facets of yourself originate from chance, at which point your whole personality starts to sway.

I tried to articulate my epiphany to Claire, tucked under her arm and facing the dark geometry of the desert at night, and later to everyone else I dated. No one seemed moved, making me wonder if the notion was self-evident enough to be cliché. When I harped on it to Randy, we were competing for warm water in the shower. "What have you learned to like because of me?" he asked. "Plenty of things," I told him, not listing any because he was being partially glib, and because I was embarrassed by how many I could pull up in no time at all.

I pass the car, walking the border of sunlight until the pavement yields to sand. The dune I choose to climb cascades under my feet, pulling me back a step for every two I take forward. Once at the summit, wind gusts hit me from all sides. They are cold and briny, ocean-chilled, and I imagine them beating the sorrow from my body. Thrown out to the world, I can no longer smell Randy on my face. It's as simple a solution as any: if suffering inside, go out.

Through bleary eyes I look toward the Pacific. Unlike the beaches of southern California, where I spent much of my childhood ambling about, this stretch of sand is devoid of humanity: no boats, no boardwalk teeming with ice cream stands and children, no army of umbrellas or squadron of surfers. All evidence of human life is secondhand. There are four beach houses including ours, as well as three kites flocking high above the water. The fading light makes it hard to trace their strings, and the bluff obscures their fliers, so I pretend they are living beings, an extraterrestrial species dropped down from the mesosphere.

A high-pitched revving turns me back to the dunes. Shade has pooled between them, forming a collection of minor islands that span the coast in both directions, providing a mile-wide barrier between the beach and trees. Another engine roar caterwauls to my left, then to my right. Eventually a lone buggy zips along the face of a distant dune before disappearing. When it resurfaces, I clock the spider decal on the rider's jacket, as well as the long pink ponytail emerging from their helmet. They come to a stop at a summit and stare in my direction.

I wave. The rider raises their arm, flips me off, and speeds away. I am so surprised I begin to laugh, hard, until I am on level ground again.

I ought to shower. I ought to unpack. I ought to sort out dinner, maybe even dessert. First I ought to see if Randy is awake, alive, scrutable. His face, stepping over me, was a vacant mask.

The bags are lightweight enough to carry in tandem. As soon as I cross the threshold, I feel it in my chest—our hour without Ms. Rourke, gone.

THE MAN OF THE HOUR

When I first met her, Ms. Rourke was sipping a Shirley Temple and eyeballing a crowded Brooklyn bar, so anachronistic to the setting she almost fit right in. Randy had shown me photos, but I would have recognized her regardless. The two shared a Roman nose, a face shape, and, at the time, a haircut. Randy wasn't with her, having run to the bathroom, and I debated waiting to approach until he was back. I was intimidated and wanting to impress. Our eyes met, hers lit up with what I took for recognition, and I crossed the sticky floor.

"Rhonda?"

"Ms. Rourke." She set her drink down and gave me her hand. "You must be Jack. It's nice to have a face for so many stories."

"Likewise." Her hand, cold from the drink, warmed in my palm. I let it go. "Where's the man of the hour?"

"That would be you, dear. It's your chance to shine bright."

I laughed, grateful the bar's low lighting obscured my flushed face, then sat. "How's your visit been going?"

"I only landed three hours ago."

"That's right." I grabbed for a menu and found none.

"And I don't like New York."

In a handful of replies she'd swept the wind from my sails. Randy had warned me she could be brusque, a claim I only half-believed, given who he was and how much he adored her.

"I would never come here if not for my son. I begged him to live anywhere other than New York. What's wrong with Cincinnati or Pittsburgh? Homestyle cities that are plenty big. When I fly into JFK I feel all the blood fall out of my head. I don't know how you stand it."

"New York can surprise you."

"Something you should know about me, Jack, is that I hate surprises. More, perhaps, than I hate New York." She raised her eyebrows. I could tell she was conveying a message, some kind of warning or threat. I couldn't gauge how thoroughly she'd already built her opinion of me, a scaffold she would fortify over the years until it was a complete structure in its own right, unyielding and windowless.

"Jack!" Randy's voice, bounding across the bar, put the tension at the table into stark relief; in our first unspoken agreement, Ms. Rourke and I smiled back at him in unison, mirroring his enthusiasm to obscure our lack thereof.

"Sorry for the delay," Randy said. "Stomach trouble from last night's food truck."

"Food truck?" Ms. Rourke grimaced, then put her hand on his. "Let's get you a seltzer."

"I'm okay," Randy said. "I've got you two in the same place for the first time." He grinned at us, placing his free hand on my knee and squeezing.

The moment was brief—the three of us sitting there with Randy's hands linking us—yet I swore I sensed Ms. Rourke sending transmissions through him, transmissions that hardened his touch. What she wanted, I became convinced, was to establish her primacy as the alpha. I fucked your son in the shower last night, I thought when our eyes met. She sipped her drink, then said, "Jack was just telling me how wrong I am about New York. I suppose you didn't mention what happened the last time I was here?"

Randy's hand fell away from me.

"What happened?" I asked.

"I was mugged." She shivered—excessively, I felt—then added: "You were right, after all. New York is stuffed full of surprises."

THEREFORE I AM

Randy's eyes are closed as the bathwater rises around him. He looks happy, or if not happy then at least less troubled than he was on the stairs. The part of me that wants to join him is offset by the part that can anticipate how his eyes, upon opening, might dim. I leave him be, unpacking our bags and returning downstairs.

Sally and Fran live an itinerant lifestyle, splitting their time between Florence, Boston, and Todos Santos. Randy has yet to give me a clear answer regarding their professional lives, so I assume they're funded by an inheritance. I pass, scornfully, by the sleek couch, an obsidian coffee table, a bookshelf organized by language. Was it Sally or Fran who described herself as a polyglot in one of their letters? One of a million lines that made my eyes roll.

The room is not without personality—a drove of ceramic pigs spread across the windowsill, a framed calendar page that reads *Wild Rose with Sally, 8 PM*, a sculpture of a thumb—but the sum of its parts remains predominantly featureless. Even Randy's photos fall victim to the flattened aesthetic, as lifeless as model home art. This gives me a dash of pleasure. Of course I am rooting for Randy's ongoing success; of course I am embittered by it.

A Francesca Woodman print hangs in the living room. This photograph, like all of her work, pulses with distress. A woman stands in a checker-floored room, looking like she is trying to sneak out of frame or protect herself from an unseen presence. She is hunched over and holding a white sphere in front of her face, her black dress melding into the shadow she casts. On the floor before her is a giant tortoise, somehow serving as the photo's most stabilizing feature. Then my favorite part: the socked foot she sticks out, arched in a tiptoe and containing, in its delicacy, the full concentration of the scene's humanity.

Randy was asked about Woodman in one of his first interviews. Famously, he needed the interviewer to tell him who she was. For all his love of the arts, photography has never been much of an influence on his own work—he'd much prefer to talk about the films of Ingmar Bergman or the poetry of Linda Gregg. My personal approach, which I saw as nobler, was to steep in plays until the tea turned black. Who deserves a stage who hasn't sat in the audience? I'm less certain now, since every decision made or unmade has felt, in turn, integral to my collapse. If only I'd read less, read more, changed the ending, rewritten the beginning, shot for the moon, for the stars, for anywhere other than where I shot, I could have been someone.

But I am someone, I remind myself, passing into the kitchen. A sad assertion that I make often. There was an awful lightness to my step in the first week I spent post-mortem (phrasing I dropped from my vocabulary as soon as Randy's mother died, although it still feels right), a lightness that emphasized how little I had beyond my career. Randy pointed out that it was a good thing, a sign I'd finally set down a significant weight. I let him tell me this, and try still to let myself believe it, though I suspect he's the one who's earned true freedom. He was the one who suggested I find someone to talk to about my career frustrations. Out of gas. That was the phrase he used, referring to his remaining capacity for my complaints. He wasn't even grieving then; Ms. Rourke wasn't even sick. My first instinct was to hit him—how terrible for him to suffer the drudgery of my career. My second was to beg forgiveness.

After quitting, I alternated between resenting Randy for his failure to see that a sizeable portion of my inner material had been cut from me—didn't he think that playwriting was vital to my genetic code?—and forfeiting myself to the likelihood that Randy's success prevented him from comprehending rock bottom. In either mood, in any mood, I drifted, my feet occasionally scraping across the sidewalk as cloudy oblivion called to me from above.

Then Ms. Rourke died and I was pulled crudely to the ground, where I've been stuck ever since, drawn down by the weight of Randy's need. Am I a sure-footed partner now? I'm walking through a stranger's house and telling myself I exist. Friends tell me work should never be the primary qualifier of life. Theoretically I agree, though at times I worry about the bar being set too low: I think, therefore I am; I drink, therefore I am; I blink, therefore I am.

Light floods through the kitchen windows, drawing me to the breakfast nook that overlooks the bluff. The departing sun has left the ocean shimmering with oily pastels. Apart from three tracks of footprints—the kite fliers, now gone—the sand is smooth as skin.

The office's drafting table holds a stack of books on art theory and a sketchpad, the first page of which features a bare foot drawn in pencil marks so fine I fear I might breathe them away. The drawing is neither impressive nor amateur. From the foot's placement, it looks like Sally or Fran planned to draw a full person, then stopped. I flip to the next page and discover a foot attached to a calf. The process continues in this way for almost half of the sketchbook, the subject drawn in limb by limb, then clothing item by clothing item, until all that remains to be drawn is the face. I do not find an eye, nose, or mouth when I turn ahead; instead, a sand dune, then another, then enough to fill the entire backdrop. The clothing gains folds and wrinkles, the dunes gain grain, and the ground gains shadows. Amid the surrounding textures, the untouched face glows. I reach the final page, no longer able to determine what minutia has been added, and all at once I recognize the figure. "Abigail?" I say her name aloud.

The water shuts off upstairs. The image, newly instilled with my knowledge of the girl, has taken on a confrontational mood. She does not need a face to shame me for having thrown a plastic bottle into an airport trash can earlier in the day. She does not need eyes to glare. I close the sketchbook and open the office's other door, expecting to be met with the living room and finding the basement stairs instead. I step back. The dark, the musty air, the tunnel Randy mentioned—it is an easy recipe for fear, which skitters across my scalp. My hesitation doesn't last long. I've always been someone who wants to yank open the closet door after hearing a whisper from within. Fear is an enticer, a seducer, a promise of stakes in an otherwise trifling life.

The basement is completely ordinary, purposeless beyond storage. Plastic tubs sit on built-in shelves; empty boxes huddle in the corner. Even the spider crawling across the floor is trite, predictable in all its erratic movements. On my second pass I notice a set of doors built into the floor. They are easy to miss, painted the same shade as the carpet and tucked in the corner, and while my fear regains some traction, it is unable to find real purchase. For good reason: I pull on the handles to reveal an empty storm cellar. There is nothing strange about it beyond its existence in a state not known for tornadoes. Randy probably stumbled down here after too many drinks and thought he'd uncovered a passage to the center of the earth.

I haul myself up to the first floor, then the second, wanting to watch the sunset from the bathroom with my head on Randy's shoulder. His clothes are scattered about the bedroom. When I collect the pieces and lay them on the bed, I feel something in the pocket of his pants. I know he would never do the same, but I can't help myself from sliding the object out. It is a tape recorder, small and plastic and as inexplicably alive as a loaded gun.

"Jack?" Randy calls out.

I fumble getting the recorder back in the pocket, my fingers tense. Randy is a devout practitioner of healthy boundaries. Not because he has always been so well adjusted, but because for a long time he was quite maladjusted, bent by the will of a jealousy that could light within him a terrifying fire. In the early years of our relationship, this second self would emerge every few months, beckoned forth by a too-long conversation at a bar, a too-late return home. A jealous Randy has black pupils and wet palms. I used to find him sitting in the dark. It didn't matter how much I braced myself—there was no avoiding the force of his accusations, which he threw like rocks.

I have to clear my throat twice before finding my voice. "Yeah?"

"Come here."

Fear sits on my shoulders this time. And with the fear, again, comes intrigue. Randy's outbursts were bad behavior. My friends said this. Randy said this, once he went to a therapist and got a grip. The jealousy, he determined, was an inheritance from his father, the last person he wanted to be. This revelation was good, and is good, of course. But sometimes I miss it. For the same reasons his possessiveness could be frightening—the magnitude, the control—it also could be perversely thrilling. Look how much he loves me, I'd think, watching him chew his knuckle until it bled.

It's surprising to find him blissed out in the bathroom, neck resting on the lip of the tub, eyes on the sunset. Whatever edge I sensed in his voice must have been projected, a psychic creation. There's relief and disappointment that he won't yell, shout, bend me over his knee and punish me for breaking the sacred laws of privacy he's tried so hard to keep up.

"Why are you standing way over there?" he asks.

I laugh, but as I approach the tub I realize that some uncertainty remains within me, heavy in my feet. "How's the water?"

"Feel for yourself."

I sit on the floor beside the tub and let Randy take my arm, which he submerges against his stomach. "You smell like stress," he says.

"I was stressed."

"I needed to get warm. It was cold out there." He pulls my hand from the water and sticks my thumb in his mouth. "Where did you go?" he manages to ask around it.

"Downstairs. I was snooping around."

Randy begins to bite me then, and for a moment I think he's lured me here for this exact purpose. My heart beats hard, two times, three times, my groin stirs—but it is only a moment.

"I'm hungry," he says, letting the finger go.

"I can order us something."

"Don't go." He grips my arm with some urgency. "Let the drowned man speak."

He sinks below the waterline, hair billowing around his face. When he opens his eyes, I am struck by the feeling that the old Randy is the one in the water, separated from me by some impenetrable boundary. A word surfaces from his mouth in a plume of bubbles.

"What did you say?" I ask, practically yanking him up.

"Pizza." He blinks water from his eyes. "I want pizza."

THE SPURNS

Randy is reading *Just Kids* aloud to me when the doorbell rings. We did this regularly in our younger years together. Then, like many habits, the routine petered out. A missed opportunity for our barren spring, I see now: Randy, handed a script, sounds almost like himself, sonorous and unstoppable.

The porch light does not ignite when I flip its switch. I am mid-apology as I open the door, then cut off by a familiar voice. "I'll be damned."

I try to place the driver beneath her oversized baseball cap. It only takes a moment to trace her back to the café, the first barista. "Fine day for an arms race, right?" I say.

"Except the day is over."

"Sure."

She shifts her weight from one leg to the other, taking the opportunity to glance into the house. "Alone out here?"

"No."

"Lonely?"

"What?"

"They're different. Being alone and being lonely."

"I know."

She shrugs, then moves the pizza box to rest it on her hip. "I've never delivered here. You'll be shocked to learn the owners aren't big pizza people. Shelby brought them Chinese once. Lo mein and fried rice and sweet-and-sour soup. We've wondered about the fortunes in their cookies. It's a nice place they have. Mind if I come in?"

"Inside?"

"Where else? The Burns ladies are riddles to me. In town they're called the Spurns since they're always spurning people. I think that's a bit unfair. I'm not one to sugarcoat, though: when they stop in the café, they're all business." She purses her lips and speaks in a strained falsetto. "Two double espressos, please," she says, waving her hand around. The only thing missing from the charade is a chaise lounge on which she might sprawl. "You get the gist."

"I do." Part of me wants to let her in, to tour through the house together and point out its various pretentions. "Maybe next time. We're winding down a long day."

She hands me the pizza. "I get it. Some days are long. Some hours are long. You wouldn't believe how time passes at the café. If not for Shelby, I'd drown myself in our frother. The deliveries are better. Time still stretches out and out like taffy, but I'm not stuck behind a laminated counter. I'm sailing through the night with a backseat full of dinner."

She moves her hand like a magic carpet, whistling for each curve. "Don't get me started on the morning."

"What happens in the morning?"

"Babysitting."

"Lots of jobs."

"Lots of wants. It's an expensive world out there. Your total, speaking of, is twenty-two dollars and fifty cents. Not bad for a hundred hand-counted pepperonis."

The smell of crisped meat and melted cheese meets me then, making my mouth water. I hand her the cash and tell her to keep the change. She bows in thanks, but still looks at me expectantly. "Thanks a lot," I say, scanning her shirt for a name tag. "Horace?"

"Oh, I'm Carolina. Horace played on the Lakers in 2001. Best season they ever had, or so our owner thinks. We start each shift by choosing a name tag pulled from their roster. Milo loves those guys like brothers. It's a little sweet, a little stupid, and, if I'm honest, a little infectious. Game two of the finals really was something. Milo has it looping at the shop, so I've memorized the whole shebang. Did you see it live? I wasn't even embryonic back then."

"I must have missed it. Not a big sports guy, believe it or not."

"You?" She lets her mouth gape. "Impossible!"

We are laughing when Randy arrives behind me.

"I thought you'd been kidnapped," he says.

"You came at the right time," Carolina says. "I was getting ready to make my move." She makes a pretend grab at me. "Did *you* see game two of the 2001 NBA finals?" she asks Randy, who shakes his head. "There's something beautiful about it, watching a bunch of overgrown men throw a ball around. Borderline therapeutic." She smacks her forehead. "God, listen to me. I've gone total jock mode."

"I'm here for the overgrown men," I say.

"I'm here," Randy says. He finds nothing to attach his presence to, making the statement hang in an ungainly way.

"Your pizza is probably in need of a reheat," Carolina says. "I recommend three hundred degrees. Thanks for chatting"—she pauses, waiting for my name, and when I tell her she grins. "Of course. Thanks for the chat, Jack. And sorry for the could-be kidnapping"—again she waits, this time for Randy—"Randy. Jack and Randy. That's nice. Very suburban."

I laugh. "What a compliment."

She goes to take her leave, making it halfway to her car before turning back. "Say, Randy? What do you think it feels like to fall through something solid?"

"A pool of sap," he says without hesitation. "You can barely move, and there's the awareness that things could solidify at any moment, leaving you like one of those poor bugs they sell in museums. Also, you can't breathe. But when you're out, when you're on the other side, there is no sticky residue. That's the biggest difference. It is sticky until it's not."

Unlike our answers, Randy's sounds less speculative than experiential. Carolina nods, impressed, then tells him she will pass on the message. We watch her taillights disappear behind a dune.

"She gave me coffee earlier," I say.

"She knows how to paint a face."

Inside, we wolf down pizza slices as if being timed, our lips greasy and our fingertips cornmeal crusted. After finishing my third, I run to grab the sketchpad from the office.

"Who does that look like?" I say, presenting the final page to Randy.

"My mother."

"What? It's Abigail." I turn the sketchpad back. This time the drawing doesn't seem to resemble anyone.

"Abigail has a face. Abigail is all face." Randy stands, briefly looking like he might be sick. "My mother is faceless. Why would you do that?"

"Do what?"

"My mother has no face." He grips the side of the pizza box. It looks like he might fling it across the room, but then he lets go and steps away. "I want you to say it."

"Your mother has no face?"

"Bingo." He laughs a terrible laugh before walking away. I can hear him marching through every room. "My mother has no face," he says over and over, as if those words, carried through the house, might sage the place of its demons.

A CHIMP IN A CHAPEL

A series of knocks wakes me in the middle of the night. Still held within the vapor of a dream, my mind conjures the woodpecker that tormented my childhood home for months before my mother finally bought a BB gun. Then I stand, and this senselessness drops.

I cross the bedroom, waiting for the knocks to come again. Randy's soft snores help ground me—my muscles, I realize, are all tense—but then another round does come, more forceful than the last. Halfway down the stairs, I'm puffed up with reproach for whoever lacks such common courtesy, having exchanged my fear for frustration. Don't you know my husband is sleeping? Don't you know my husband is grieving? My fear returns at the next bombardment, stopping me three steps from the bottom. A vision of Ms. Rourke fills my mind.

There is little doubt the dead, given the chance, would knock loudly. There is no doubt Ms. Rourke would knock loudest of all. I know she is ash, yet in my head she is dirt-clad and decomposing, a corpse rubbed raw from the many miles spent crawling over state lines.

I crouch down, unable to see anyone through the door's upper window. Then I hear whistling. It's not so much a song as a show of impatience, something to hurry along a friend. The probability that Carolina is the one at the door suddenly seems so likely that I go straight there, only recollecting my wits when the handle is in my grasp.

"Hello?" I say. "Who's there?"

"Hello?" a man answers. "I'm here."

I peer out the window and see the crown of his head, bald and shining in the moonlight. He is standing close to the door, his nose almost against the knocker.

"Can I help you?"

"Help me?" He laughs. "I'm here to help you."

"With what?"

"Randy!"

I drop the door handle. An unnatural coldness moves up my arm before spreading through my chest, as if put there intravenously. "Randy?"

He thrusts an object against the window, making the door shake. I recoil from the impact, then see the bottle he is holding. "Brandy," he says, dragging the end of the word into a nasally whine. "Libation for the goods, the bads, and the very uglies."

I remain cold, though there's relief in the likelihood that he is drunk rather than deranged. "We're asleep," I say. "You'll have to drink on your own."

The bottle disappears from the window. All is quiet for a spell. I try to deepen my breathing and swallow the bitter spit in my mouth. When I take a step back, I hear him scratching a fingernail against the wood. "Fran warned me you'd be like this," he says.

The comment jabs me, a prick followed by a swelling burn. In radiant technicolor I see Sally and Fran ridiculing my career and fashion sense, my occasional rashes and my mouth full of fillings. There is no telling what all Randy has shared with them. But as soon as I think of Randy, it occurs to me that he is the likelier subject of the man's remarks.

"You know Sally and Fran?" I ask.

"Know them? I've been next door since before they got here. Even seen them screw a few times, not by any choice of my own. There's this thing they do on the deck. I don't stick around to watch, if that's what you're thinking. I'm the opposite of a pervert. Asexual, in fact."

I turn the deadbolt and open the door. It's not the man I want to let in so much as the information about Sally and Fran. That they sometimes have sex on the deck is the most relatable detail I've yet to learn about them. The man enters like a greyhound through a starting gate, kicking off his shoes before heading for the kitchen. I follow his mothball scent through the dining room. He is already pulling two glasses from the cabinet when I enter the room.

"Two fingers?" he asks.

"One."

He makes a pouting face. He is older than I might have guessed, liver-spotted and sunken-eyed. As I take the offered glass, I see his coat is covered with enough white cat hair to obscure the fact it is black.

"Thanks," I say. "I'm Jack."

"Jack. Remind me the mister's name?"

"Randy."

"That's right. I had brunch with Sally and Fran before they jetted south. They told me you'd be coming. I was excited to finally meet the man behind all the photos. He's the patron saint of this house, except living." He fills his cup halfway full. "I won't lie to you, Jack. His stuff isn't really for me. It's no offense to your husband. I've never had an artsy eye. It's a wonder Sally and Fran have me over here. I'm like a chimp in a chapel." He sips his brandy. "Yummy. My name's Claude."

"Cheers, Claude." I take a sip and the brandy blazes through me. That Claude is not in the arts warms me to him. I'd prefer every new person I meet to be an accountant or social worker.

"Tired?" he asks.

"Always."

"I know that gig. Before this year, I figured it was the modern condition. Lug yourself to work, lug yourself to the bowling alley, lug yourself into your wife and out of her again. Wash and repeat forever. You know the drill. But then"—he taps his temple while draining his glass—"I figured my shit out. And you can, too, for only twenty-nine dollars and ninety-nine cents a month."

My expression makes him laugh.

"I'm tugging your tongue, man. I wish it were that easy. What I did was flip the hourglass. Or smashed it. I quit my job at the salmon farm—you can't imagine how long it took to stop hearing their bodies slapping against the gates, like Clarice and her lambs—and I divorced my wife, who signed the papers without a single moan because she was also lugging herself to work, to the shooting range, onto and off of my body. We loved each other in the way cows love heat lamps, and that does not a happy marriage make. Am I killing you with these metaphors? I'm in a memoir class and the teacher says it's my Achilles' heel."

"A metaphor against metaphors."

"What?"

"Nothing."

He blinks, either trying to sort out what I said or to find his way back to the story. I decide I might actually like him. He lacks the self-concern that's corseted my social sphere for the past decade, keeping us from saying what we mean.

"Your divorce," I say.

"Right. Cows, lamps, and Claudia. She's a wonderful lady. Well, mostly wonderful. I won't tell you about the time she Frisbeed my favorite CD off the balcony. She's free now and so am I. I work down on the beach, making sure folks stay away from the snowy plover nests, and I spend my spare time doing whatever the hell I want. Are you a hobby man?"

"Trying to be," I say, thinking of the pastimes I've picked up and dropped since stopping playwriting. Gardening. Baking. Jogging farther than a mile. "I like swimming."

"The ocean here is freezing, best left to the whales. Go for the lakes. I'd take you, but I don't pair well with wet. Claudia guesses I died of rabies in a past life. I'm writing about it now, in my class. It's a horrible thing for a human to suffer." He shudders, reaching for the bottle. Somehow my glass is empty. He pours us both more. "The point is I've found life in all these new pockets and crags. I'm writing my story, collecting my shells, making my way through *The*

Golden Girls, and studying the bats that live on the face of the bluff. Have you seen them? Gorgeous species ruined by vampire movies. Movies can ruin anything."

"They can."

Claude leans back, studying me. "Well, Jack, that's enough about me and mine. What's your sob story?"

"I'm also going through a transition," I say. "But the jumper cables are missing."

"Jumper cables? You need to swap that sedan for a sports car. Better yet, a horse. Giddy up and go!" He leans forward and sets his chin in his hands. "Tell me everything."

I wish I had more restraint, or at least more decorum, but my failure spills out of me. It's embarrassing. It's exhilarating. I detail the decision to quit and the two years beforehand, a gummy stretch of successive flops. For a while I believed the plays were too novel, hence the disinterest from my agent and the lackadaisical response from audiences when small production companies did take them on. Then, accepting that they were not working, I decided the issue was that I'd lost the fuel present in my early work. When I came up with *Parthenon*, I thought I'd broken the cycle, writing with a fervor I hadn't felt in years. Who better to turn to than the Greeks, spearheaders of tragedy? I believed in my Hail Mary until the night of the read-through, when my year of work crashed on its face.

"There was no question it was over," I say. "I heard the play and knew the best I had to give was not very good. So I stopped. Now I'm lost. That's the problem with pouring yourself into one thing. Eggs and baskets. I was scraping yolk over cement for the longest time." My mouth is dry from talking. I go for more brandy. "Sorry to rant. You see what I mean about jumper cables—apparently I'm still stuck." I laugh. Claude frowns.

"That was some of the most depressing shit I've ever heard," he says. "I hate to break it to you, pal, but we're not in this together."

"What?"

"I'm not divorced, not a salmon farmer, and definitely not asexual." He glances at his crotch as if to verify this. "My name isn't even Claude. Can you imagine? My name is Clarence."

"Clarence?"

"Clarence Freeman. And you have bummed me the hell out." He laughs in a shaken way. "I'm a method actor. Claude is a character I'm working on. A guy who's hidden his misery behind a bunch of sham happiness. Would a normal person show up drunk in the middle of the night? No chance. Claude would, because Claude is desperate for human contact. Or at least that's how I'm interpreting him. The script sucks."

"All of that was a lie?"

"Not everything. I do live next door. I haven't been there very long. And I do hate swimming." He smiles. "Sounds like you believed me?"

Where the cold crept through my blood, heat surges. My veins feel acidified, my skin feverish. "I think you should go," I say, imagining how easily the whisky glass would shatter.

"I wasn't planning to break character!" he pleads. "I just couldn't pretend we were buddied up on the same team. It would've felt like I was scamming you, saying how great it was that you gave up on playwriting. It's not great. It's a shame." He pauses, appears to read the anger in my eyes, then holds his hands up in forfeit. "All right, all right. I'll go. I've got leftover cordon bleu with my name on it anyway."

His shuffle to the door is slow. As he crosses the threshold, I have an urge to shove him.

"Your coat is covered in fur," I say. "It's disgusting."

"So gross, right?" He holds his arms out and spins. "I don't even own a pet!"

I close the door and take several deep breaths in the dark. I am verging on drunk, wobbly and disoriented. Something tells me to chase him, tackle him, pin him to the sand and make him tell me—what? Whatever he might owe me is indistinguishable. When I look out the window, all I see is the rental car and the dunes beyond, swept by the wind into entirely new shapes.

DAWN PREMISE

I wake up with the idea for a play sitting square in my head. Friends are in a restaurant, eating brunch and speaking in vapid non sequiturs. An earthquake hits, and the group's response is to speak louder, more vapidly. One is named Fabio. This is where the story blurs. I have yet to open my eyes and find it easier to maintain concentration with them shut. *I wasn't born for this,* Fabio says—the play's opening line—while he gestures at a too-runny egg. It must be his birthday. Should the entirety of the play happen here, with the earthquake's magnitude increasing over time? And what is the point of the earthquake? The birthday? Fabio?

It ends as easily as it started. I open my eyes to a room

full of tempered light, cringing in a precise emulation of how Beatrice cringed while reading her lines. I have recreated this face in the mirror many times. Randy is rummaging around downstairs and I am grateful for his absence. I probably would have told him the idea if he were in bed. I probably would have told Clarence, too, had it come to me last night, eager to prove that I still had something in me. Most humiliating would have been the hopefulness in my eyes.

I resign myself back to exile, where plays are not written and joy is not reaped. Rolling over, I press my face into the pillow until it becomes difficult to breathe, then get out of bed. A headache hits me from behind once I'm upright. While I brush my teeth, wash my face, and let loose a stream of dehydrated urine, I envision the marvelous catastrophe of my skull exploding.

Randy is talking to someone in the kitchen. I can't make him out from the staircase, though I can tell from his inflection he is asking a series of questions and not waiting long for answers. Clarence. My anger at his prolonged lie reboils. I hurry down, clipping the wheel of the drink cart on my way through the living room. The rattling bottles quiet the rest of the house. When I enter and discover Randy sitting alone at the table, my energy has nowhere to go. I pace the length of the room, glance into the office, then pause, directionless.

"Were you talking to someone?" I ask.

"I was." On the table is the tape recorder, as well as Ms. Rourke's ashes, the baggie opened to the room. "And I would have kept talking had you not come in like that."

He is tense when I touch his shoulders. "Forgive me, my liege," I say. "I shan't dare make a disturbance again."

He laughs, albeit reluctantly. "I'm trying something Abigail suggested. She's the one who gave me this recorder."

"What are you trying?"

"To talk to my mother." He glances at me, then quickly averts his eyes. "Abigail does it with her friend. He died when they were in sixth grade. She says he responds, sometimes. The frequencies can't be picked up without a device, so you have to use this." He taps the recorder. "He sang along with her once. Her friend. That's how it first happened."

"What were they singing? 'Candle in the Wind'?"

Randy pushes himself up from the table. "You don't have to be an asshole," he says. "Some of us actually like our parents and friends."

"Just because I don't need—"

"You don't like your parents, Jack. They invited us to Spain and you laughed at them."

"Randy." I try to give him a look that communicates how ridiculous this is. "They invited us to cut costs on their Airbnb. We talked about this. I didn't laugh at them. I laughed with you."

He shakes his head. In any dispute, Randy is all motion and I am all stillness. He laps me twice as if in search of something, talking as he goes. "I would have gone. I like your parents. I write them cards at Christmas. It isn't fair, Jack."

"What isn't fair?"

He pauses by the table, where he retrieves the recorder. I try to make a move of my own—a single step to the left or right—but my limbs have fully calcified. Between us, dozens of answers to the question swarm, just as they have swarmed before. It isn't fair that he puts effort into a relationship with my parents when I hardly put effort into a relationship with Ms. Rourke. It isn't fair that he likes them when I disliked her. It isn't fair that my parents are alive while his mother is dead. Our eyes meet in the flurry. My righteousness softens, seeing how lost Randy looks. The desire to run across the room isn't enough to make it happen.

"I'm sorry," I say. I mean it, or think I do. When Randy has a softening of his own, some worse part of me seizes the slip. "I'm sorry my parents don't love me like your mom loved you, and that I didn't want to go to Barcelona with them three fucking years ago."

"Fuck off, Jack. You're not a victim if you shoot yourself." He goes into the office, closes the door halfway, then adds, "Breakfast is on the stove. You're welcome."

I stay in the middle of the kitchen after he closes the door, the abrupt arrival of guilt further entrapping me. When I do free myself, I find a pot of congealed oatmeal on the stove. It is a flavorless paste that I choke down penitently. On the refrigerator, a postcard of a felled pine is hung up by a translucent magnet. The note is from Randy, penned at the close of his last visit.

Sally & Fran—

What a pair of weeks I've had! I read Gadamer! I swam! I went to the sea lion caves! I walked in the woods! I stepped on a slug! I finished my essay on

> *Merleau-Ponty! I started my essay on Renee Gladman! I edited forty photos! I tanned on the deck! I drank the wine you left! I kayaked to the ocean! I touched a dead jellyfish! I bought tuna from the dock! I ran in the sand! I slept like a babe! And I owe it all to you!*
>
> *With love and thanks,*
> *Randy*

I read the postcard four times as I continue to shove oatmeal into my mouth. Both things are heartbreaking: the effort, however weak, of Randy cooking for me, and the coordinates, however faint, of who he once was. I remember how Gadamer and Gladman enthralled him, how Merleau-Ponty tasked his patience. ("Say *proprioception* five times fast," he said to me one night, *Phenomenology of Perception* dropped over his face.) We talked on the phone after he saw the jellyfish. I remember his delight, how the waves rumbled behind him.

I drop the pot into the sink, fill it with soapy water, and go to the office door, ready to beg forgiveness. He is muffled through the wood. I press my ear against it until a question comes clear: "How did you feel about milk?"

Something unfastens within me. I see myself from across the room, then across the house, then farther still. What fate has put me here, listening as my husband tries to commune with the dead about dairy? I shove away from the office, hurrying through the house and to the front door. The illusion that it is shrinking only breaks when I push through it.

The day is damp and cool, the fresh air making me feel instantly saner. Fog tickles my lips like static. Through its wooly dome, large swatches of blue sky have been cut. I follow a sloping path to the beach. My descent is slow, the grass beneath me slippery. After almost falling, I focus on the ground, seeing a set of barefoot prints before me. My first thought is Clarence, no matter that the feet are child-sized. "It's a shame," he had said about my quitting. So what?

The grass thins as the hill levels. I walk toward the water until the wave breaks threaten my shoes. When I was young, staring out at the ocean made me feel ill with insubstantiality. Today I welcome the diminishment. I look at the insects scuttling over a crushed crab, the beached kelp that must have been tugged loose by a storm after years of determined growth. Who could lose sleep over a badly written scene? A negative review? A mother-in-law? Who could see the entirety of human culture as anything other than an extravagant effort to deny our actual circumstance? We are drops on a pan living, like everything else, in an ambivalent world.

I pick up a bottle cap wedged in the sand, wondering if there is an article within these ruminations. "God Will Not Save You, and Neither Will Art: A Former Playwright on Life Beyond False Saviors." I debate the headline and my preferred media outlet. Then I stop. The true absconder would not spend their time pitching *The New York Times*. Besides, I do believe art saves us. Not from hunger or thirst, but from our more nameless needs.

I walk for a while longer, grow bored, then start to make my way back up the beach. When my phone rings, I'm sure it is my former agent, or another agent eager to resurrect my career, or a production company wanting to produce one of my old plays—the same delusion sequence I suffer every time a call comes.

"Hello?"

A robot tells me I have a significant amount of medical debt. I hang up, then scroll to my father's name and dial. The movement feels inevitable, put into motion back at the house as a response to Randy's accusations. A similar impulse took over in the week after Ms. Rourke died, motivated by guilt and retaliation and the lens of mortality, which did make me wonder if I ought to try harder to forge a meaningful bond with my parents. The calls sputtered by the end of April, then stalled out altogether.

"Jack?" My father's voice sounds far away, like he's standing a room's length away from the receiver.

"Hey, Dad. Can you hear me?"

"Loud and clear. Why are you shouting?"

"I'm not." It occurs to me I might be. I face away from the ocean. "I'm at the beach. I'm not trying to yell."

"What beach?"

"In Oregon. Randy and I are on vacation."

"Glad to hear it. I can't remember the last time we took a trip. You think you'll go everywhere once you retire, and then you go nowhere. What's Oregon like?"

"Beautiful."

"Very good."

"How are you two? I've been meaning to get the update on the neighbors."

The neighbors were touchstones of our spring dialogues. They were disputing the placement of a new fence, a subject my parents and I found easier to broach than whatever was significant to our lives, the true respite from sorrow revealing itself to be inconsequence.

"The neighbors are fine. They had us over for paella the other night. Peace through shrimp and sausage. Your mother and I are also fine, although she took a bit of a tumble on our bike ride this morning."

"A tumble?"

"A fall on Orange Grove. One minute she was pedaling beside me, the next she was not."

"Is she okay? Why didn't you call?" I feel slightly lightheaded imagining her injury and crouch near the sand to steady myself. I know she is no longer on the pavement, yet that is where I imagine her, sprawled and helpless.

"She's fine. Currently sleeping like a goose. The doctors want to keep her here for the night to monitor her head. It looks like the biggest damage is a wrist fracture. Small potatoes for a woman with osteoporosis." He pauses, then says, "You want to know something I've noticed?"

"What?"

"The chairs they have in hospitals have not improved one iota in the course of my life."

I pinch the bridge of my nose. "So she's okay?"

"She is okay."

"What can I do?"

"From Oregon? Give the Ducks a finger for me. I'm still not over their Rose Bowl win."

"Dad."

"You could call again," he says. His voice is suddenly close to the speaker. I can't tell if his somberness is new, or if I couldn't hear it because of the bad acoustics. "I'm sure Mom would appreciate it."

"Really?"

"Of course! Who doesn't want a chance to brag about their big crash?"

I hear a new voice, likely a nurse or doctor, and he tells me he should go, and au revoir.

The line dies. The fog has accomplished its departing trick and, although no one is here, I feel exposed beneath the blue sky. I wish Randy had been present to overhear our conversation, and am also glad he wasn't. Such graceless intimacy is embarrassing to have made public, no matter how long I've come to expect it. I go to rub away a twitch that's begun fluttering my right eyelid. Forgetting the bottle cap between my fingers, I nick my cheek with the serrated edge. "Fuck," I say, dropping the trash back to the ground.

I get all the way to the house before remembering I'd planned to trace the small footprints on the path to their origin. For now they remain Jane or John Doe's, origin unknown.

HONORÉ DE BALLSACK

"You haven't seen any of his photos?" Martina asks, passing me the joint we have been sharing on her fire escape. "What if he's rotten?" Like most of my friends, she is dubious of Randy, whom I have been seeing for a month and whom they have yet to meet. Soon they will love him. Soon they will say he is a certified keeper, a cut of grade-gay beef. For the time being, we have our doubts. Randy is Midwestern and mild-mannered, untattooed, unpierced, unwedded to the color black; he is the kind of person you might describe as unassuming if you have not yet learned that presence exerts itself in manifold ways. Later tonight we are exchanging work for the first time, a dozen of his photos for a one act of mine. "He might be," I say, sucking on the joint until it burns my tongue. "And if so?" Martina raises her eyebrow.

"Bad art isn't a dealbreaker," I say. "Really?" Martina laughs. "Tell that to Kat." "Poor Kat," I say. As we recount the infamous evening—a spoken word at Bottle Shop, Kat caressing the microphone before screeching into it—I drift from the memory and the fire escape and toward Randy, feeling defensive of the criticisms lobbied against him, no matter that they started with me. "People forget the importance of Honoré de Balzac," he'd said to me last night, his face between my thighs. "What?" "Honoring the Ballsack." A grin, a laugh, a lick. Did I love him then, without knowing it? Martina flicks the finished joint off the fire escape, its embers shooting out like fireflies. "I should go," I say. "I need to get wine." She nods, reaching over to tuck my hair behind my ear. "Here's hoping he's the next big thing," she says. "That's what my Jackie deserves. A star for a star, amen."

FROM THIS TIME FORTH I NEVER WILL SPEAK WORD

Randy has found a new mood by the time I return. He is on the couch, laughing into the cordless house phone with his legs tucked beneath him. Joy, once a hallmark characteristic, now seems misplaced on him, as artificial as a neon-green sweater.

"Here he is," Randy says, waving me closer. "I'll put you on speaker."

"Jack?" I recognize Sally's voice from our last call, when she got in touch with me to encourage our visit to Florence, having heard news of Ms. Rourke's passing. I'd been surprised by the distance between her voice on the page—intense, cerebral—and her voice on the phone, which was quilted over with plainspoken kindness. "How are you liking our little town?"

"It's lovely," I say. "I was just down on the beach. You have the most beautiful home."

"You must not have looked too closely at the walls yet." Fran's voice is lower than Sally's, made of more solid substance. "We've been meaning to repaint for longer than I can remember. Execution is not our strong suit."

"You fooled me."

"Then the art is doing its job. Randy's photos are there for the exclusive purpose of distracting from the spackling."

"And the bad beige," Sally adds.

"And the bad beige. Our collection is all smoke and mirrors. It makes you wonder what Peggy Guggenheim might have been hiding. Nail holes? Kandinsky-sized cracks in the wall?"

"A depressed daughter," Randy says.

"Oh, Pegeen!" Sally wails. "I forgot about her."

"Just like Peggy." This is Fran.

"And to think people say art has no practical function," Randy says.

He smiles at the handset, pleased by the laughter coming from Sally and Fran's end. I laugh, too, despite knowing nothing of the Guggenheims.

"We won't keep you longer than necessary," Sally says. "Call if you run into any trouble. And say hello to the neighbors if you see them. They'd be happy to meet you both."

"I did meet one of them," I say. "Claude?"

"Clarence?" Fran asks.

"Right. Clarence. He came over late last night."

Randy puzzles his face.

"Sounds like Clarence," Fran says. "Did he bring brandy?"

"He did. And pretended to be someone else for an hour."

"We should've given you a warning. He's harmless, if eccentric. A surprisingly good actor, too. We saw him in a local production of *Othello* last summer."

"'Demand me nothing: what you know, you know: From this time forth I never will speak word.'" Sally quotes Iago's final line with bravado, then laughs. "He is good, and harmless, and very weird. The same goes for Polly and Paul. They're in the north house. You're guaranteed to see them naked at some point. They lived in a nudist colony for a while."

"A naturist colony," Fran corrects, her tone indicating that they have been corrected on this before. "You will see both bush and tail. They own the bookstore in town."

"I do need something to read," Randy says.

"We've got plenty of books!" It is slight, this plea from Sally, but within it I hear her amassed adoration for Randy. I am reminded of when we were visiting Ohio for the first time and Ms. Rourke tried to prevent us from going out to eat the state's famous Skyline chili by insisting she could make it herself. I thought she might cry when we went anyway.

"No offense, Sal," he says, "but I'm not looking to think so hard."

Again they laugh, again Randy smiles, and again I feel that while I am near their warmth, I am not within it. This time I fail even to smile. I want to be the one bringing Randy the dumb joy currently spread across his face. I built a fire over here. I built it in the corner of our bedroom four months ago, wanting to keep you warm. Why are you turning to other flames?

Sally and Fran give the bookstore's location—Bay Street, the same riverside strip we were on before—suggest a restaurant, then bid us farewell. Randy's glow continues to radiate after he hangs up the phone. "Come here," he says.

I go like a dog, forfeiting my sourness for his affection. "They're sweet."

"You sound surprised."

"I didn't know what to expect. A conversation about Foucault, maybe."

"Those happen at night. Tell me about this mysterious Clarence."

Randy is a rapt audience as I describe the whole scene to him. His focus makes me want to perform—hand movements, vocal impersonations—to spin a yarn of the richest possible material, a modern day Scheherazade, if attention were the sole thing she was after.

"Why did you let him stay?" he eventually asks.

"The brandy," I say, unable to admit the peace I found in the salmon farm, the memoir class, the snowy plovers—evidence, eventually falsified, that settling could be liberating. "I felt like an idiot. You should have seen how let down he looked after I told him about my life."

"I'm sure he wasn't let down. And who cares if he was?"

"I care."

Randy's sighs have a distinct timbre of agony, at least on some subjects. "Oh, Jack," he says. "I wish you lived somewhere else."

"What does that mean?"

"Don't go tense on me." His fingers massage my spine. "Close your eyes and imagine a world where the opinions of others pass by like cotton on the wind. You see them go? Isn't that nice?"

I want to reject this paltry and patronizing effort at consolation. I am immobilized by a second feeling, a stronger feeling, one so desperate for Randy's comforts that what might typically make me gag with sentiment feels medicinal. When I close my eyes, I do see it, sort of. Not a free ego, but cotton floating in the sky like snow.

"You should wake me up next time," Randy says. "I want to see the Clarence show."

"I don't like waking you up. You're happy when you're sleeping."

"What do you mean?" Randy sounds concerned. "You can't see me when I'm sleeping."

"Of course I can see you when you're sleeping."

"Not inside. You can't see inside." He touches his hairline, as if inspecting for a bump. "Right?"

It takes me a moment to realize he means this question seriously. "Of course I can't."

He relaxes. "That's good."

Neither of us reacts when my phone vibrates with a text in my pocket, the screen's light shining through my worn denim. I'm afraid to push and make Randy scamper away, and so I try to sound lighthearted when I ask, "What's happening inside your sleep that's so undercover?"

Randy's laugh jumps out of him like it's been spring-loaded.

"I want to know," I say, poking his ribs. "It must be good. You seem happy as a clam."

Randy continues laughing as he says, "It's terrible. I'm

being served a meal in a pitch-black room. They keep bringing me food and I keep eating it. The food is like a sponge with bones in it. I want to chew carefully but their hands are always at my mouth, pushing more in, so sometimes I have to go fast. And I always end up eating my tongue. I chew too fast and eat my tongue. None of it is good. Nothing is good. Happy as a clam"—he shakes his head—"I wish."

His grin and breathiness are almost as disturbing as the dream.

"That's terrible," I say. "You dream this every night?"

"Every night. And that's not even the worst part. The worst part is what I do after I swallow my tongue. That's what I don't want you to see."

My phone vibrates again, and this time I welcome the getaway. "I should check this. My mom fell off her bike."

"Oh no, is she okay?" His concern returns him to normalcy at a remarkable speed, as if the dream was only ever external to him, a light foundation rubbed right off.

The photo my father sent loads slowly. Bedsheets over the faint suggestion of a body. A hand draped across the waist, pulse oximeter on the pointer finger. Then, more rapidly, an arm, a hospital gown, a neck. She must be okay—why else would he send a picture?—but the final moment of loading is unbearable. I open my mouth to explain, then the rest of the image arrives. My mother smiles with a chipped tooth, her casted arm held high, the thumb up.

"Wow," Randy says. "She looks like a potato chip."

TEARLESSNESS

A week before he met them, Randy asked me to tell him more about my parents. He was holding a frame to the wall while I instructed him on where it needed straightening. I hadn't liked the painting when he pointed it out at the flea market. Now I had to admit the piece worked, the earthy ocher corresponding nicely with the bureau. I couldn't determine if the painting intended to represent something—a field, maybe, or an unbodied dress—and would wonder about this intermittently for three years, at which point we would gift it to our friend Jamel, who believed it depicted the door to a bathroom stall. "And you still want it in your bedroom?" I asked him. "Some of my best nights happen in bathroom stalls," he said, fishing an olive from his drink and popping it in his mouth.

"I've told you about them," I said to Randy. "Higher on the right."

"Only the broad strokes. I want the grease in the hair, the grime beneath the fingernails. I want to know what combination of people could have possibly formed someone like you."

"Am I so awful?"

"Yes. How's this?"

"Good."

He made pencil marks at the top of the frame, then set the painting down. "Come on, Jack. Give me a piece or two."

I flopped onto the bed, exasperated by the task I've struggled with for most of my life: how to explain our neutral relationship, unmarked by the fierce devotions held by half of my friends, nor the bitter resentments held by the other. My dodginess read as avoidant—friends from both camps were always looking to unearth the terrible truth they assumed I'd hidden. The reality was I didn't have much to say.

"Bill is a landscape architect," I said. "He likes to golf, garden, and sing in the church choir, even though he isn't religious. He puts peanut butter and tomato on his bagels. He watches the Jason Bourne movies every year. People like him because he's frictionless. As agreeable as a chess piece, my mother likes to say."

"Agreeable?" Randy joined me on the bed. "That must be an uninherited trait. Have you seen him cry?"

"Cry? Once."

Four years ago, I recounted, I told my parents about my first boyfriend, Thomas. My father patted me twice on the back, then fell toward me, resting his head in my lap and proceeding to weep. I sat motionless, unsure of how to respond. Eventually I put my hand on his head. The silky texture of his hair surprised me. I pulled away immediately.

"I suppose you should tell him about Andrew," my mother said. She stood, brushed nonexistent crumbs from her pants, then added, "Thank you for sharing, Jack. I'm happy for you. A boyfriend is a big deal. I should get to the store before it gets busy." She began to leave, then came back, stroking my father's head and emphasizing, in so doing, how clumsy my own effort at affection had been.

When my father calmed down, he told me about Andrew, the childhood friend who had died of AIDS-related complications when he was twenty-nine. I assumed he was going to relate his friend's death to me, and was preemptively offended by the collapsing of our experiences, the half-informed missives he might give me about safe sex and drugs. Instead, he went on describing Andrew until I could practically see the man standing at the opposite end of the room. Bell-bottoms and an eyebrow ring, crooked incisors and a goatee.

"I haven't thought about him in a long time," my father said. "He was my best friend. And his boyfriend was named Thomas, like yours."

I expected questions about Thomas, my Thomas, then. We were back to the way we always were, the frayed wires of vulnerability patched back to their state of inertia. "I hope we're having chicken for dinner," he said before wandering off.

"Were you jealous?" Randy asked.

"Of Andrew?"

"The whole conversation became about him."

I shrugged. If anything, his rare emotional display, and

my lack of response to him, underscored the distance between us. We did not feel causal to one another in the way I figured most family members do.

"What about Mom?" Randy asked.

"Molly is pricklier," I said. "Devotionally independent. Impressive with ceramics, jewelry, carpentry, violin, and cooking. Not a fan of asking for help, and rarely in need of it. Most of my friends were afraid of her. She can be abrasive. Plus, she's beautiful. I'm sure you could have guessed that." I pointed at my face and fluttered my lashes.

"Never," Randy said, though the joke was undermined by the way his gaze lingered—lovingly, longingly—on where I'd gestured. "Have you seen her cry?"

"What's with this fixation?" I pushed him onto his back and straddled his stomach.

"My parents cried all the time. My mom still does, and I assume the same for my dad."

"But you don't."

"I don't."

Randy had never cried in front of me. The joke was that he'd exhausted his store of tears during his parents' divorce. What would push him over the edge now? We offered guesses back and forth—the death of his family dog, the breaking of his favorite camera lens—except then those things would happen, and he would not cry. "What about when your parents die?" I asked him once. "My mother," he said. "I'll cry for her." He sounded so certain about this, and when he did start crying about Ms. Rourke, which happened not at the time of her dying but on the day of her diagnosis, he'd looked at me as if to say, See?

Like my father, my mother had cried in front of me just

once. Where his tears had been emotional, hers were physical, the result of a saw slip while woodworking. "I need a ride to Huntington," she'd said matter-of-factly, standing at my door with a tear-streaked face and a hand held out before her, dripping blood through a clutched wad of paper towels. She would not face me on the drive to the hospital, possibly worried I would confuse her pain for something other than it was. Emotions were inarticulable to our family. From afar we could see them, then they would enter our house and transform from solid to gas.

"Are you okay?" I asked her when her breathing suddenly sharpened.

"No," she said, turning up the radio.

Randy tugged me down after I'd finished the story. Recently we'd begun aligning our bodies as if to transpose them. My forehead to his forehead, my belly to his belly.

"Do you ever wish it was different?" he asked. "Things with the two of them?"

"I don't think about it very often, so I guess not."

"Not thinking about something isn't always evidence of ambivalence." He tipped me off of him. "For someone who grew up with aliens, you write human emotion well."

"You think?"

"I know," he said. "Or maybe it's your alien outlook that lets you see emotions for what they really are."

"And what are they?"

"Fallen angels."

I laughed. "Fallen angels?"

"Yes. Some want to get good with God, others to get down with the Devil." He yawned. "I'm excited to meet them. Maybe we'll bond over tearlessness."

I looked at the painting behind him. A square of afternoon sunlight had found it, illuminating new strokes within, surprising shades that heightened the aesthetic appeal while further obfuscating the subject—blues and golds, a slash of green.

"You were right," I said.

"Of course I was right," Randy replied, not clarifying what he might have been right about. He got up from the bed and pulled off his shirt. "What should I wear tonight?"

"Blue." I was staring at his chest, waiting to see if his nipples would harden. The room was cool enough. In a week he would mock me for my Freudian fixation. In a week I would spray him with Windex. Today he looked where I looked, then teased each nipple with a hand, knowing I loved them but not knowing precisely why. I hadn't told him that it was in their sensitivity, how they served as keys to undoing his composure when I had them in my mouth.

"Pervert," he said, the word like any endearment, only better.

Honey, bunny, baby, mine.

BRUISER

We drive to town with the windows down, Randy's hair flying freely around his face. A loose strand floats in front of me before getting sucked out of my window. I wish I'd grabbed it. I wish, sometimes, I grabbed every hair that's ever come loose from Randy's body.

The bookstore is beside a hair salon called U R Worth It. A wind chime made of sea glass hangs like a dead fish before the entrance. Randy stands beneath the chime, then reaches for it. "Where did the breeze go?" he asks, knocking two polished shards together.

"It's taking the afternoon off. Big day tomorrow."

"What's tomorrow?"

"The day after today."

Randy looks perplexed, then, noticing the sign for the

bookstore, delighted. "Books 'n' Bears. I wonder if all the booksellers are going to be beefcakes."

The store's interior is quaint and grandmotherly, a surplus of teddy bears scattered through the stacks, including one as large as the woman behind the counter. She makes a noise of acknowledgment upon our entrance without looking up from the sock she is knitting. Her white hair falls in a braid to her lap, where it coils around itself, and, apart from her Bluetooth headset, she looks dressed for colonial times.

"Afternoon," Randy says. "Are you Polly?"

The woman lets out a single, barking laugh. "Do I look like a fifty-three-year-old bombshell to you?" Her eyes snap up.

"I guess not."

"Guess not? You sure know how to make a lady feel special."

He begins to apologize but she waves him down.

"Relax. I know my worth. Polly and Paul are almost never here. They're long-distance overseers. Kind of like my first boyfriend, who tried ruining my life all the way from Texas."

"I see," Randy says. "We're guests of Sally and Fran. They recommended we stop by. I can see why." He looks around, perhaps for a specific detail to compliment.

"I can't. This place gives me the creeps. Too many eyes made out of marbles." She turns to the largest bear and shakes her head. "I'd blindfold them if I could."

The bears, which had not bothered me, gain a sudden malevolence. The feeling I have staring at the big one is both familiar and unplaceable, which makes it all the more disconcerting.

"I think they're cute," Randy says.

"How nice. You know, Sally and Fran only ever come in to whisper about the poetry selection, so I'm not sure what lie they're selling." She pinches her face into a terrible expression. "No Clifton? No Celan? What savagery, Sally! What debasement!"

"They had no complaints about the poetry when we talked," Randy says. "I'm Randy. This is my husband, Jack."

"I'm Lisa. You look familiar, Randy. I can't say why." The knitted sock has finally dropped from her hands, joining the braid in her lap.

"I visited a few years ago. You may have seen me walking around."

"That's not it."

"He's a photographer," I say, expediting the revelation I suspect she is headed toward. "You've probably seen him in *Artforum*, or *The New Yorker*, or *The Atlantic*."

"I don't read that crap."

"Maybe you saw the documentary he was a part of last year, or the Whitney show. They kept that up for a long time."

I can hear myself, can hear the hostility of my tone, a hard grind on the ears. Randy is clearly uncomfortable with my relentless pursuit and Lisa's relentless refusal—with each suggestion she shakes her head hard enough to make her earrings swing—and my compassion for his discomfort is not yet outweighed by my distaste for it. He has been everywhere. Is it really so hard to be a public figure? Yes, but knowing that and believing it are different, and while I've known it for years, I haven't believed it for longer. What is more infuriating than a self-conscious star? A self-loving one, I suppose.

"I'm not thinking of some article or interview," Lisa says. "I'm thinking of a movie, and not some dried up documentary. A real one. Your head was shaved and you had a beard. In one scene you dance in a red room with a sexy robot."

"You're thinking of Oscar Isaac," I say, the answer coming suddenly to me. "*Ex Machina*. He's in that movie. Randy is not."

"Oscar Isaac." Lisa pronounces the name skeptically, then says it again with more certainty. "He's the one. Now that's who I'd like to come through my door."

"You and me both," Randy says. "Can you point me to the mysteries?"

"What's with the world and mysteries?" she asks. Something about the question makes her face undergo a transformation, the door she's held shut to us abruptly falling open to reveal a frightened person inside. For several moments she's doe-eyed and open-mouthed, and then she blinks herself back to composure.

"Near the back," she says, picking up her sock. "Shelby can help if you need."

At the mention of Shelby's name, I look to the back of the store, recognizing the other girl from the café, her blond hair a jolt of light in the dim room. She is kneeling near a shelf of books and trying to jam a large hardcover in. Walking toward her, I try to decode the arrangement of books, finding no genre indicators on the towering shelves. By the time I reach her, I've spotted only one piece of paper: *Very Cheap Westerns*, it reads.

"You may need to give it a kick," I say.

"Kick a book? You're not some kind of fascist, are you?" She leaves the book sticking an inch outward.

"That depends on the book."

"*Don Quixote.* Thick as a brick, and for what? A man to fight windmills? It's on my short list of worst books to shelve. Second only to Dumas. Maybe I should be kicking them after all. It's not like the authors are around to stop me." She pretends to wind up her foot. "Who's the plus-one? Your hubby?"

Randy has stopped midway between the front desk and where we stand, distracted by an oversized art book. When he notices us looking at him, he waves.

"My hubby."

"Carolina told me he was a hunk, but I didn't buy it. Now I see. How was the pizza?"

"Greasy."

"We eat leftover slices for lunch six days out of the week."

"Good life."

"It's more about saving. Carolina and I live to budget. Do you know what the average American spends on food every week?"

"I don't."

"Me neither. I assume it's a lot." She slumps against the shelf. "Are you rich?"

"Rich?" My automatic position is one of refusal, given the many years I spent broke. "I guess technically, yes."

"What does that mean?"

"It's not my money."

"Well played. I'm looking to find a Daddy Warbucks for myself. Some people think that's anti-feminist. I don't. Who says independence needs to come through work? I want to do things I love without needing to worry about paychecks. Is that what you do?"

"It's what I'm trying to do."

"You should try harder. I don't get why you're so sad."

"Sad?"

She looks at me like I've asked a stupid question, maybe the stupidest of all time. "The sadness is on you like a tick, my friend. You know you're actually not supposed to burn them off like everyone says. Anyway, your sadness is vociferous."

"Good word."

"The SAT gave me one thing."

Though embarrassed by Shelby's read of my emotional state, I am also validated by it, as when you go to the doctor with a mysterious set of ailments and leave with a diagnosis.

"There are plenty of reasons," I say.

"Name one."

Randy arrives behind me.

"Randy, this is Shelby," I say. "She works at the coffee shop with the girl who delivered our pizza last night."

Shelby salutes him. "We prefer to be referred to as women. It's a pleasure, Randy. Your husband was just beginning to enumerate for me the reasons why he is so sad."

"Oh?" Randy turns toward me. He looks me up and down, scanning for this sadness. His expression remains doubtful, and this frustrates me, tempting me to continue my list, to prove that my reasons for sadness are plentiful and valid. Then Randy pats my head and says, "It's his hair. A recession unlike any this country has ever seen."

"You ass," I say over Shelby's laughter. "That is one reason I'm sad. There are others."

I wait for either of them to ask me to elaborate. When they don't, I consider offering answers unprompted, except then Randy is touching my side—a touch he always does when he makes a joke at my expense—and Shelby is verifying that the mystery section is what he is after. In an instant they are beyond me and my problems, heading for the back row of books.

"What kind of mysteries do you like?" Shelby asks. "Crime procedurals? Capers? Or how about the cozy mystery? Carolina and I are obsessed with the titles in this series." She points to a row of books by Spencer Quinn. *Heart of Barkness. Paw and Order. The Sound and the Furry.* "We've considered getting *Of Mutts and Men* as a friendship tattoo. Thoughts?"

"Give it more thought," I say.

The two of us fall silent, made aware of the intensity of Randy's focus. Facing the wall of spines, he has withdrawn from the world, scanning the shelf as if reading for a coded message there.

"Do you want a recommendation?" Shelby asks.

He doesn't answer. I shrug when Shelby glances at me. Overhead, a ceiling fan revolves at a purposeless speed, a pair of flies weaving in and out of their rotation.

"Here," Randy eventually says, bending low and freeing a paperback from the shelf. The book is nondescript, a blue cover with *Bruiser* embossed on the cover.

"What is it?" I ask.

Randy opens to the first page, where the title is printed in a Gothic font. He touches the ink as if it might still be wet. "This is what I want."

"What is it?" I repeat, looking at Shelby to see if she might know. She is on her phone, fingers pecking against the screen.

"It's a book I've been wanting to read forever," Randy says. "A book I've wanted to read for longer than Shelby's been alive, probably. The author died on February 6, 1954, after a telephone pole fell in his swimming pool." He brings the book to his face, smells it, then walks away.

"What a way to go," Shelby says. "Do you like this?" She turns the phone toward me. On it, two arms are held together. Each has a tattoo of half a wishbone; pressed together, the bone is meant to look unbroken.

"It's a little on the nose."

She takes the phone back. "That's what I told Carolina. She claims nothing is original, so why bother pretending? What do you say? Are all of these books telling the same ten stories?"

"I used to think that. Then I thought the opposite."

"And now?"

"Now I don't really care."

"I'll add that to the list," she says.

"The list?"

"Of reasons you're sad." The way she looks at me then is with actual sympathy, something I want to run from as much as I want to hold on to it. She nods behind me. "You better hurry. You're about to get left in the dust."

Randy is walking out the door, *Bruiser* in hand. The eyes of the bears are on me again as I follow after him, and this time their familiarity becomes clear. Years ago, Randy and I went to an art installation that featured a household of mannequins. The artist had filled each room of a foreclosed house with the furnishings of their childhood home. The transplant was total, down to a miniature spoon propped against a sugar bowl, yet no sentimental quality had carried over with them. Perhaps, Randy suggested, it was the naked mannequins who blocked it. One stood in the kitchen, its hands submerged in the sink's soapy water; one lay in a bed upstairs, a Playboy magazine beside it and its hand angled over its smooth crotch. Strangely, each new mannequin felt more real than the last, as if they were sapping the objects around them of their life. By the time we reached the basement, the mannequin hanging by a noose from the rafters may as well have been human for the way it made me recoil, making me race back upstairs. *Family Life*, the installation was called.

The mannequins did not have eyes like the bears, but that didn't stop them from looking at me with the same scrutiny.

Lisa is talking to someone on her Bluetooth. "You won't believe who just came into the store," she says. "Yes, he's famous." She pauses. "Yes, he's handsome." Her wave, responding to mine, is more of a shoo. "Oscar!" she announces. "Oscar Isaacson!"

DEATH IS NOT A CONCRETE WALL

From behind, I can't determine if Randy is upset. His abrupt departure suggests so, plus the way he barrels down Bay Street like a man on the run. I hustle to catch up, calling out when I reach the hem of his shadow. "Can we slow down? Your legs are longer than mine."

He is not upset. Turning back, he looks exhilarated. "It's nice being chased," he says. "My parents were both so short. They saved the leg for me."

"Where are you hurrying to?"

"Abigail's boat," he says. "Promise you'll be nice."

My pace slows at Abigail's name, then further at this remark. "When am I not nice?"

"Pretty often."

"Pretty often?"

Randy steps closer, smiling, then lightly flicks my ear. "Feel these ears, Jack. They're red as beets. Hot ears don't lie."

"I'm nice to you."

"Usually."

"Usually? Almost always."

Randy puts his hands on my cheeks. "Almost," he says.

I fall behind as we pass by a store selling salt water taffy and orca-shaped driftwood, then a boutique with sheer gowns hanging in its window. When I spot the gallery with the painting of our apartment building, I approach its window eagerly, as if the painting might tell me something. Looking again, however, I see that it isn't our apartment at all, but a block of honeycomb. I lean closer, willing it to transform, and then the gallery owner—hidden behind a cement pillar—yells out, "Back it up! You're smudging my view."

At the end of the street, vendors fill the grass again. I watch Randy accept a mango slice, thank the seller, then slip the dripping fruit into his pocket as he carries forward. The giddiness in his step is bordering on ridiculous, as if he might soon start skipping.

I wander grumpily beneath the seagulls, who swoop and squawk in the air overhead, my comrades in contempt. A man sings Creed to a circle of veterans while a group of friends trade barbs in mock British accents. The sonic pair is enough to make me want to stuff my ears with clay. Then, beneath their cacophony, I hear a mother explaining menopause to her children. "That's why I sometimes need to sit," she says from her spot on the grass.

"Is that why you don't eat fish?" her daughter asks.

"That's because I'm a vegetarian."

"I think I'm in menopause," her son says. His voice is a perfect distillation of puberty, brassy and haphazard as an elementary school's horn section. It is a great line, something Fabio of this morning's imagined play might say. The thought takes me back to the diner, to the birthday party, where Fabio is lamenting his twenty-six years.

I'm menopausal, he says, fanning himself with a laminated menu. *Another barren boy. You'll lay my soul to rest, won't you?*

The friend beside him bows her head. Who is she? Sue Ellen. Chic and austere, a chemically manufactured blond, paler than marble, glassy as a pool at dusk. She begins her eulogy. *Fabio: tolerated friend, toxic lover, abandoned son. Like champagne, he bubbled briefly. He is survived by his friends, Sue Ellen, Julian, and Ray, ranked here in order of attractiveness.*

No need to degrade yourself like that, Ellie! Fabio says, patting Sue Ellen's head. *You're at least a four. If I were straight, maybe even a four point five.*

She pulls away from him, spilling her water across the table. *If I'm a four, you're not even numerical. Look what you did. You got your birthday all wet.*

The four watch the water spread. Who are the others? Ray goes as if to grab a napkin, picking up a syrup-soaked strawberry from Sue Ellen's plate instead. *I'm the ugliest, aren't I?* he says, throwing the strawberry into his mouth.

You're not ugly, Fabio says. *You're a hippie.*

A hippie without a cause, Sue Ellen adds.

I'll get it, the last one, Julian, says, pulling the napkin from his lap and dabbing it on the table. It is such a feeble gesture, and its meekness makes me love him. Who is he, this last-to-arrive, cleaning up the mess of his friend's making? He's only just entered the play and already I know he is its real center, a nobody protagonist whose identity is forever being flayed by his own compliance. Is it here that the earthquake begins? And why does the earthquake matter? And what am I doing, writing plays in my head again?

I return to the boardwalk, where a dog lopes toward me, dropping a ball at my feet. Its adoring face and wagging tail are nearly enough to break me. Almost always, Randy had said. Almost. I kneel down and scratch the dog's ears, making its back paw thump. Maybe we love them because they are easy to please in a way so few things are. When the dog turns from me, called by its owner, I have to keep myself from restraining it.

Below me floats the *Sea la Vie*. A buoy designed to look like a submarine sandwich is slung over its side and a Yale sweatshirt is slung over its steering wheel. Randy and Abigail are not on the dock where they were yesterday. There's a man bashing a tuna's head with a hammer and two women feeding each other crab chowder with chopsticks. "Shark!" a boy squeals from the prow of a yacht. His family does not even glance at the water, so obvious is his lying. Even from afar I can tell he is pointing at a clump of trash.

Eventually I see Abigail standing on the stern of the boat she retreated to yesterday. Hands on hips, she looks like the heroine in a seafaring adventure, proudly overseeing Randy's ungraceful boarding. Neither look to see if I might be following and, by the time I navigate the marina's maze, they are already belowdecks.

The boat sways beneath my weight when I get myself on it. The dipping motion, paired with the deck flooring painted to look like a chessboard, make my stomach tighten.

"Will you hurry?" Abigail calls from the cabin.

The adult in me prevents me from calling out something about niceness, and her clear deficit. The steps to the belly of the boat are narrow and numerous. Where I expected three or four, there must be at least fifteen. This interior strikes me as incommensurate with the exterior, a ratio akin to an iceberg's insofar as what is above the water line proves to be nothing at all.

"Hello, Jack," Abigail says from an oversized beanbag. "How's your giant?"

She and Randy face one another in beanbags that rest in a sea of loose packing peanuts. The walls and ceiling are overlaid with thousands of bottle caps. Each catches candlelight—there are a dozen tapered candles lit, the room's only source of illumination—and the effect is of steady movement, like confetti drifting down from midnight sky.

"Nice armoring," I say, tapping a cap with my finger. "Did you rob a recycling center?"

"I did."

"Really?"

Abigail shakes her head, exasperated. "Adults ask all the wrong questions. Do you have any idea how much recycling ends up in landfills? God help you if you're plastic. If you think you are helping by putting your water bottles in one of those blue bins, think again. Different chutes to the same graveyard. Have you ever been?"

"To a landfill? No."

"After you see a landfill, you don't stop seeing it. Landfills aren't just the fenced-off mountains of waste you see on TV. They're wherever humanity has put its foot. I can hardly stomach living here in Florence. I might die if I had to walk through Portland. Human refuse keeps me awake at night."

Randy is not facing me, so I cannot see his expression while he nods at Abigail. I'm sure it is full of reverence.

"Your commitment is impressive," I say, the packing peanuts squelching beneath my shoes. "Very inspiring. We'd be lucky if more of the world saw things like you."

"All I'm doing is making a home for things we decided should be both immortal and disposable. Imagine being created to live forever, only to be used for a day. How awful. I could cry for what we call 'single-use.' I have before."

"Right."

"Would you like to take a seat? There's room for all four of us."

Several sculpture-like objects materialize from the shadows then—three to four feet tall, each built from a mélange of recyclables—but I don't sense she is referring to them. The honeyed scent of the candles becomes sickly another step deeper. Joined with the undulations of the water, the smell reignites my nausea. I hurry to Randy's beanbag, where he shields the tape recorder and baggie of ash in his lap as if they were baby birds. Of course. We were never three, just as Randy and I are never two.

"We were about to listen to Randy's tape," Abigail says. "It's helpful to have an experienced listener with you. No offense, Jack. You don't seem like someone who has spent much time with the dead. What is death to you? A broken circuit? A concrete wall?"

"I don't know. No one knows what death is." As I speak,

Randy's grip on the recorder tightens. "Right?" I try to sound less defensive. "No one can say for sure."

"Maybe not," Abigail says. "But I do know that death is not a concrete wall."

"I agree. Death is immaterial."

"Well, I'm not sure about that. Let's let bygones be bygones. I don't want to distract from the process with more shots in the dark. Randy, are you ready?"

"Will you tell me how it happened again?" he asks. "With Dallas?"

"The whole thing?"

"The whole thing."

A flicker of impatience crosses her eyes, but then her gaze softens. "Of course I can do that," she says, adjusting her posture and taking on the kind of position that is difficult to stage direct but that good actors naturally assume before giving play-defining monologues.

She first met Dallas at a cocktail party hosted by Mr. Steve. How to best describe that man? Walking barnacle, disgraced sea captain, pothead. Always smoking spliffs, playing with his earlobes, hosting backyard events for the town drunks to come and get smashed. "Cocktail party is a misnomer," Abigail says. "I knew that back then, and I was twelve. It's like calling a rag a caftan. A baby could see that. I was a baby and I could see that. People piss in the yard until the whole thing gets soggy. Bottles roll down the slope of the lawn and into the lake, which continues lapping beautifully in spite of this injustice. It's hideous. Cocktail party my ass."

Mr. Steve's property stands on the shore of Siltcoos Lake. When dragged by her parents to these events, Abigail would spend her time wading in the shallows, intermittently tossing beer bottles back to shore and fixating her attention on the lake's rippled surface until the party abstracted behind her. The night she met Dallas, the water was milky with moonlight. She was on the verge of losing herself in it when a cattail knocked against her face.

"I didn't mean to do that," the boy standing beside her said. "I only wanted you to see it. Don't you think it looks like a corndog?"

In spite of his boyish dishevelment—bedhead and a spit-soaked shirt collar, a bad habit from babyhood he couldn't and wouldn't have the chance to break—something about his bearing made Abigail remember a painting she'd seen on a field trip, a painting she'd thought of as beautiful, of another boy in another place at another time, a painting she could not and is still unable to recall in more specific detail but that opened her toward him.

"You shouldn't pluck living things," she said.

"I found it floating by the dock, probably cut by a propeller. I'm giving it a second chance to be something tasty." He grinned, pretended to bite the cattail, then laid it in the water.

"Now it looks like poop," Abigail said. "I liked it more as a corndog."

Dallas laughed hard, smacking his hip with a muted whack. He retrieved the cattail and held it below his chin. "A corndog," he asked, "or a microphone?" Then he sang a melody so lovely Abigail had to turn away in order to endure it. Did we know how that felt? Painful beauty? "I haven't experienced it like that since," she says. "I hope I never will."

Their solitude was broken by the arrival of Mr. Steve. The man stood at the water's edge with a joint hanging from his lip. Abigail could smell him from where they stood, a skunk on fire. Whereas she was typically repulsed by the man, she had a moment—inspired, she was sure, by Dallas's song—of sympathy for him, or if not sympathy then genuine curiosity. As his eyes rolled and his body swayed, she wondered where it was they went, the die-hard drunks, when the alcohol took charge. From the outside it looked like an ugly place, but maybe the interior was not. Maybe that was why her parents pursued it so ceaselessly, night after night. A blacked-out space of private rapture, cavernous and calm.

This spell ended when Mr. Steve unfastened his belt to pee in the water.

"Dallas was trying to pull me up the shore," Abigail explains. "I couldn't stop myself from looking at the thing in Mr. Steve's hand. It was the worst shade of white. I don't know why I felt like I had to look at it. Or actually I do. I just don't know if it makes much sense."

Her rationale had to do with innocence. In life it seemed you had two options: to cast off your innocence or to have it wrenched from you. Why not opt for the former? And so she let herself be pulled away by Dallas only after watching Mr. Steve's penis dribble out all of its toxic urine. "I waited for the sensation of un-innocence to arrive while Dallas led me to the neighbor's. It didn't come. I'd lost my innocence years prior, probably when I watched my father put out his cigarette in that tide pool. I still felt depressed, something Dallas saw right away. After opening the back door of the vacation home with a key from under the mat, he offered me a candy bar. When I refused, he offered to sing."

This marked the first of many nights to come. While their parents chased oblivion, Dallas and Abigail entered the neighboring house, where he would sing to her. Her favorite songs were the ones he improvised, the wordless melodies that moved smokily through the air. They began to worry about where they would go when the weather warmed, knowing the vacationers would be arriving sometime in June. It didn't end up mattering. On the last day of May, Dallas and his mom were on their way to the grocery store when a truck crashed into them. "The driver wasn't drunk, just suicidal. And Dallas's mom wasn't drunk, either, for whatever that's worth. Dallas was still holding the magazine he was reading when they pulled him out of the wreck. No one can tell me what magazine it was, only that he was holding it."

Abigail leans back with a mystified expression on her face. She attempts to regain her grasp on the narrative thread, then loses it. What clouds her cheeks is something I know well: the disbelief of having grief plunge in so painfully, even after the hundredth time. When she leans forward, I think she might get sick on the packing peanuts. Instead she grabs the recorder from Randy's hand. "Dallas found his way back to me on here. I sang and he sang back. There's not much more to it than that, so why don't we listen to your tape now?"

She attempts a smile and the motion knocks her further askew. She looks concussed, finally her age, which I now see must be around fourteen.

"You can cry," Randy says.

"I know I can." Her tone is harsh in a reflexive way. "Why can't anyone tell me what magazine he was reading?" She asks this and then she drops her face into Randy's outstretched hands, where she does cry.

The desire to disappear is a strong one. I am the itch in the room, the scratch on their tenderness. Unworthy, certainly, of being an audience to Abigail's tragedy. That I did any comparing between us fills my chest with mortified guilt, which threatens to erupt in a cough. She was a baby. She is a baby. I try to put on a compassionate face, or at least an approximation of one, in case one of them looks at me.

They don't. Eventually Abigail sits straight, releasing Randy's hands to dry her face on her sleeves. "I haven't cried this much since I read the IPCC's latest climate report," she says before smacking her cheeks. "Should we get on with it?"

"Let's wait," Randy says.

"What's wrong? I cry for my dead friend and suddenly you treat me like a flower petal? Don't do me like that, Randy." She can't hide the smile beneath her frown.

"Who says I'm doing this for you? I'm tired of this smelly boat. I'm tired of your plastic creatures. You live in a recyclable nightmare."

Abigail grins. "It's an honor to be recognized in this way. Ready to go, Jack? You can let the blood back into your face."

I laugh, try to stammer out a response, then give up. She leads us out of the cabin. How Orpheus ever looked back when he had so much promising daylight ahead is an utter mystery to me. I nearly cry out in relief when we meet fresh air.

"Come back soon," Abigail says. "I promise to not be so

blubbery." She turns to me. "You've got a night's worth of sleep in your eye."

She leaves before I can respond, disappearing down the stairs. The doors she shuts over herself remind me of the basement's storm cellar. The checkered floor reminds me of the Francesca Woodman photograph in the dining room. There is no tortoise here, no woman with a white orb held before her. There is, however, a strong weather of uncertainty. Randy is down on the dock, shielding his eyes to look at the mass of trash out in the water.

"I thought that was a body," he says once I join him.

A dark patch stains his pants pocket.

"Hold still," I say, reaching in and removing the mango. Although lint is stuck to it, the slice is still slippery, like a cut of raw chicken. "Gross." I toss the mango off the dock.

"Gross."

"It was sweet, what you did in there."

"Sweet as a mango?"

"Sweet as a mango. You've always been the nicest one."

LIST OF FIRSTS

What compels me to start it? To keep it going? To stop? I'm not one for keepsakes, not a hoarder of mementos, yet after my first date with Randy, I return to my apartment and write, *First date (6/12/2007)* in my notebook. A draft lifts the page, then settles it. Outside, two women argue over the durability of a tote bag. I almost cross out the note. The words, looked down on just a moment later, exude sentimentality. It is why I am suspicious of the diaristic mode in general: Does anyone really write for themselves alone, or is every diarist secretly appealing to their posthumous audience? What else accounts for the stylistic flair, the intellectual posturing, the general verve? I keep the note. Later, I add to it. *First kiss (6/17/2007; cherry lip balm). First handjob (6/21/2007; rocket). First handhold (6/30/2007; callousless).* I like the constraint, which lessens my embarrassment with its minimalism without losing the memories' luster. With a few words I am drawn back to wherever we were. *Crawfish. Sazerac. Deep (deep) end. Aloe lube. Nail file. Sing-along. Phantom.* Here might be proof that you can write for yourself. The stranger sees *First sleepover (6/29/2007; hotdogging)* and knows nothing. I see the same entry a week, month, or year later, and am again being rolled onto my stomach, again feeling Randy's weight on me, again feeling him grind his erection into the valley of my ass. "Do you want to fuck me?" I say. "Not tonight. Tonight all I want is to dog your bun." What came first, the laugh or the moan? *First swallow (7/19/2007; fire hose). First road trip (8/22/2007; Outer Banks). First fight (8/24/2007; motel sheets).* When did I stop, and why? Possibly when I lost interest. Possibly when I bought a new notebook. Possibly when we'd spent enough time together that the firsts became less meaningful than the seconds, thirds, and fourths.

THE MR. ROURKES

Randy's phone rings once we are back from town and settled at the kitchen table, where I am working on the crossword and he is examining *Bruiser.* He is not reading the novel, only turning it over in his hands and flipping through the pages. Absentmindedly I am plotting what I might say to him about this—a joke about books starting on page one, a question about the novel's significance. For now it is nice to be sitting quietly, focused on our own projects while our legs are overlapped beneath us. The phone breaks our peace.

"Hello?" a breathless voice asks as soon as Randy accepts the call. "Is this Mr. Rourke? Mr. Randy Rourke?"

"Yes, speaking."

"I'm sorry, Mr. Rourke. Can you repeat exactly what you just said?"

"Yes, speaking?"

"You'll have to pardon my rudeness, sir, but I do believe I spoke with a different person when we last talked. This is Allen from Portland International. I called two days ago in reference to your lost-but-soon-to-be-found bag."

"Jack," Randy says. "You spoke to Jack. My husband. He's right here." Randy holds the phone toward me.

"Hi," I say. "This is Jack."

"That's the voice I heard. You know it is illegal to pass yourself off as someone else, particularly in matters as important as this? Regardless, I'm calling with good news about your bag. The contents have not been dispersed nor destroyed, in spite of our standard policies. The reason for this extension has to do with a clerical mistake on our end."

"We asked about the bag yesterday," I say. "They didn't have it."

"That's where the clerical error comes in, Mr. Rourke and Mr. Jack. Or should I say Mr. and Mr. Rourke. The Mr. Rourkes." He pauses to catch his breath. Between his words lies a silence impossible to find within an airport. Where is the shuffling of feet, the murmuring of voices, the dull drone of engines?

"We were told you were let go," I say.

"Let go? I wasn't let go, Mr. Jack. Or I guess I was let go for fourteen hours. That's how long it took for the authorities to determine that the untoward activity happening on my server was in fact happening in my next-door neighbor's apartment. We share Wi-Fi. You think you know a guy, and then you don't know that guy."

Randy picks up the pen and pulls the newspaper toward

him. I think he might write a note to me in the margin, then watch as he fills in the answer for eight down: *CROATIA*.

"Are you there, Mr. Rourkes? My hand is on your bag right now. R-A-N-D-Y R-O-U-R-K-E. I'm tracing the letters. I'm thinking of your faces upon being reunited with whatever you've been missing. It's so special to see. Hundreds of people I've brought back to their possessions. Did I tell you I've been employee of the month more often than not? Do you really think they would fire someone like me?"

"Sunday," Randy says. "We fly out Sunday. We can get the bag then."

"I'm afraid that won't do, Mr. Randy Rourke. A significant reason the bag still exists at all is that I've chosen to take matters into my own hands. It's this kind of above-and-beyond care that has led to my monthly badge."

The silence thickens in the gaps between his words, becoming gelatinous, radioactive. I feel it in my body in the way I feel sirens: an alarming tickle in the nerves. Because Allen sounds nowhere, he could be anywhere.

"Well, what do you suggest?" I ask.

"I thought I might bring you the bag, Mr. Jack and Mr. Randy. I thought I might bring it to wherever you are."

"No," I say. "Thank you, but no."

Allen clucks his tongue. "It's always struck me as a shame how rarely people know what they want." Finally, at last, a sound from his end of the line. The meow of a cat. It opens his life—Allen in an apartment, Allen at a foldout table, Allen rubbing the side of a tabby with his sockless foot—and I want at once to be rid of the image. When Allen says, "Don't worry, Count Countess, kibble is coming," I hang up the phone.

"That man needs help," I say, kneading my jaw unclenched.

"With what?"

"Were you not just on the phone? He took your bag home. That's insane. You really have no idea where it's from?"

"None."

"Are you curious?"

"It hasn't hurt me so far."

"Not that you know. Maybe there's a hundred dollars in there. A thousand."

Randy picks up *Bruiser.* "Maybe." When he stands, his shirtfront is caught in his waistband. I can see the outline of the tape recorder in his jeans. I don't think of Ms. Rourke, seeing the recorder. I see Abigail standing on Mr. Steve's shoreline, alone, and the image brings the weight of her story down like a wet duvet.

"I could use some air," I say. "Will you walk with me?"

Randy glances toward the office. How did Ms. Rourke feel about milk? How did she feel about bookstores? How did she feel about sailboats, or checkered floors, or dead children?

"Yes," he says.

"Yes?"

"You could use some air. I could use some light."

"Really?"

He points to his face. "Have you seen me? I'm whiter than white."

"Whiter than white, prettier than pretty. A face to launch at least one or two ships."

Randy kicks my leg, then kisses me. "You taste like turkey," he says.

"You taste like mustard."

"Another?"

We kiss again. "You're thinking the same thing I'm thinking," Randy says. We are bent forward, close enough that Randy's blinking tickles my cheek. "I can taste it. We're having the exact same thought."

"Is that right?" I put my foot on his. Hobbit feet, he calls them, for their furriness. The only ones I've liked in my mouth. "What are we thinking?"

"We're thinking about Dallas's voice, and how amazing it must be if it made someone like Abigail go soft. I'm glad he's still singing at the end of things."

I close my eyes disappointedly, then realize he is right, at least on some level. I was thinking about Abigail, and Dallas's voice by proxy. Plus, I want him to be able to taste my thinking. "Yes," I say. "Exactly."

Randy looks unsure when I open my eyes. It is a hopeful uncertainty, the kind of expression he makes when confronted with a beguiling piece of art. "Try me," he says. "Taste for what I'm thinking now."

His tongue fills my mouth. It is almost funny, the way he pushes himself so fully in, then almost arousing. As I begin to move my tongue over his, the task sheds all frivolousness. I focus on each detectable flavor—the mustard and poppy seeds, the turkey and, somewhere behind it, the coffee—waiting for them to part, allowing a breach into Randy's consciousness. The more I suck, the more the flavors wash together and dilute. Soon, it does not even feel like I have Randy's tongue in my mouth, but a disembodied piece of flesh.

I let go, or Randy pulls back.

"Let's walk," he says. "I haven't touched the ocean yet."

"I didn't get to guess."

"It's not about guessing." His smile is sad, but then he takes the recorder from his pocket, places it on *Bruiser*, and leaves both behind. I try to hide my surprise at this, and my excitement, as I follow him to the door.

"You're wrong, by the way," Randy says once I reach him.

"About what?"

"Four across. *Villette* was Brontë's 1853 novel, not *Jane Eyre*."

I make a face at him. He is right, like always. Right about names, right about dates, right about the biography of this artist or that one. And it is not just trivia he knows, either. Randy can talk to a friend about their worrisome drug use, set boundaries with a landlord, and be a consistently decent person in an indecent world. It was one of the first things I described to my friends about him, his essential goodness, and while we'd all pretended to gag, we knew it was a stroke of fortune for me to have found him.

"Congratulations," I say. "Your loner youth wins again."

He smiles, opening the door to a perfect afternoon. Windless, sunny, and hushed. In the distance I hear the whine of an ATV, perhaps the same rider who flipped me off yesterday. It means nothing to me, and less still when Randy puts his hand on my ass. "I'm glad you tried," he says, guiding me into the bright light.

FORLORN PANTS, FORLORN SELVES

The beach is a different place than it was this morning. Gone is the fog, the chill, the sheen of dew. Gone are the troublesome footprints, mucked by wind and other feet. I am happy to leave it all behind, to roughhouse with Randy beneath a warmer sun and bluer sky. We take off our shoes so the cold water can meet our ankles; we take off our shirts so the sun can alight on our skin. Randy's silver streaks extend to his chest hair, threading through the black like bursts of lightning in the night sky. I used to think it would be all bad, aging. Then I saw changes like this and realized how wrong I was.

For the next hour we wander. I tell Randy about how, as a kid, I made my mother carry me from the water back to our towels to avoid getting sand stuck to my skin—a task she was willing to indulge only twice per beach visit. He tells me about the time his father drove him to Lake Erie and told him it was the Atlantic Ocean. “Hardly his worst lie,” he adds.

We trip each other, kick up foam, stand in the surf until we are sunken to our shins in freezing sand. At one point, Randy gazes at my midriff longingly. “I wish you wore Speedos.”

“That makes one person on the whole West Coast.”

He laughs, his limbs loose. Randy’s gait always transforms into a teenage slouch when we riff off of one another. “How about the East Coast?” he asks.

“Same situation. Worse, possibly.”

“Midwest?”

“I’ll give you that. There’s probably a small group of Midwesterners who would enjoy the view of my body stuffed into a Speedo. You can be their leader.”

“You’re right. Only for my boorish upbringing do I find you irresistible.”

I wave him away, though I would attach myself to an IV of his attention if I could. His compliments have eternal heat. When the men on Scruff praise me, the glow is a flint spark, only amounting to anything in profusion. Randy’s admiration is molten in quantities large and small.

“Why are you looking at me like that?” he asks, narrowing his eyes.

“Because I love you. And I love when you do that with your hand.”

His hand is on his belly, a habit developed when his dad told him too much laughing would make his stomach fall out. “I’m glad you find me so amusing,” he says.

Amusing isn't the word, I think, watching Randy as he prods a dead crab with his toe, points to an osprey in the sky, and brings me a shell that time has smoothed down before making me kiss it. *Exhilarating* might be better.

"Let's go in," Randy says when we reach a tidal river that splits the shore.

"What about your pants?"

"The thing about pants, Jack, is they're made to come off." He undoes his belt, button, and zipper. He is wearing the same black briefs I am, bought in a jumbo pack at some point down the line. "Coming?" he asks as he steps down the riverbank.

Would I go anywhere Randy asked me? I've asked myself this question many times. The answer hasn't changed, but it has stopped surprising me. Where before I wouldn't follow a partner three blocks astray from where I was already headed, with Randy I would go all the way to Harlem for a sandwich, to Ohio for a holiday, to hell—or halfway—for a mother.

He stands in the middle of the river, the water midway up his thighs. The cold doesn't seem to bother him. My legs tighten at once against the chill, skin and muscle holding close to bone, the hair on my thighs stiff as corn stalks.

"The water doesn't know which way to go," Randy says once I've fitted myself to his backside. He's right. The intersecting currents push and tug between our legs. They've carved ridges in the silken sand, the fragile structures giving way with every shuffle of our feet.

My teeth chatter. Randy puts his hands over mine, then passes us over his stomach and the hem of his shirt. The guidance reminds me of an early night with Kat when we faced each other on her bed and she brought me to each place she liked best to be touched, then showed me how to touch her there. After, she offered me her hands, saying it was my turn, and don't be shy.

The remembrance draws a flicker of arousal, quickly lost to the cold. Randy slips us beneath his shirt, where the skin is warm, then ducks us beneath his waistband, where the skin is warmer. He flinches when my hands reach him. "I'll be your hand warmer," he says. When he withdraws his own hands, the motion momentarily threatens our balance.

"I should start saying I'm cold more often."

"You can put your hands in my pants anytime." Randy traces the river's charcoal surface, creating delicate furrows with his fingertips. "There's a lighthouse in Cleveland that looks made out of ice," he says. "My father told me it really was ice, and that if we'd come in the summer it wouldn't be there, it would be melted into the ground. I believed that for years, way after I knew we hadn't actually gone to the Atlantic. It wasn't until I went to Erie one July during high school that I saw it is not ice. It's stone. It just seems that way because of the weather."

"Bad weather."

"Very bad. When I saw the lighthouse, I cried. I stood on the beach while my friends stood behind me, eating hot dogs and probably wondering what the hell was wrong with me, and I cried and cried." He shakes his head. "I wish I could go back and hit myself."

"Why would you do that?"

"That was my last time. I wasted my final cry for years on a white lie. My father had done a million terrible things by then. For some reason that hurt me in a way that made it hard to come back. My friends practically carried me home."

I open my mouth then find myself afraid that any consolation I offer will be inadequate. I press my lips to the back of his neck instead.

"I need a shave," Randy says. "I'm all overgrown."

"I like it."

He relaxes as I knead his inner groin, a motion learned from Kat, one I knew I would take with me as soon as we broke up. Should we feel honored or cheapened to know the tenderness we bestow is later bestowed onto others? I think honored. It means we did something right.

Voices reach us from down the beach. A family of three is moseying their way in our direction, their outlines still indistinct with distance.

"The book was his," Randy says. "*Bruiser.* It was my father's favorite novel. He must have read it twice a year. He kept it in the glove compartment with his protein bars."

"So you're going to read it?"

"Yes. Or maybe. I might."

"Do you think it's a good idea?"

"It's a book, Jack," he says.

"It is a book. But your dad is also your dad."

I once thought Mr. Rourke was dead, given how rarely Randy mentioned him. Then, over time, stories started leaking out. Dennis the Menace, Randy called him. Ruiner of childhoods, of marriages, of family vacations to the Florida Keys. The one, Randy and his therapist concluded, who had given Randy all that terrible jealousy.

"He is my dad. For so long I've thought the best thing

about him was how close he made me with my mom. Now that they're both gone, I feel like I can look at him again. I don't know anymore. I'm not done with either of them."

He turns around. My hands, free of his briefs, are immediately swept up in his. I know what he wants, what he is offering me, and together we put our noses to my fingers and breathe. This is the smell I love, the smell of a lively Randy, an alive Randy, a Randy who gets easily out of bed each day.

"I know you're not done," I tell him.

The Rourke parents, expelled, float between us like stillborn calves. I wonder what Randy makes of them, seeing them out in the open like this. I wonder how he reabsorbs them into his body, yet I know that's what he's done once the family's laughter comes again. Its proximity wrenches the door of our privacy open, drawing us back to our forlorn pants, our forlorn selves. We share a final smile as we re-button, shy, almost, then the trio is upon us.

"Why were you hugging in the water?" the first, a boy of about eight, says.

Landing beside him in a cartwheel is a girl who must be his twin. "They're gay," she says, blowing hair from her lips. "Homosexuals. Like Uncle Ted. Remember what Mom said?"

"'All love is beautiful, meaningful, and none of your bloody beeswax.'"

Their mother wears a red sweatsuit, a red headband, and red flip-flops. "Sorry about these two," she says. "We've been learning about different family structures. The next lesson will be on civility." She squeezes their ears, making them squirm away.

"It's okay," Randy says. "We are gay."

"Mostly."

He stops an eye roll midway through its rotation. We've been here before. For Randy, I am inconveniencing conversational flow with a needless correction. For me, Randy is ignoring the full scope of my sexuality. In a gesture of forfeit, kindness, or apology, he puts a hand on my back and says, "Yes, mostly. We're three-quarters of the way. A solid C." Then he adds, "We've been together for ten years." He says this for me as much as her. The implication, I believe, is not that a decade of being with a man tilts the scales of my sexuality. Instead, it is that we have been together for ten years, so what does the rest of it matter?

"Your relationship is the same age as them," the woman says.

We all turn to where the siblings spin circles nearby. On them, ten years looks like no time at all.

"They're cute kids," Randy says.

"I see too much of their father in them. My whole life I imagined passing down my curls and jawline. They got cowlicks and close-set eyes from some minor league hockey player I shacked up with when I was driving through Toronto. It was the coldest night of the year. He had a snakeskin pinned to the wall above his bed. Every time I breathed it moved."

She glances upward and I wonder if she is seeing it again—the snakeskin, and with it the whole of the night. Green walls, the bedspread pilled, the floor cloudy with dust bunnies. Randy says I have a talent for imagining bad things worse. We've debated whether this falls under the domain of empathy or misanthropy, settling on something like misanthropic empathy.

"The guy did know how to use his tongue. I asked if it

was a Canadian thing, what he was doing, and he said he was from the Hague. I'm not sure if he would remember me if we ran into each other at a bar. It was one of those kinds of nights." She pauses. "The kids are what matters. I would've slept with the devil if he promised to knock me up."

Randy and I laugh.

"I mean it. I thought pregnancy might never happen for me. I was jealous of every big belly. I hated the dog that walked by my house with swollen teats, dripping milk on my sidewalk. Talk about a bitch. I was the wretch back then. It seems like another life. Do you all have kids?"

Randy shakes his head. "We're artists."

"So what? You think artists can't parent?" She crosses her arms across her chest. On her left forearm, a misshapen elephant with a tremendously long trunk has been drawn in blue ink.

"Of course they can," Randy says. "It's just harder. Or would be harder for us."

"How do you know? Kids might be the best thing for you. Sure, they take all your time. Sure, you stay up late some nights trying to figure out who you were before them. And sure, there are times when you'd like to leave them behind, to un-nail yourself from whatever floor or wall you've been pinned to and walk away. But kids also set the mind on fire." She taps her temple. "I never even painted before them."

"You're a painter?" I ask.

"Don't sound so excited! Yes, I paint. And I never touched a brush until I let these two loose on the world. It turns out life is much more amazing when you're seeing it for the first time. That's one thing kids remind you. You think I would've painted a piece of bark if they hadn't spent an hour passing it back and forth? No. I wouldn't have painted anything. That's what I'm saying." Her arms fall to her sides. "Sorry to soapbox. What kind of artists are you?"

"I'm a photographer."

"I used to write plays."

"And now?"

"Now I write grocery lists. There's an art to it."

"There is," the woman says without irony.

"He's the one you should be talking to," I say. "He's had enough success for the whole state of Oregon."

"Is that right? What do you photograph?"

Randy thinks on this for a while, then says, "I hardly know anymore." A deep fatigue sweeps the smile off his face.

"You should borrow the twins," the woman says. "An afternoon with them will open up your skies. Both of yours, maybe."

We are all distracted for a moment by the children's shrieks—they have found dentures near the waterline, the boy clapping the teeth together.

"Do they ask about him?" Randy asks.

"Their father? Of course. And every time I tell a different story. Stuntman, astrophysicist, sea monkey. They're going to be so let down when they learn the truth."

The twins run circles around us as we march back up the beach, sensing in some animalistic way that our mood has shifted toward the melancholic.

"He's gone!" the girl shouts when we reach the turn to our house. "I wanted to give him this." In her hand is a snapped sand dollar.

"Maybe we'll see him again," the woman says. "We met

the most interesting man when we first got here. He taught us all about the snowy plovers that nest on this beach, didn't he?"

Her kids nod, taking turns to recite several facts about the birds.

"And he had a dried alligator foot tied to his vest," the boy says. "For luck."

"That's right." The woman puts her hand on her son's head, then on her daughter's. Both kids swing into her, fixing themselves to her sides.

"Was his name Clarence?"

"Something like that."

"Claude?"

"That's it! Claude. You know him?"

"He lives next door to our place." I consider telling her all I know about our fraudulent neighbor, then realize it would serve no purpose. "Can I ask you about the red?"

Both kids giggle as she looks down at her outfit. "I lost a bet. These two claimed they could eat an entire rack of ribs and I didn't believe them. They picked every bone clean."

"We love meat," the boy says, holding the dentures in front of his mouth and making them speak with him.

"Can you put those down, please?" the woman says.

"She says she doesn't want to be left here." The boy holds the dentures to his ear and begins nodding sympathetically. "She says she's been here so long. It gets cold at night. People step on her. She says she wants to see the swimming pool at our inn. She's tired of the beach."

"You see what I mean," the woman says to us, pretending to ignite a lighter near her head. Then, to her son: "She can come to the inn. She isn't coming on the plane, though."

The twins squeal. We say goodbye after the boy struggles to shove the dentures into his pocket, their turn still a ways up the beach. On the hill to Sally and Fran's, I step in each place Randy steps, enjoying the illusion of being untrackable.

"She's a good mother," Randy says at the top. He does not turn back to see if I agree because it is the kind of observation that prompts no friction, as when, staring out at a beautiful sunset, someone says, "That is a beautiful sunset."

TOURIST, TRAPPED

Randy is gone from me by the time we enter the living room, distracted by whatever the mother and her children dredged up in his head. He laps the couch I sit on twice, gives me a robotic bow, then retreats to the office, from where I soon hear the low murmuring of his voice.

It doesn't take much to imagine what Ms. Rourke might say to him. What begins as a sort of interior joke quickly gives way to something more stressful, and soon Ms. Rourke's voice is swarming me. *That Jack is a try-hard. A flirt, a cheat, a wannabe, a social climber, a liar, a mooch. That Jack is made of tissue paper. He'll melt in your hands if he doesn't leave you first.* I pull my feet out of the sun, for they have begun to sweat. "I don't think I trust you," she said to me during our second meeting, where she was wine drunk. "I do love your cheeks."

Sweatier than my feet are my hands and neck. Imagining Ms. Rourke's accusations has summoned an old worry: that Randy, given enough phone calls or time alone with her, would be convinced he was better off without me.

I shake my head with some aggression, more like a wet dog than a man. Anxiety is one of the only feelings I've always believed I can jostle free. Jostle and distract, the method goes. And so I shake my head again, hard, before locking my focus on Randy's photograph on the opposite wall. In it, a man stands in the center of a bathroom. He faces away from the camera, shirtless. The hair on his back is lush, fanning out from his tailbone and up to his shoulders, an aspiration of wings. There is only one strip of bare skin a few inches above his left hip. The hand that shaved it, as well as the razor, can be seen at the edge of his body, suspended in midair and uncertain of what to do next. *Maintenance #2*, the photograph is called.

My body begins to relax into the cushions. I keep myself focused forward, knowing that the fastest way to undo peace is to preemptively celebrate its arrival.

Maintenance #2 was taken a few months into our relationship. "I'm shooting Wayne while he shaves his back," Randy told me while snapping apart his wooden chopsticks. "Wayne?" I asked. I was deciding whether or not to use chopsticks myself, knowing my ineptitude with the utensils, so did not immediately think of Randy's neighbor, whom I had met a few times in passing. I should have guessed. Wayne's hair swallows the figure of his body like ivy. In the thirty photos *Maintenance* comprises, he tries to rid himself of it to no real success. If you scroll quickly through them, he jerks around disturbingly, looking, in the end, like a mangled tiger.

At the gallery debut, I felt smug as the crowd wandered from frame to frame. It was not simply about knowing Randy. It was that they were seeing the art while I had seen the pre-art, the post-art, and the art-in-between. More specifically, I knew the art's subject inside and outside of the lens. The photos were different if you knew Wayne, I was certain. The timbre of his voice, the habit he had of bringing Randy the paper once he'd finished reading it. Who was he to them? Not a person, not really. That's what art can do: strip someone of their real-life humanity and imbue them with an abstract kind of humanity, one built by whomever is seeing the work. Wayne was not even at the debut, and I felt glad about that. That I alone knew him made me feel close to Randy.

I close my eyes and elongate my breathing. I feel calmer, and aware that my fears are still stalking about the room, biding their time. I toss myself new distractions, but nothing sticks. I think about children, how all-American Randy would look holding a baby, then my parents, and my mother on the pavement, fallen, then the woman on the beach and her all-red getup, how fashion can be a shorthand route to characterization, especially on the stage, and then I'm back in the diner of my imaginary play, wondering what Fabio, Sue Ellen, Ray, or Julian might wear that would convey something essential to their personalities, then I'm thinking about *Ballast*, what *The New York Times* said about Artaud, about gay bars, what they might say about this new-and-never-to-be-written play, and then I'm watching Beatrice cringe as she reads from *Parthenon*, and my eyes are open again.

My father doesn't answer when I call. I leave a meandering voicemail asking for a progress report on my mother. Then I open Scruff. Since arriving in Oregon, I've gotten twelve woofs, four messages, and one private album. There are woofs from Portland, from Bangkok, from Paradise, Indiana, from New York, and from Florence. None of the men are particularly attractive to me. I send back three woofs anyway. The two Florence profiles don't have any photos. The one that is five miles away is blank; the one that is seven miles away has the kind of manifesto common on hookup apps. *NO GAMES. NOT HERE TO PLAY BY ANYONE ELSE'S RULES. LIFE IS FOR THE LIVING. NO DRUGS. NO BAREBACK. I'M A SUCCESSFUL ATTRACTIVE MAN WHO IS NOT GOING TO BE YOUR SUGAR DADDY. LOOKING FOR REAL MEN WHO DON'T GIVE A FUCK ABOUT TECHNO OR DEODORANT. HIKING, CAMPING, FISHING, CRABBING, FUCKING. LIFE IS TOO SHORT TO WASTE ON BAD SEX. BRUCE SPRINGSTEEN. QUENTIN TARANTINO. CULTURE. CAN'T HOST.*

The first message is from a widow's-peaked man in Maine. In one photo, he sits next to a woman whose face he has covered with a moon emoji; in the second, he has hidden her behind a ghost. *Hey, handsome.* The second man has only one photo, a mirror selfie in which he flexes his bicep. He is attractive in an everyday way, someone you would cast as an extra for your insurance ad. *Yo.* The third is from Dr.Dragon, who has sent me a photo of his erection, bejeweled at one end by a cock ring and at the other by a drop of precum. *For you.* What got me off yesterday has become boring, a casualty of him laying all of his cards out so quickly. Still, I feel obliged to respond. *Yes please,* I write alongside a drooling emoji.

The final message is from another anonymous profile, Lake&Bake, whose bio reads: *people fly . . . dogs die . . . you ride . . . on my guy?* He is two miles away. *What brings you to Florence?* he asks. *Italy's better in spring.*

I heard the food is good year-round.

He responds right away. *Hate to break the news, but you're a tourist, trapped. Nothing is always good.*

Lonely Planet owes me a big refund.

Haha.

What's up with the town motto?

People fly and dogs die?

Ay.

He is typing, then not typing, then typing again. I check the private album from the man in New Mexico. Seeing no nudes, I'm tempted to message him regarding the meaning of *private.* Then a string of messages from Lake&Bake arrives.

There was a bad winter a few years ago. Bad bad. Carbon mono leak in the nursing home, gonorrhea outbreak at the high school, dead whale in the river, etc.

In Feb like ten dogs died. No clear cause, just laid down. I saw three near the water.

When the paper wrote about the dogs, there was an anonymous op-ed on the same page about seeing people in the clouds. Or maybe it was shadows of people.

The bumper stickers came fast. Reclaiming the tragic by leaning into the absurd. Of course dogs were dying and people were flying. We'd had the shittiest year of our lives.

The dogs are what I see most clearly, their tufted fur blowing in the wind.

Not sure if the motto is more or less creepy now, I message back.

That's for you to sort. What brings you to town?

Love of dune buggies and tacky souvenirs.

That's my hometown you're talking about.

It's lovely, really. I'm escaping my own bad year. Friends have a place on the beach, the rest is history.

Bad year? I can think of three ways I could make you feel better.

Only three?

Conservative estimate. Low expectations yield high rewards.

I feel it in my lower stomach first, the rub of arousal. I listen for Randy, making sure he is still rambling away.

Hard to imagine rewards when I don't know what I'm working with, I write.

Expecting a photo from beneath the beltline, I'm surprised when he sends a shot of his face. The picture is close up and blurry. Silver stubble covers his chin and cheeks, adding a wintery effect to his sharp features. He is someone who exudes authority, the kind of person your eyes would gravitate toward in an emergency, believing he might have the power to save you.

Wow, I say. *The finest of Florence.*

Until you arrived.

Haha, no. But thanks.

I listen again for Randy. My heart rate rises when I don't

hear anything, the organ itself clenched by guilt, then returns to normal when he laughs. It is faulty thinking, but I use his laughter to justify my conversation with Lake&Bake, as if Randy's fidelity to the dead warrants me some infidelity with the living.

Can I see more of you? I ask.

The next picture shares in the graininess of the headshot, taking on the retrograde aura of my favorite pornos. He's naked in a corduroy recliner, ankles crossed, arms behind his head. He looks at whomever is behind the camera with one of those love-drunk expressions anyone would feel lucky to receive. From his neck down, he is covered in tattoos, an unexpected departure from his neat face. Most are faded to the point of indecipherability. The name *TRISH* is clear on his right clavicle.

Jesus, I reply.

He sends back a winking emoji, then tells me it's my turn. I don't review my album before sending it out. My photos cannot obscure my self-consciousness, clear in the concerted angles and generous lighting. I unlock the album, then turn my gaze to the beam of sunshine coming through the skylight, which looks nearly solid, a column of gold.

Nice, Lake&Bake writes.

I wait to see if this is our conversation's death rattle, rubbing an itch on one foot with the toes of the other. This type of rejection does not hurt me, not really. Possibly because I have Randy. Possibly because rejection on Scruff is ubiquitous, doled out with no real rhyme or reason. And possibly because, on the matter of my body, I've beaten any feasible insult to the punch. The itch moves from one foot to the other, and then my phone buzzes.

So, when are we going to get those legs over my shoulders?

My waning erection swells, demanding an adjustment of my pants. *That's a little complicated.*

Not very flexible?

I'm very flexible when I want to be.

Is that right?

My free hand goes to my lap. I scroll back to the photo of him on the recliner, zooming to crop out his face. It feels too compromising to touch myself while looking at such shameless adoration. On his right thigh are tattoos of a liquor bottle, a trout, and a mandala; on his left, a liquor bottle, a poorly executed *Vitruvian Man*, and the words *NO SNAILS*.

So it's not a problem of flexibility. Married?

I debate whether or not to be honest, knowing it will sully whatever fantasy we've been building. Before Randy is acknowledged, I am anyone who can do anything. After, the conversation invariably changes. Some men block me, some get excited at the idea of my disloyalty, some confess to being in committed relationships themselves, some want to know more—Man or woman? Open or closed?—and some want to know less. In each instance there is a tilt, the boat that held two now bearing three.

When I dodge the truth, the chance of a plan developing increases, resulting in nights like the one where I circled someone's block four times, wondering what he was doing up there, if he had cleaned the place, if I would smell what he'd eaten for dinner, if he had had to restock on condoms, if he'd shaved his face, his neck, his shoulders, and if he would kiss me right away, or if he would be too shy. Each unknown carried its own erotic pulse because I'd been living in a world where so little was hidden. Ten years had stripped the mystery from between Randy and me. The only surprise he'd brought in recent months was that of his depthless grief. When I left our apartment that night, he was sitting on the floor with the photo album he'd been flipping through for the last week. "It's cold in here," I told him, closing the windows he'd opened during my shower. Outside, winter had ambushed the nascent spring with one final shock. He looked at me, puzzled. "There's snow in your hair," I said. "I don't feel that way," he said as I brushed the snowflakes out, noticing while I did how greasy his hair was, unwashed for weeks. "What way?" I asked. "Old."

Married, I write. I want Lake&Bake to fight for my betrayal, if only so I can entertain, then deny his temptation, feeling better about myself every time I approach the edge and retreat.

What's that like?

The question makes me laugh, given how impossible it is to answer with any sort of brevity, or to any completion. What is marriage like? It is like nothing. It is like everything. *It is*, I write, *not what I expected.*

What did you expect?

Not sure. A slow march toward death with someone you like less every day?

Romantic.

Very. I've always grouped marriage into monotony, and monotony into misery.

Sad parents?

Surprisingly, no. My parents are very keen on one another.

That's sweet.

Sometimes. But there's not much trickle down.

Ouch, Lake&Bake writes. *That's no fun.*

I've seen worse. And they do love me, in their way. I think it might be ideology that made me so resistant to marriage. Dominant culture gives me the creeps.

But now . . .

Now I'm married. Tamed by a wedding band. So much for my countercultural aspirations. I spent my whole life changing shapes only to end up a square.

I'm sure you're not a square. Maybe a circle.

So generous. What about you? Married or divorced?

You never told me what changed.

You mean why I got married?

Why marriage hasn't felt like a slow march toward death.

I don't know. It is monotonous, but rarely miserable. Being married is the easiest thing I've ever done.

Such a simple sentiment, but one, read back, that fills me up with enough sentimental affection to run me to the office, lift Randy in my arms, and kiss his blocky head a hundred times. Almost.

Easy is good, Lake&Bake writes. *I've been looking for easy all my life.*

Any luck?

With some things. Cooking and swimming. Dreaming. I'm very good at dreaming.

What do you dream about?

I dream about my sister Patricia. I dream about tropical beaches. I dream about fucking men like you. Name something good and I've probably dreamed it.

Marriage?

I said something good.

Zing.

Kidding. I don't think I've ever dreamed about marriage. Never really thought about it, either. Only recently have I started wondering why that is. Not in a regretful way, just curious. It's strange to not want what so many people want.

Randy's voice reaches me again, breaking my focus, and with his voice comes his dream, the one that ends with him swallowing his tongue. The distance between that world and the one Lake&Bake dreams of fills me with an overwhelming sense of injustice: to be so deeply trapped in Randy's derangement that at times it becomes my own—who could survive it? I grip the couch cushion, needing Lake&Bake to say something to keep me free of my life for a few minutes longer. I want to know about Trish. I want to know about the person who took the photo of him. Any fact that will help clutter my vision.

I should probably go, he says.

Even if I tell you I'm undoing my belt?

Ha, yeah. It's been nice chatting. But I usually only talk with guys who I can actually bend over my bed frame.

The urge to get in the car and go to him possesses me with startling force. I type the word *I*, then the office door swings open and whatever route that word was going to take is diverted. *I'm Jack.* Randy emerges, stepping into the kitchen and stretching his arms above his head.

"It's muggy in here," he says. "Where's the AC?"

Nice to meet you, Jack. I'm Steve. Mr. Steve to most.

The message knocks against me like a rock. Mr. Steve. I read the name several times, hoping it might change. Each pass generates another detail from Abigail's story: the backyard benders and the sodden lawn, the peeing and the spliffs. I set the phone down carefully, as if the device might otherwise detonate.

Randy is saying something to me. The words fail to assemble until he is directly before me. "Jack," he says. "Are you going to get that?"

"Get what?"

"The phone." He reaches over me, grabbing the landline from its cradle.

"Hello?" Randy says.

"Who do you think you are?" The woman's voice is loud enough on the speakerphone to crackle.

"Sorry?"

"You let a whole day pass without coming over?" Her accusatory tone begins to break, giving way to a more playful chiding.

"Sorry, but who is this?" Randy asks.

"Polly! Of Polly and Paul! The Double *P*s, your charming and intrusive neighbors!"

"Emphasis," a man, Paul, adds, "on intrusive."

"What's a little fun?" Polly says. "We heard you two were at our bookstore today."

Randy's face relaxes. "We were."

"And? Are you more book or bear?" Polly asks.

Randy nods at me, inviting me into the conversation. "It's a tie," I say.

"Right answer!" Paul shouts. "Now you've earned your spot at the table. Or I guess I should say jacuzzi. Can we interest you in some dinner?"

"Dinner enjoyed in the glow of an Oregon sunset," Polly says.

"And with jacuzzi jets blasting your back. We're making kebabs. Come over at seven. We're north of you. Swimsuits optional. Unencouraged, even."

The line goes dead. Randy sits on the couch beside me, reaching over and pulling on my ear. "Kebabs," he says.

"I guess so."

I look at him, then away, worried that Mr. Steve might be breaking the blood vessels in my eyes. Back in his jealous days, Randy was often reading my eyes and I was often averting them, knowing he would find trouble whether there was any or not. My reflexive avoidance brings with it a thrum of excitement, a hot pulse in the navel.

I reverse course and stare at him straight on. I try and open my eyes to him, my mind, to broadcast every wayward thought, ready for the taking, the punishing. There is a lightlessness to Randy's envy that is totalizing. I miss the feeling of meaning so much to someone that a craven part of them wants to remove you from the rest of the world. At least that way you know you won't be left out in the yard.

Nothing happens. Randy moves his hand from my ear to my jaw, where he rubs my stubble with his velvety palm.

"Remember Wayne?" I ask, pointing at the photo. "You and I stayed up all night after the debut. When is the last time we did that? Don't you miss it?"

Randy's hand leaves my face for his "Miss what? Staying up late?"

"Not just that."

He waits for me to clarify. I don't, and he doesn't ask me to. Then I see that he doesn't actually appear to be waiting at all. He's picking at his tooth and beginning to laugh.

This time when I look at him I imagine Mr. Steve's cock

bannering across my eyes over and over again, like a message on a blimp. Randy's laugh grows.

"What's so funny?" I ask.

"I was just thinking about Wayne," he says. "He could never finish the sudoku."

STRANGER STRANGERS

It takes an hour for my stomach to unwind, and even then my insides feel tender, run raw by guilt. I try not to seem so desperate for affection when Randy invites me to take a shower with him, but I am desperate for affection. I beg him to scrub me with Sally and Fran's many products, then to dress me for the evening ahead, then to sit close enough on our patio that I can fit my whole arm inside his shirt. We are laid out on a wicker couch, margaritas in easy reach.

"According to Clarence, Sally and Fran fuck out here," I say.

"I think those two fuck everywhere. You can tell by the way they stand."

I laugh. "The way they stand?"

"You'd know if you saw." Randy brings some of his still-wet hair to his lips, then wags his eyebrows at me.

"I'm glad the life of the mind hasn't made them forget their pleasure," I say.

"Not as glad as them. She died at the start of part three, you know. The first page was in the typewriter when she dropped flat. December 4, 1975."

"What?"

"Arendt. *The Life of the Mind.* A heart attack at a party—bam."

"I didn't even know there was a book with that title," I say. "Good thing you married me for my body."

"A very good thing."

An acorn-shaped cloud drifts by overhead, catching the sun behind its tattered stem and instantly stealing the day's warmth. Randy pulls me closer, loosening his hold when the sun surfaces again.

"Have you heard from your mom?" he asks.

"Nothing new. I left her a voicemail."

"We're always one step from the end." He holds out his hand, extends the fingers, then quickly balls them into a fist. "Is she still a part of that pickleball league?"

"I'm not sure."

"What about the community garden?"

"I don't know. We haven't caught up in a while."

"So her life is under a tarp."

"Her life isn't under a tarp, Randy." We've both stiffened, making my extraction from his shirt an ordeal. "We're different. You and I are different, our parents are different. It's great that you and your mom had what you did. There's no reason for me to call mine every other day."

"Have it."

"What?"

"Me and my mother have it," he says, his lower lip trembling slightly. "We're still talking."

"And she's talking back?"

It's sad, almost, to see this gibe pass so cleanly through Randy. He's neither hurt nor offended, only eager to answer. I wonder if I haven't somehow misheard myself. Maybe the question was asked, at least on a certain level, in earnest.

"She's finding her way," he says, his trembling lip gone, replaced with what I think of as his golden child face—a cherub eager to please. "My mother is in a forest. She's in a forest and I'm at the edge of the trees. I can hear her moving."

"What does she say?"

"She isn't speaking. All I hear is the sound of her moving. Rustling. Abigail told me it could go like this. It's confusing for them. Dying scrambles up your senses. If she is talking, I can't hear her yet. I hear her pushing through pinecones and leaves."

"Who knew your mother was so outdoorsy," I say, hoping to offset the ice cube–like feeling his words have created in my chest.

"My mother was outdoorsy," he says. "She took me to Hocking Hills after he left. My father and I camped there when I was a kid and she wanted to show me that it didn't matter so much, him being gone. She wore these wedge heels. All of our veggie dogs fell in the fire. But she was very happy when the stars came out." He isn't looking at me when he smiles. "She kept asking if this is how Dad did it. If this is how he lit the fire or pitched the tent. I'm sure it was for her, too, wanting to prove his absence wasn't a disaster."

Randy flinches when I take his hand. "I was just kidding," I say.

"She woke me up in the middle of the night because she was too cold," he says, still swept up in the memory, or trying to be. "We drove home at two in the morning. So maybe she wasn't outdoorsy. But that's not the point."

"You're right," I say, hoping to sound more encouraging. "That's not the point. Is your father in the woods?"

"He's not in the woods. Whatever's on the far side of the woods—that's where he is."

"But he's coming to the woods?"

"I don't know. We didn't speak for seven years. I don't know where he is. I'll know when he's in the woods, though. He put his full weight into every step."

I sip my margarita, watered down by ice melt. The pause sobers me, making me self-conscious about what we have been saying. To pursue a fantasy is to risk becoming contaminated by its illogic.

"What do you want from all of this?" I ask.

"Answers."

"Answers to what?"

Randy closes his eyes in frustration. Except he is not frustrated, I see once he opens them again. He is sad. "Every five minutes I think of something I don't know," he says. "They feel like strangers to me. Strangers becoming stranger."

"They aren't strangers. You know them better than anyone."

"That makes it worse. I'm the last thing tying them to the world and can hardly remember what they liked."

"Maybe that's okay. Or normal. It's impossible to know it all."

He laughs. "Is that supposed to make me feel better? The great unknown of human life?" He continues laughing when I tell him yes, I was hoping so. "Your consolations have always been unorthodox, Jack."

My own laughter fades almost as soon as it starts. I think of Sally and Fran and Abigail, all of whom Randy looks to so eagerly; I think of the tape recorder and the ash and *Bruiser*, lifeless objects that Randy clutches like totems.

"I'm trying," I say. "I'm trying to make you feel better all the time."

"Right, sure. I know you are," he says flippantly, his face still flush with silliness. "Everyone is trying to make me feel better. Blah, blah, blah. But I don't think that happens."

"You don't think you're going to feel better?" I ask, my head growing heavy.

"I don't want to feel better," he says, smiling widely. "What would that even mean?"

Then he kisses me, and our heads together have an unbearable weight, nearly impossible to hold, though his lips are plush and pliant, keeping me there.

"Why is your mouth closed?" he asks, wiggling a finger between my teeth.

I try to let his deeper kiss coax me toward a lighter state of being.

"Do you think your parents like kissing?" he asks.

"I know they like kissing."

"You should make a note of that. It's so much easier to keep track before they're dead." He pushes off of my chest to stand, leaving me briefly breathless.

"Jesus, Randy."

"What? It's time to meet the neighbors." He beckons me up. "I've never been so hungry for home cooking."

"I cook for you," I say. It feels untrue as soon as it's out, as if all the meals I've prepared—simple, to be sure, but not entirely lacking—amount to little more than the packaging from which the ingredients came. Randy is already inside in any case, searching for his shoes.

DIET OF CORPSES

The passage to Polly and Paul's is cold in our swimsuits, the wind provoked by the approaching night. As it lashes our legs, Randy's hair flies about, mirroring the beach grass's restlessness.

Beneath the door knocker, a Post-it flaps like a demon's tongue. *What are you waiting for?* the message reads. *The door's unlocked and the water's very warm!*

The interior of Polly and Paul's house is so unlike Sally and Fran's that it takes a moment for my senses to adjust. On the living room walls, a mosaic of mismatched frames are interspersed with woven baskets, tapestries, and taxidermic animal heads. I can't help thinking of Mr. Steve's tattoos as I divide the cramped decor into individualized parts. For his *TRISH*, trout, and *Vitruvian Man*, Polly and Paul have a painting of a foot, a photograph from the 2008 Olympics, and a warthog head left to squeal for eternity. I wonder if it is a localized condition, this interest in pandemonium, one Sally and Fran have skirted by only living here seasonally.

I shut the door behind us. "Name five things you see."

"Deer hooves, pineapple lamp, shag rug, college diploma, hookah. You?"

Randy's answers open me to the rest of the room. Polly and Paul have squeezed two couches, two love seats, and three armchairs into the space. There is a shag carpet. Also a Persian rug, a floor runner, and a rubber mat with dog bowls on it. "Fern," I say. "Record player, dream catcher, *Guernica*, Mr. Potato Head."

"Mr. Potato Head?" Randy laughs. "Where?"

I point to where Mr. Potato Head has been affixed to the wall, his nose missing. "Imagine what Sally and Fran think of this," I say.

"I think they'd just have aneurysms."

We step deeper, entering a haze of incense. "Is that sandalwood?" I ask.

"It's smothering." A peculiar look passes over Randy's face. Maybe he's remembered the same thing I have: a joke I used to make about Ms. Rourke putting the *mother* in *smother*. If so, he takes the memory in stride, resolving his face before leading us forward. "Let's find fresher air."

We cross through the dining room, where the stateliness of the Edwardian chairs is offset by the fake palms standing in each of the room's four corners, and the kitchen after that. There are two refrigerators here, and a table large enough for ten. Paul's voice finds us through the open window. "Follow the teriyaki trail!"

The patio is a stark contrast to the house, barren except for the jacuzzi at its center and the grill abutting the jacuzzi's southern side. It does smell of teriyaki. Also, chlorine. The wind carries a cloud of steam and smoke toward us and then dispels it, leaving Randy and I bared to the world. Facing Polly and Paul, who grin at us from the water, I feel embarrassed by this revealment. I step behind Randy as if to hide, then recover my wits.

"Smells like chicken," I say.

"Tastes like it, too," Polly says. "I hope."

Polly and Paul's skin is pink with heat, their hair damp. Paul's head is bald in a rarified way, made better by hairlessness rather than a victim of it. He has the benefit of a full beard—this being the hair of his the water has dampened, droplets inset within the curls like jewels in a fishnet. Polly, meanwhile, has a full mane, with thick, mythological coils falling from her head. Her face is freckled, pale, one eye lower than the other, which gives her a look of perpetual slyness. There is something familiar about her, especially when she slackens her smile, that I can't identify.

Their nudity should not surprise me, but I am taken aback when they stand to greet us. Perhaps it has less to do with their nakedness than their brazenness. Sleek with water, they are each a paragon of how averageness, given a dose of confidence, becomes exemplary. None of their features would be notable in isolation—not the stretchmarks on Paul's hips or Polly's breasts, the slight paunch of their bellies, the smattering of downy hair beneath their navels—yet the way they carry these things makes them virtually incandescent.

"Nice to meet you all," I say, trying to keep my eyes up. "I'm Jack."

Polly swats my offered hand away. "In the age of handshakes, I'm all hug." She opens her arms and waits for me to lean forward, at which point she wraps them around my neck. "I'd apologize for getting you wet, but you're on a slippery slope there anyway. Jack. And you must be Randy."

Randy has just separated from Paul's hug, and now we swap, Paul squeezing me hard enough to crack my back. "Ouch," he says. "That sounded overdue."

"By about seven years."

"Seven!" Paul lets me go. "Don't let our chiropractor hear that. She'll have a cow."

"And, in the ever-wise words of my father, why have a cow when you could just eat one?" Polly laughs. "It's no wonder Mom went vegan."

A fresh gust of wind surges over the patio wall, pooling near our ankles before rising higher, making my and Randy's shirts billow.

"Lord," Paul says, clutching himself. "I'm freezing my balls off out here. Look at my guy. He's nearly inside out." He looks down at his shrunken penis. "Such a sensitive organ." He flops back into the jacuzzi and sends a cascade of water over its edge. "You two must be freezing. Get your asses in here."

"Yes, come in!" Polly joins Paul, sinking down to her neckline and releasing a moan. "Life is good at one hundred two degrees."

I follow Randy's lead while disrobing, relieved when he keeps his swimsuit on. We lower ourselves into the water's heat and release an involuntary groan in tandem—the same groan as Polly's, the same groan as any middle-aged person's, maybe. The heat shucks away my cold shell, leaving me soft and formless.

"The price is right, isn't it?" Paul says.

"Very right." Randy has his head back and his eyes half-closed. He looks like any man in any hot tub, unbereft and uncomplicated. His relaxation helps me welcome my own. The four of us all adopt similar positions, sinking into a timeless stupor.

Eventually Polly reaches over to the grill, throws back its covering, and presents a row of sizzling kebabs. Each has pierced the same order of chicken, peppers, onions, and mushrooms. The flames lick at the food through the bars below.

"Nice char, P," Paul says. "Polly's a real grill master. Her dad had her flipping burgers when she was five years old. He didn't believe in childhood."

"Childhood, American schooling, or the need to drink so much water." Polly transfers the kebabs to a metal platter. "Such a twit. But he gets sweeter every year. Aging has drawn the sap out from the stiffest tree. He even makes veggie burgers for Mom now." With the tray full, she lets the grill's cover drop. "Hope you came hungry. We've got enough to feed the whole ark."

While we eat, we exchange the rudimentary facts of our lives. Paul is from Washington. His parents separated a week after he was born, so he spent weekdays with his mother in Tacoma and weekends with his father in Seattle, an inverted schedule from his brother, whom he failed to bond with for this reason. Before moving to Oregon, he traveled up and down the West Coast as a touring musician for a small-time jazz act. It was during these years that he met Polly in Sausalito.

Polly was born in Arizona. She was the youngest of five, the only girl, the only one not to go to college, and the only not to return to Arizona after leaving. "It's all still right here either way," she says. "I close my eyes and it's all red desert." It is unclear whether she feels resentful or nostalgic when she says this. Paul rubs her neck while he gnaws at a mushroom. He and I are at the same point in our kebab. The mushroom, garlicky and moist, squeaks between my teeth. Randy is occupied with a bell pepper, which shreds like braised meat when he tears into it.

He and I speak next. His Ohio and my California. Our doomed fates, as only children, to be insufferable. We both enlist our standard shorthand to capture ourselves: Randy always says he was raised in a suburb of frat houses, in the shadow of a football stadium, in a state flat enough to sleep on; I always say I was raised in Los Angeles County, not Los Angeles proper, believed myself too artistic for so much sunlight, in need of the turbulence of seasons, and moved to New York on the same movie-fueled delusion that shuttles many young people there.

We get sidelined from these sketches when Paul jabs his lip with his kebab skewer. He is fine, his bleeding brief. The unexpected violence reminds him of a film, something French and brutal that I did not see. How does art relate to cruelty? This question takes us through our second kebabs, and is largely convivial, for none of us is staunch enough in an opinion to generate friction. This kind of dialogue would drive many of our friends crazy—Martina in particular, who accuses contemporary criticism of creating mazes from its surplus of hedged statements—and might drive me crazy on a certain day, too. Today I find the delicate prodding to be the superior mode of inquiry. Perhaps it is the evening light. Perhaps it is the bodily buzz coming from the drink Paul procured from behind the jacuzzi after telling us about his love for Puget Sound. Perhaps it is the intoxication of unexpected ordinariness—to see that our hosts are more sensible and funny than I imagined, to see Randy providing deep and idiosyncratic insights, revelatory of his singular mind. Whatever it is makes me feel suave and Socratic.

Only after Paul collects our stripped skewers does he realize sunset is imminent. "Hey!" He wields the four rods in the direction of the ocean. "The sun tried to sink without us. Good thing I looked in your eyes." He nods at Randy. "Your pupils are lovely little mirrors."

I can't tell if Randy is blushing, or simply red from the water. "Happy to be of service," he says, and then I know it is a blush, for in his words there is the diffidence that follows flattery.

"Nice work." I palm his thigh, a gesture of possessiveness, or encouragement, or both.

Paul replenishes our drinks while Polly asks if we know about the green flash that sometimes accompanies sunset. Randy says yes, that he looked for it last time he was here to no avail. Polly explains the science behind the phenomenon, but Paul's position becomes increasingly distracting as she goes on. In an effort to reach more ice, he has bent himself over the jacuzzi. His ass bobs in and out of the water, facing us from only a few feet away, and the movement sends ripples over the water's surface. Polly only registers her husband's compromising position when Paul lets out a series of grunts.

"Dang, Paul," she says, spanking him. "Save a little for the imagination."

Paul smiles over his shoulder. "Imagination is overrated."

There is no real scorn in Polly's eye roll; she follows it by scooting closer to Paul and hugging his leg. "What I wanted to say about the green flash is that we've only seen it a few times. Those nights we've had the best sex of our lives. I don't know what it is about the cosmos, or the color green. We get electrified. I hope you don't mind my candor. We like to live our lives unfenced."

Paul turns, finally, and distributes our drinks. "You can see why I watch for it every night," he says with a wink.

I work to catch Randy's eyes, to see what he makes of our hosts. His sight is fixed toward the horizon, and so I turn myself there, too. The gales have calmed, gone to some mysterious place. Now, seabirds slice through the sky, oranges and pinks lie heaped on the horizon like stacked sorbet, and the surf's radio-rumble rises up the cliff. If the ocean seems austere, the extravagance of the light is enough to offset that austerity, or to complicate it by reminding us that even the grim unknown can be beautifully lit.

"No green," I say once the final wedge of light disappears.

No one responds, making me wonder if I've said the words at all. After a period of silence, during which the blue night begins to convene, Polly asks, "Do you know what Mom calls nonvegan eating?" She lowers herself into the water until only her face remains at the surface, turned up like a lily pad. "She calls it a diet of corpses. Isn't that awful?"

She smiles, closes her eyes, and sinks below the surface. Her hair slips around my knees and shins, even curling into the palm of my hand. Then she surfaces and it is all pulled away. "No green," she says. "We'll have to electrify ourselves."

"I can do that." Paul reaches to the side of the jacuzzi and the jets burst alive. Our warped bodies disappear beneath the roiling tumult. We all release another involuntary groan, the jets kneading our lifetime's worth of knots and aches. There is one skimming my left ribs, one at the center of my spine, and one—the strongest—between Randy and me. With some force, the latter forces my hand off his thigh and into the bubbly turmoil.

DON'T CRY FOR ME, POLLENTINA

By the time the full shawl of night falls, we are properly tipsy, easeful with each other in a way that suggests old company yet giddy in a way that suggests new. Polly wants us to compare hand sizes. Have we seen how large Paul's are? Randy wants us to admire the way he can create a geyser by squeezing his palms together. It is impressive, the fountaining water. We watch it crest and fall, its heat lost by the time the water lands back on our heads.

I'm surprised by Randy's ready flirtations, intrigued by them, and cautious that I might be misreading them as something they aren't. Apart from a halfhearted threesome attempt a few months into dating—a night that began at an ABBA-themed dance party and that ended with all three of us shrugging our way toward orgasm—we have only attempted group sex once. It happened some six years later. Our sex life was in a rare ebb state then, and I'd begun masturbating with a teenager's frenzy. I missed sex with women and soon became fixated on this absence. When I watched porn, I turned to straight couples and then to women alone. I talked with Randy about this when the feeling became too much to leave unspoken. I didn't want to open our relationship, I explained, and I didn't want to have sex without him. I did think it could be fun to try something new.

"Meaning sex with a woman," he clarified, holding a dripping sponge in his hand.

"Meaning sex with a woman, together," I said. I'd been drying the dishes he was washing, except the operation had come to a halt.

"Interesting."

"Interesting?"

He squeezed the sponge, wetting the stacked mugs below with soapy water. "Yes," he said. "Interesting. Who did you have in mind?"

Later he would ask me if it was the threesome I wanted, or sex with the person we had the threesome with—Leila, whom I'd grown close to after she was cast in my fourth play. Was it Leila I wanted? In some ways, sure. We have always had good chemistry, and she is stunning, one of the more free-loving and intelligent people I know. In other ways, my desire had become so acute that it was seeking satiation wherever seemed likeliest. Leila's love life reminded me of mine, pre-Randy, which made her a feasible candidate.

Randy and I went back and forth for a month, and then he agreed, and I chose to believe his agreement was not simply a forfeit to my wants. I talked with Leila, who was excited by the idea, and we all met for a drink before going back to our apartment. Then there was kissing. Then there was undressing. Then there was an hour of absolute euphoria. To go down on Leila while Randy went down on me, or to watch Randy tease Leila's left nipple while I teased her right—they were all embodied there, the various subjects of my desire. I reveled in the company.

How I missed Randy's discomfort is one of several shames I keep with me at all times. Only when Leila said, "Are you okay?" did I really look at him. He was beside me, one hand on my ass and the other stroking himself. Although he smiled, I could see that he was not there. It was not jealousy that pulled him away—that I could always recognize. It was some other feeling.

"I'm fine," he said.

Leila sat up. "We can stop."

Randy demurred at first, then nodded, saying maybe we should just relax for a while. I felt jolted by this shift, nearly asking why we would do that. I felt it truly, for a flash—the priority of my happiness over anyone else's. We lay there for a while, gazing at the ceiling, and then Leila said she should head out, she had an audition in the morning. I walked her to the door, then made a slow return to the bedroom. Randy was sitting on the bed, his pajama pants on.

"Should I be sorry?" I asked.

"Sorry? No." He would not look at me, even after I touched him.

"Did you have any fun?"

His laugh was painful to hear. "I don't know, Jack."

"Do I need to be sorry?"

"Stop asking that. I have to pee." He closed the bathroom door behind him while I sat in the bedroom feeling increasingly ill. How did it enter my mind at the same time, then, the image of Randy's face between Leila's legs? How does it ever happen that lust gains traction in moments of strife? I felt like a person divided. My stiffened briefs versus my wallowing mind. Hearing Randy flush, I climbed quickly into bed, not wanting him to see me in this state.

"Going to bed?" he asked.

"It's late."

He left the bedroom and I did not follow him. I still return to that evening. I would like to say it is always for penance, but it is just as regularly for pleasure. The image of Randy between Leila's legs, his mouth pressed against her spread sex and his eyes wide. I believed it was a look of wonder. I believed it was one of the most sensational things I had ever seen, and still do, so long as I pretend to not know all that came after.

This experience hangs over the hot tub like a cloud of cautionary gnats. But the more I watch Randy, the more certain I am that I am not projecting pleasure onto him. He laughs, sticks his foot into the air to show the odd lengths of his toes, tells the story of his first time giving someone a hickey, a story that is funny but not entirely lacking in eroticism. Then, as if to vanquish any lingering question, he takes his swimsuit off. It rises like a trash bag from below, ballooning in the jets. "I thought I'd join the party," he says.

Polly and Paul clap. It occurs to me that Randy might be getting drunk when I clock my own inhibition. "These drinks are strong," I say, sliding out of my suit. It does not rise with the showiness that Randy's did, and so I coax it upward. "Voila."

"Voila!" Polly throws her head back. "I love that."

"Everyone knows *voila*," Paul says.

"It's less about knowing than doing," Polly says. "You never say *voila*."

"That's true." Paul touches Polly's cheek. "I'll voila you any time you want."

"Maybe I don't want your voila." Polly gives him the stink eye before leaning against him. "Let's get back to your story. You were about to get to the good part."

We had been telling them about how we met before being sidelined by a joke that led to the remembrance of a song popular in our teenage years, the chorus of which we sang as a group. Then the conversation lapsed back to its two primary refrains: the comfort of the hot tub and the beauty of the night.

"Right," I say. "Where were we?"

"You were up against a tree," Paul says.

"Right. I was at the park, reading a book and eating a jar of olives, when my light was taken by this total hunk of a man. I thought he was going to ask me about my book. Instead he held out his hand, smiled, and said, 'Mark?'"

"Mark!" Polly shouts. "Who is Mark?"

Randy takes over. We haven't told this story in a while, and it's nice to see that we both remember our lines. "Mark is the man I was supposed to be meeting for a blind date," he says. "My friend described him poorly. Or maybe I was just hoping it was you." He puts his hand on my leg and I can feel the pruning of his fingertips even underwater.

"To Randy's credit, they were supposed to meet near to where I was sitting. Mark was just a few trees north."

I never saw Mark clearly. I stayed at the park for the duration of their date, stealing occasional glances in their direction. It was impossible to focus once Randy walked away, the poems I'd been reading looking like hieroglyphs on the page. Randy and I had hardly spoken before he left to find Mark, but his gaze during our brief exchange had rendered me into something higher than what I'd ever seen myself to be. I leaned back on my blanket and stared at the green canopy overhead. It felt painted. I felt painted. That, I was already discovering, was the Randy effect. I wanted him to come back.

"And he did come back," I say. "He came back and asked me for an olive."

"Only he'd already finished the olives," Randy says. "And I'll never forget what he said when he showed me the empty jar. He told me that it was one of the only things he'd inherited from his mom, this bottomless hunger for green olives." Randy shakes his head. "I thought that was so sad. That all he'd taken from her was that."

"And what about you?" Polly asks me. "Did you think it was sad?"

"Not really. I've taken things from her, and from a thousand other people in my life. I like it that way. I'm egalitarian."

Paul laughs. "As someone who's taken everything from his father, I think your way sounds smart," he says. "Give me the olives and spare me the mental health crises."

"Paul's got a troubled family," Polly says. "The most troubled ever, maybe."

Paul raps a knuckle against his head with some force,

then says, "Don't let us distract you. You're all out of olives"—he looks at me—"so what do you do?"

"I offer to buy him a martini."

Paul and Polly laugh, commending my quick thinking. The mood remains light, though Randy's comment has stuck to me like a burr. It's never come up in our telling of the story, whether to ourselves or to others. His stance isn't the surprise—he believed his parents had given him nearly all of himself, sometimes for better and sometimes for worse. The surprise is that this disconnect between us was there from our very first day.

"Let's hear about you," I say to Polly and Paul. "Sausalito, you said?"

"Sausalito," Paul confirms. Then, in a tune like a commercial jingle, he sings, "Gotta go to Sausalito, where they know where the dreams go."

"And the breeze is the sweetest thing," Polly jumps in. "For it frees all of everything." When she lets her last note drop, they both laugh.

"That's a P and P original," Paul says.

"Written from the lofty heights of a mushroom trip."

Paul grins. "If there's one thing we loved in Sausalito, it was eating dirty dried caps while Richardson Bay kissed the bottoms of our feet."

"That," Polly adds, "and singing each other love songs on the community karaoke machine. Paul's got a great voice. We both have great voices, actually."

What brought Polly and Paul to California was a flyer. Paul found his taped to the bathroom stall of a music venue in Olympia. Polly found hers under a bench in Arizona. The flyer's text was scant—dates, an address, a line drawing of a houseboat. At the center, this question: *Homesick?* And beneath, the entreaty: *Come home.*

Polly and Paul were homesick, except not in the standard sense of the word. Polly lived at home, after all, and Paul did not have a home he wanted to return to. The feeling, then, was closer to the spiritual unhousing Heidegger talks about, or was it Nietzsche? Who knew—their passion for philosophy lasted no longer than a summer. The point is their unrootedness left Polly intermittently angry and Paul intermittently suicidal. Here was the unfortunate truth of his inheritance: nearly every man in Paul's family had dug his own grave. "I didn't want to follow them," he explains. "But sometimes the knowledge of a path's existence is all it takes to find yourself three miles down it. Playing jazz was the best distraction I had. Once the music stopped, I had no good defense. My forebears always came knocking."

"What did I say about a troubled family?" Polly asks. "Paul's universe isn't turtles all the way down. Paul's universe is trouble all the way down. I could feel it when I first met him. I want to loosen that rope, I remember thinking the moment I saw him."

"Don't cry for me, Pollentina!" Paul says, though Polly doesn't appear to be crying. "We're years later. You did loosen that rope."

"Sorry, sorry." She puts her face in her hands, then drops her face to the water. Whatever sound she makes down there—a scream, a shout—becomes distorted and whaleish at the surface. She reemerges with water dripping from her chin. "I'm a very empathetic person," she says. "Would I trade it? On some days, yes. Then I remember that it got me Paul. Empathy hooked me the catch of the century."

Paul pulls Polly in for a kiss that quickly escalates into a full-mouthed affair. I almost laugh, the display of affection is that uninhibited. Polly's tongue is deep in Paul's mouth, then his in hers; at the waterline, he squeezes her breast like a ball of dough. Randy does not look surprised, instead watching with his telltale signs of arousal: slackening of the jaw, glossing of the eyes. His arousal jolts my own, and I shirk my misgivings, finding Randy's hand again and leading it up my thigh. It is exactly when we meet my rising erection that Polly pulls herself from Paul, wiping saliva from her lips and letting loose a full-throated howl.

"Animals!" she shouts. "We are animals." Another howl, this one longer and louder than the first. I flinch at the sound, which is funny enough to be frightening, or frightening enough to be funny. "I was going to tell you about my anger," Polly continues. "My trouble wasn't like Paul's trouble. He was another link on the family fence. I was a mutation. Angry as an armadillo in a family of peacekeepers. My mother and father both worked in harm reduction for addicts. My brothers are all school counselors. There was no such thing as an argument in our household, only a discussion. The raised voice, my father likes to say, is the dazed voice."

Like a black hole, Polly's anger was born from nothing. She awoke one day with gripped fists and a pounding heart. She was fifteen, a swimmer. She liked braiding hemp necklaces and playing goalie while her brothers shot pucks at her. That morning, something in her disposition had been altered. "It was as if someone had been whispering horrible things in my ear all night," she says. "Except when I woke up, I couldn't remember what they'd said."

She did not at first know to name the feeling as anger. Getting dressed, she thought it might be a fever; then, going downstairs and finding herself tempted to knock down the family photos, a possession. "You look pissed," her second-oldest brother said as he poured himself a bowl of cereal. "If it's something I did, I'd love to talk through it." As soon as it was named, she felt it. And as soon as she felt it, a terrible shame swept through her, not allaying her fury but further toxifying its fumes. Angry was the worst thing you could be in her family.

So what could she do other than bury her anger behind a civil veneer? Soon she was a swimmer, a goalie, a necklace maker, a chess player, a flautist, and a table tennis champion. Her parents worried she would burn out, not seeing that she was already burning out somewhere only she knew. "Part of my shame was in how baseless the anger seemed," Polly explains. "Nothing terrible had happened to me. I had friends. I had ambitions. I had parents and brothers whose kindness was so profuse that it actually began to sicken me. I wondered if I weren't evil. That's how confused I was. Poor thing. Poor Polly. Evil. Can you imagine?"

The desert and its furious geography became a harbor for her. There are few places as punishing. She would go there and scream, or run herself into cactus barbs, or throw rocks at the scampering lizards. In this way she was able to maintain a façade of stability through high school and several years beyond. When she saw the flyer, she felt all at once that she was on the verge of cracking, that it was a miracle she hadn't yet; too, she felt the closest to an answer she'd ever come. Homesickness felt right in an essential way. It was the first afternoon in a long while that she didn't punch a cactus.

"You punched a cactus?" I ask.

"I punched a hundred cactuses. Look." She scoots toward me and offers up her hands, the knuckles richly scarred. "But none after that day. I moved to Sausalito and I found happy."

"Happy." Paul points proudly to himself. "If God were real and here right now, I would shake his hand for giving us such poor lots. If we'd been more content people, we wouldn't have followed a piece of paper and joined a cult. We would've been parallel lines."

"It wasn't a cult," Polly says, reading the question on our faces. "Or it was, depending on your standards. Mostly it was a wellness community with some bad sexual politics. It really wasn't all bad. We even liked some parts of it. The karaoke machine, for instance. The daily yoga. Right, Paul?"

"Right."

"We stuck around as long as it took to fall in love. Then we boogied south. Then we boogied east. Then we boogied north and west and got ourselves here. It's been twenty years of beachside living. How could we ever leave behind sunsets like these?" Polly stretches her arms over her head and yawns. "I wonder what time it is."

"If you're tired—" I start.

"You'll know when I'm tired, Jackalope." She leans forward and holds me in her gaze. "The night is young. I want to play a game. I want another big drink. I want to feel like all the crap in the world will turn to roses. Let's go inside."

"That's a great idea, P," Paul says. "I love that idea."

The suddenness of Paul's response, plus the acquiescence, tells me what I need to know: that Polly's mood is at risk of turning. We all stand.

"It's freezing," I say, hugging myself and clambering from the jacuzzi before helping Randy do the same.

"Inside will be warm," Polly says from where she and Paul continue to stand. "Give us a minute. You'll find robes in the bathroom. First door to the left. Look, Paul's pointing the way." She nods to Paul's fully erect penis. I can't decide what's most amazing: that Paul has an erection after Polly's story, or that Paul has an erection, in spite of the cold, and is standing before us at all.

"Warm robes dead ahead!" he says, bouncing his hips.

By the time we reach the door, the jacuzzi's jets have shut off and a fibrous silence has taken the place of their roar. It takes everything in me not to turn around, especially when I hear movement in the water. Only when we are inside do I sneak a glance out. Polly and Paul are not kissing or groping one another. They are holding each other in a tight hug, faces burrowed in each other's necks.

"Who knew Paul was so hung," Randy calls from the bathroom.

This makes me laugh harder than it should, less for its content than for the release it provides. Randy emerges from the doorway and tosses me a plush robe. I try to read how he is feeling and, seeing nothing clear, say, "Those two have some serious history between them."

"They're monuments. You can see the way living has piled up on them."

Our position and the overhead light makes it so all I see, looking past Randy, is our own reflection in the patio door. "Do you think they're cute?" I ask.

"I think they're combustible."

The sliding door scrapes open, replacing our reflection with Polly's grinning face.

"Peeping Jack!" she says cheerfully. There are tears on her cheeks. "You like?"

She poses, thrusting out her hip as Paul shivers behind her. I am only able to focus on her, seeing now why she first looked familiar to me. Polly is how I imagined Rex's sister in *Parthenon*. The hair, the age, the mannerisms. Would it be a thrill or a nightmare to meet one of your characters in real life? I'm sure my first instinct would be to apologize.

L'ORIGINE D'ELIZABETH

Paul makes a fresh round of cocktails while Polly heats a coal for the hookah on the stove. In the warmth of the living room, beneath the blur of incense, I try to settle the low-grade nerves Polly and Paul's stories brought out in me. The two can be heard singing down the hallway. Beside me, Randy hums along. It is so soft a sound, so internal, that I only know he is making it by the vibrations I feel through our touching shoulders.

"Name five more things," I say.

"I like them," Randy says. "Polly and Paul."

"Me too." I wonder if he's said this because it doesn't seem to him that I'm having a good time. "Do you remember Agatha from *Parthenon*? Polly is exactly how I imagined her."

"Agatha," Randy says. At first I think he's forgotten her, forgotten *Parthenon*, forgotten that I was ever a playwright. "I don't see it." He twists a lock of his hair into a coil then lets it unravel. "I like them," he says again. "They live close to the root."

"Close to the root?"

"You know. Down low."

Polly materializes, holding a glowing coal with a pair of thin metal tongs. "I'll open the flume," she says, setting the coal on the hookah's foiled bowl and taking five deep pulls. Fruity smoke pours from her mouth, briefly obscuring her entire head. "Yum. Paul just finished this shisha batch. Let's see if you can guess the flavor."

Randy takes a modest hit. "Strawberry?"

"Let's let Jack guess."

The smoke makes me cough immediately.

"Don't tell me the coal's already gone harsh," Paul says. He puts the tray of drinks on the ottoman and takes the hose, sucking in a massive pull that overcasts the whole room after he expels it. "Nope. Jack must have sensitive breathers."

"It's been a while." I grab a drink to soothe my throat. It tastes like a martini stirred into a piña colada. "What's in here?"

"You're better off asking what isn't," Paul says.

"So, what's your guess, Jack?" Polly asks.

I try to remember how the smoke tasted before I hacked it up and, failing, go with Randy's suggestion of strawberry.

"Strawberry lemonade," Polly says. She rubs Paul's shoulder. "I'm getting some lemon, hon. You still owe me five bucks."

They lower themselves to the floor, transforming at once

into the subjects of Courbet's *L'origine du monde* and ORLAN's *L'origine de la guerre*. Paul is no longer aroused like the man in the ORLAN painting, but his reddish body hair and general shape are nearly identical. Polly's resemblance to Courbet's woman is uncanny—and more exact, even, than hers to Agatha. It is in the body, and also in the face, missing from the painting for a century before resurfacing in 2013. I remember the night the discovery was announced, igniting a lively conversation around our dinner table: Did the painting, seen as a whole, offset accusations of the work being objectifying? Was the work objectifying? And was objectification inherently bad, whether in art or life? To the last question I said no, having been made an object and having loved it. Friends' eyebrows raised around the table, but soon everyone agreed: subjecthood is a blessing and burden, worth casting off now and then.

"I get so stiff the second I'm out of that water," Polly says, stretching her neck. "Now I know why my cat stopped going upstairs when I was a kid. I used to take it personally. I used to take everything personally. I've ended up just like him."

Paul meows. "We're all just like him."

"How do you two fight it?" Polly asks. "How do you stop your creaks from creaking?"

Whatever we do, we haven't done in some time. Those parts of our lives—the Pilates and diets, the chiropractor and the acupuncture—died their own deaths when Ms. Rourke went.

"We languish and toil," I say. "A method recommended by no one."

"I saw that when you first came through the door," Polly

says, her voice made deep and prophetic by a fresh hit of tobacco. "I saw your languish and your toil. You boys are walking around with cement backpacks. You came through the door and I saw that."

"My mother died," Randy says. He sounds excited, as if he's been waiting all night to offer forward his misery. "All I do is miss her."

"I thought that was it, that you might be missing Mommy. What is her name?"

"Rhonda."

"Rhonda. What a beautiful name." Polly's smile grows wide. "I love beautiful names. I love beautiful things. I can tell you do, too."

Randy nods like a kid. I'd choose Polly's soothsaying over her howling, but her sonorous tone is grating in its own way, especially when she starts asking Randy about his familiarity with certain Hindu texts. Paul seems to be asleep, although his fingertips are busy tapping on his sternum. I let my gaze wander south. My eyes don't linger on his thighs or stomach, and certainly not on his penis, passing over everything as directionlessly as a paper airplane.

The origin of the world. The origin of war. ORLAN's piece was created in response to Courbet's—who brings about life but women; who brings about war but men—though the opposition is generated largely through the names of the paintings. Untitled, you might think the artists were trying to demonstrate the shared qualities between naked bodies at rest: how soft they are, how marvelous in their unbothered ease.

"Tantric massage?" Randy asks, pulling me back.

"It's a weekly ritual for us," Polly says. "The primary way

we keep ourselves physically and spiritually limber. These days the spirit is easier to bend. We can show you, if you like."

Paul heaves himself up with the help of the ottoman. "It's the best thing we took from the wellness community, besides each other. Those people love tantra. The first time I saw everyone laid out on the floor, I remember wondering what the hell I'd gotten myself into. Then this guy massaged every question, comment, and concern away." He steps back. "I'll get the coconut oil."

Tantric massage, Polly tells us, is about the union of mindfulness and pleasure. The goal is not orgasm but expanded consciousness. "Not that those things can't coexist. I certainly saw plenty of *O*s on that houseboat." She pauses, touching a finger to her lips. "Admittedly the wellness community was not the model for true tantra. We aren't, either. Tantra is about what works for you, the individual. That's how I see it."

Paul returns with the oil and an oversized towel, which he spreads on the carpet.

"You go first," Polly tells him. "In another life, I'm sure I was a shepherd. There's something about guiding that feels natural to me. Sometimes I dream of sheep in distress."

Paul hands her the oil then positions himself faceup on the towel. She drizzles an excessive amount over his belly, chest, and legs, the smell cutting through the other aromas in the room. "Tantric massage is all about the erogenous zones." She places her palm on Paul's stomach and begins to rub. "But you must build to those areas." Her circle widens, and soon Paul's whole stomach is shiny. "There are paths running through the body. By mapping them, you show your consciousness all the places it can explore." Her hand moves up to Paul's sternum. She oils his pecs, leaving a one-inch boundary around his pink nipples. Then she works his arms, attending to his biceps, forearms, and hands before lifting them over his head and rubbing oil into his armpits. Paul, who has his eyes closed, smiles as she does this. Already he seems far away, tucked beneath several layers of invisible drapery.

The massage feels simultaneously intimate and clinical. Intimate for the way Polly is touching Paul and the way he is responding to her touch—occasional moans, a returned erection—and clinical for the way Polly narrates her actions. I try to focus on the mechanical elements, still needing to cross my legs and adjust my robe after she begins rubbing his legs.

"Paul carries his darkness here," Polly says, addressing his thighs. "At least usually. That's why I pay special attention to the quads." She bends closer to him, pressing her elbow into his muscle and tracing it toward the knee. "I'm not getting rid of the sadness because there is no getting rid of Paul's sadness. What I'm trying to do"—she changes to his other leg, repeating the elbow technique—"is loosen the body so the mind can follow. Paul sees his sadness as a field of poppies. On bad days, the poppy stems are rigid and brittle, the blooms made of glass. When we keep things loose, everything can sway."

I feel like I am there, in the field of Paul's psyche, with glass blossoms chiming off of one another like bells. I try to visualize the geography of Randy's grief, to guess where it might be within him. But it seems impossible that Randy's grief is localized to any one place.

Paul groans. Polly has reached his crotch, maintai the same one-inch gap she did with his nipples. "Erogenous zones are important because of how much they contain. That's another reason you can't go straight to them. Imagine skipping over the front yard to get to the solar system." She shakes her head, then says, "You'd never be ready for the stars," before grabbing Paul's penis. I watch his mouth open, hear his breath tug into his throat. She strokes him. I adjust my legs again and, when I do, Polly glances at me.

"It's okay. Collective arousal is precious, largely neglected in our culture." She pours more coconut oil on him, then continues her caressing. "Think of church or baseball games, minus the dogma and the idiot fans. Humans gather in search of porous borders, then clutter the airspace in unnecessary ways." She drops Paul's penis, which twitches against his belly, and smiles at us. "My highest self is the one that's massaging Paul, because she knows she's doing something vital for someone else."

My erection does a twitch of its own. "Do you think energy gets passed between people?" I ask.

"Of course. Everything is contagious. That's not a bad thing, by the way, so long as you know how to receive and redirect."

I nod like a disciple. I want to receive and redirect. I also want Randy to hear that his grief is not harmless, that I am regular collateral. Reverently I watch Polly handle Paul's nipples, mouth, and scrotum. More reverently, I watch as she tells him to roll over and begins to oil his broad ass. She is so unabashed in what she does, so expert, that I am not surprised when she spreads his cheeks and pushes a finger inside of him. I remember Randy and I on the stairs. So close to succeeding, to meeting in the ether. "I love you, Jack," he had said, and I felt it within me, his love, right before he left me lying there like an open gate.

Polly presses down on the base of Paul's back to steady his shuddering body. I sip my drink, feeling fuzzy, horny, enlightened—or on the verge of becoming so. Randy's robe is bunched up. I have the urge to reach inside, to see if he is half as turned on as I am. He's stayed quiet beside me, but seems equally transfixed.

"You found his heart," he says then.

"Exactly, Randy." Polly sounds proud. "This is the heart of Paul's galaxy."

I want to add something to show that I'm also a quick study, but there isn't more to say. She is in the heart of Paul's galaxy, and continues to work her way deeper, only stopping when he seems on the cusp of an orgasm, a breakdown, or both. Then she withdraws and lays her body over his. It is a swift deflation, almost disappointing. But then they begin to breathe as a single being and my disappointment disappears. I imagine Polly's body subsumed by Paul's, then mine subsumed by Randy's, then all four of us puddled in a boundaryless heap. The vision is beautiful, nearly tear-inducing, and semi-squandered when I burp up a ball of alcoholic fumes.

"Who wants to do me?" Polly asks, rolling off of Paul.

"Me," Randy says at once.

"Attaboy." Paul's voice is surprising to hear, like someone speaking after a months-long coma. "I won't tell you where she keeps her anger. It isn't where you'd guess." He laughs as he hoists himself up. "I hand the towel off to you, dear," he says, kissing Polly's cheek. "Sorry if it's a little wet. My consciousness spills." He wanders off, dazed as a newborn.

"I always start on my stomach," Polly says. "In this way Paul and I are different."

"Where should I start?" Randy asks, braced on his knees beside her.

"You decide. Your exploration guides mine. It's part of the reason I wanted one of you to massage me. You don't have me mapped like Paul does." She reaches up and touches the belt of Randy's robe, turning it over in her fingers. "What's a tide pool with Paul could be a canyon with you. We won't know until you touch me."

Randy nods. A moment of private inquiry, a conversation had only with himself. I am the combustible one, I think suddenly, watching him. At risk of exploding if he touches her, at risk of exploding if he doesn't. My whole body feels ready to come. The feeling pulsates when Randy finally pours oil down Polly's spine, where it spreads venously. I want to lick it, not just the snaking fluid but the whole tableau, the room itself.

"What is this?" Randy asks.

I adjust my position and see a rectangular patch of skin on Polly's side, so distinct from the rest of her back that it appears to be made of a different material entirely. Paper, perhaps, or marble. It spans her entire right ribcage.

"That's my graft," Polly says, craning her neck to look back. "That's Elizabeth."

"Elizabeth?"

"Elizabeth, Lizzie. It's the name we gave her, years and years ago. The cadaver. The name we gave the cadaver who got me this skin after my motorcycle accident. The hospital wouldn't give her information, so we made up a life."

Randy traces the graft's outline with two fingers. "Tell me," he says. "Tell me her life."

"It was so long ago."

"Please." He presses his whole palm down, then blinks in astonishment. This is what wonder looks like. A far cry from the face he made with Leila, yet the remembrance still redoubles my arousal. I want him on top of Polly, beneath her. I want Polly moaning in the same way Leila moaned—a whinnying sound, yet lovely.

"Paler than Elizabeth," Polly says. "That's where it all started. I woke up after my surgery and the first thing Paul said is that I'd been given royal skin, paler than Elizabeth's." She rests her head on her hand, settling into the memory. "Queen Elizabeth I, that is."

The fuller writing of Elizabeth's life began later, once they returned home. They were living in town then, new to Florence and without friends or community. This was before the bookstore, before the wedding, before almost everything that came to define the current era of their lives. Paul worked days and Polly, homebound during recovery, had to fill the hours. It was the first time in her life she felt uneasy with solitude. The unease did not have to do with the weather or the apartment, though both were dreary, and even less to do with the pain or painkillers, though both had a history of destabilizing her. She was hardly experiencing pain, in fact. Why, then, could she not sit still, not read any of the books she owned, not dial back any of the friends who'd called to check in on her? "The answer should have been obvious," Polly says. "It was in retrospect."

"Elizabeth." Randy sounds starstruck, saying the name. "Elizabeth."

The graft did not itch or burn, sting or ache; once the initial tenderness was gone, she actually could not feel the patch at all. "That's what bothered me. How other it felt. I didn't feel alone. I felt watched. Scrutinized. My life was inhabited by a stranger whose name I didn't know, whose face I'd never see. I started having dreams where I pulled the graft off, filled with the same anger that used to run me through the desert. That's when Paul intervened. He said she didn't have to be a stranger."

Every day, they would each invent a detail for Elizabeth's life and join the two facts over dinner. Elizabeth was from an imaginary place called Draconia, allergic to the sun, in love with a boy she believed could turn into a fly. She had a middle part and eyes like pennies. She had a healthy relationship to her parents but not her pets, who gathered at her door every night. During her senior year, she was nominated homecoming queen (she needed some tie to royalty, obviously) and became a tyrant during her reign. In Elizabeth's world, whatever that world was, the homecoming court was a real monarchy. "We never decided when she lived," Polly says, "and we never decided how she died. I needed her real and not, like a fairy tale about a friend."

Within weeks, Elizabeth existed to them and so stopped haunting Polly. The story had served its purpose, and over the coming months, feeling began to emerge in the skin graft, proof to Polly that her body was reclaiming the portion of itself that had been lost. "I can feel your hand now, almost completely," she says. "It's funny to think about all of this. It's been a long time. I'm surprised I remember so much."

The oil has dried on her back, making it look as if a snail made a winding tour between her neck and hips. Randy has both hands on her side. Worry creases his brow and his jaw is tightly set. "But she's still here," he says, parting his hands to look at the graft. "Right? She's here."

"It's a story. She's just a story."

He looks at Polly as if she's just hit him. "She isn't. She lived. And you needed her."

Polly shifts away from him. "I needed her for a while. The story of her. But it was also fun. She was a teenage tyrant, for heaven's sake!" She smiles, attempts a laugh.

"It's not funny," Randy says. His voice is subterranean. When Polly rolls onto her back, the urge to turn her back over is clear in his eyes.

"Randy, relax," I say. I shift forward, and this time my burp brings bile up with it, the sourness sticking in the back of my throat. "We're having a good time."

"You're not even here," Randy shoots back.

"What?" I laugh, but feel exposed, caught in my daydreaming.

"She's not real," Polly says, sitting up. "There's no Elizabeth."

"There's someone," Randy says. "You made room and then took it away."

"It's skin." She slaps the graft. "Skin."

"And it's Polly's body," I say. "So let it go."

Randy's expression darkens. From somewhere above us a dog barks once, twice.

"We woke up Diesel," Polly says. "He's sick and old and picks up on bad energy faster than I do. Can we call a truce, Randy? Agree to disagree?"

For a moment I expect Randy to burst out in laughter, his expression suddenly full of bizarre light. "It isn't just your body," he says. He isn't yelling, but he is quite loud. "I felt her. You can't throw the dead away."

The dog's barking picks up.

"Please stop that!" Polly says. "You're upsetting him! I told you that he's old and sick, so please stop!"

She looks like she might cry. I scoot down the couch as if my proximity might help in appeasing the situation. Randy is silent, and soon the barking sputters, ending with a single agonized hack.

"Phew," Polly says with a small smile. "I feel his coughs in my chest. Awful."

Paul resurfaces, standing at the threshold of the room in a robe. "Cover yourselves, lady and gents. We've got unexpected company in the form of wasted teens."

Polly leaps up, collecting the towel and wrapping it around herself. "Are they okay? We have that focaccia in the kitchen."

"They're fine. A tough night between Carolina's folks, but they're laughing. I found them in the hot tub. Luckily I was able to put this on before they saw me." He yanks open his robe then closes it again. "I got them water and told them to stay put."

"Carolina?" I ask.

"Best friend to our niece, Shelby," Polly says. "I think you met them in town." She has shifted into another new persona, this one motherly and concerned. "I hate to kick you out. We should probably get them sorted." She's already walking from the room by the time she finishes speaking.

"Rain check?" Paul doesn't wait for an answer before leaving us.

Randy is still on his knees, breathing like a bull and not appearing to have registered what's happened. All at once I'm appalled by his grief, the depravity of it. He looks like a creature, bent and ghoulish. I could kick him. What gives him the right to pull the rest of the world down? What happened to the good time we were having?

Just as quickly as I have these thoughts, I am pulled by the exact opposite, the pitifulness that made me resentful now filling me with mercy.

Randy's robe has fallen open. Before going to help him stand, guiding him back to our house and into the living room, where he will not speak to me, instead grabbing *Bruiser* and disappearing into the office, I look at his penis, more withdrawn than I've ever seen, pulled back from the world as if scorched by an unbearable heat.

MY BEST THING

Leila and I do not speak for a month following the botched threesome. When I call her, walking home from my first and final pottery class, she answers right away. "Jack," she says. "I thought you'd put me on the No-Fly List."

"Definitely not. It's been a busy month."

"For me, too. Have you worked with Nigel Reed? He's a total twat."

I laugh, tell her no. It is the day after Halloween. Candy wrappers are strewn across the sidewalk, a colorful imitation of fallen leaves. We get to talking about Reed, who has told Leila she's doing Halie all wrong, then about *Buried Child* itself.

"I'm worried he's going to kill it for me," she says. "If Nigel Reed kills Sam Shepard, I'm going to kill him. I hope you'll help."

In a café window, I look happy. Happier than I've been looking. Randy and I are still out of sync. We are not miserable. We are not thriving. Leila, like many actors, has the capacity to make you feel like you are thriving. It's what first drew me to her, how effortlessly artful our conversation felt.

Over the next seven blocks, we lob topics back and forth until we are juggling a dozen between us. Have I ever gotten my hair cut in Manhattan? Has she seen the Nan Goldin exhibit at MoMA? When I reach our street, I turn left instead of right. Sometimes, when you don't want something to end, it is as easy as carrying it elsewhere. We go to Eastern Parkway, then to Brower Park, where a kindergarten class is doing yoga. The kids giggle in downward dog. Leila tells me about her cousin's marriage to a gay republican. I tell her about my resolution to drink more kombucha. We laugh, grow somber, impersonate a friend who has taken to mysticism after a car accident. When Leila has to go, I feel an immediate, plunging loss.

"Can I call you again?" I ask.

"You can always call me. I was a little peeved you let me sit for so long, if I'm being honest. No one talks like us."

I turn my back on the park, shy of my blushing face. It is embarrassing to have your pleasure so readable. And this, no doubt, is pleasure: to have Leila affirm for me what I've long felt about her. "I won't let it happen again," I say. "No one talks like us."

At home, Randy asks if I got lost and I tell him yes. Leila and I keep talking, calling each other almost every day, and because I don't tell Randy on the first day, I don't tell him on any day. I take the calls on the street or on the fire escape, the roof or the corner coffee shop. Our conversations are gab sessions, then roundtables, then therapeutic back-and-forths. Sometimes we joke as if preparing for a night at The Bell House. Sometimes we rant about politics, or parents, or exercise, and how much more of it our bodies require lately. In our canvassing of the mighty and the microscopic, we somehow avoid the night of the threesome, and our dating lives in general.

I don't let myself think about why this is the case. In my eyes, Randy and I are airtight, unbreakable, destined to grow old in bed together. Despite our offseason, there is never a question of wanting to leave him, for what constitutes stormy weather for us is still mostly mild. He toasts my bread in the morning; I rub his feet at night. As for Leila, I'm glad to be the one she calls when she's had a bad day or a good one. Sometimes she retreats—unexpectedly clipped, or avoiding my calls for a few days—but more often she is there as I am there, which is to say eagerly. "Are we ever going to hang out?" she asks one day.

"In person?" I realize the question is ridiculous as I say it.

"That is typically how it goes," Leila says. "A thing friends do." Her playfulness doesn't quite shroud the exasperation lying one level lower; it moves through her voice like a mouse under a towel. I apologize, say of course we are going to hang out, then I let another month of calls pass.

Then, out with my college friend Diego for drinks, I run into Leila on a date. She beams, lights up the room, invites us to join them. We politely pass, or rather I do. Seeing a stranger's arm around her shoulder has made it difficult to breathe, my throat tight with envy. I'm so rocked by the encounter that I end up telling Diego everything at the next bar. "This doesn't sound good," he says, licking the salty rim of his margarita. It doesn't. I don't need to see his worried eyes to recognize that. We split a beer before heading home.

Is it possible I am on the same block where I called Leila on Halloween when she calls me tonight? That is how I will remember it. The sidewalk is covered in a fine layer of snow. A miracle in New York City, Randy always says, to find snow that hasn't been trampled on.

"How was the date?" I say by way of answering.

"Jack. What are we doing?"

"I don't know. Walking home?"

She laughs. There is a moment when I think she might invite me over. Except then she laughs again, and I realize she is not actually laughing. She is crying.

"I'm drunk, so don't make fun of me sounding like an absolute loser. What are we doing, Jack? I've told you everything. Why have I told you everything?"

"What do you mean?"

"You know what I mean. I saw your face at the bar. What are we doing?"

"I don't know. I like it. We like it. We're friends."

"Friends." Now she laughs. "We're doing friends wrong, then. Friends don't talk like we talk. I don't talk with friends like that. I've told you everything."

I stop walking, looking up at the streetlight to see if fresh flakes are falling. I can't make out more than the light's orange glow. I am also drunk, I realize. The cold finds me in my stilled state. I should keep going, yet can't convince my legs forward. "Don't you like it?" I ask.

"Of course I like it. I love it."

A siren fills her end of the line. I lean against a brick wall that reeks of urine. The word's invocation has ripped a hole in the sky. Love. There are few instances when the unsayable is able to enter the world without shredding some part of it.

The siren wanes. Leila is still talking. "That night with Randy—"

"We don't have to talk about it."

I feel dizzy. It is snowing. The flakes land on the nape of my neck because I am so far hunched over. A group of college students wobble past me, unbothered to ruin such a perfect stretch of white.

"I want to talk about it. Or I want to tell you that it's stayed with me—something you did. Can I say this? I'm sorry, Jack. I'm drunk. My date sucked. Can I say this to you?"

I tell her yes, my fear of dissolution replaced by the need to know what mark I've left.

"You put your fingers in my mouth after having them in yours. It was such a small thing. I didn't even think about it much until we started talking again. I think about it all the time now. Do you even remember?" I hear a door close, the ding of an elevator. "When I'm in bed, or out with friends, or talking with you, I think of your fingers in my mouth and how good it felt. It's too much, Jack. Whatever we're doing is too much. I had to tell you that."

"Where are you?"

She hangs up. Again, the plunging feeling. A worse version of it. I don't remember getting home. I do remember calling Leila back until her phone went straight to voicemail. "You're my best thing." I said that in a voice message. My best thing.

I don't tell Randy that detail when I confess the next day. I do tell him about the months of phone calls. I am too bereft not to name my sickness. At first, the loss of Leila is the greater source of suffering than the hurt I have inflicted on Randy; soon, this will flip, and flip again.

"My mother thinks you've cheated," Randy tells me a few days later. He sits in our most uncomfortable chair, the one we say is for undistinguished guests. Back in his eyes is the old envy, black marbles staring out at me. He holds his fury in for a week, and the waiting is unbearable, the anticipation of damage being its own damage. Then he cracks, throwing a glass between me and the door when I go to leave one night. He begins to cry at once, and though the hand that pulls bloody slivers from my feet is repentant, the hand that steadies my ankle is not. "Don't go," he says repeatedly, both plea and command. Beneath his grip, my bone aches.

Throughout this time I am righteous as I insist on my innocence, and angry with Ms. Rourke, who should know what actual cheating is. Cheating is slipping on your husband's used condom on the kitchen floor. Cheating is a scratched-up back, a sweat-moistened car. Cheating is not a phone call. Cheating is not a hundred phone calls.

Then I remember the voicemail. My best thing. And how I would have gone to her that night, had Leila invited me.

ARTIST IS PRESENT

Tonight it is not Clarence's knock that wakes me, but his laugh. I am somewhere between drunk and hungover, and initially believe Randy is the one being so loud. He never came to bed after Polly and Paul's. I reached for him around midnight and found only bedspread. I felt sad, then bitter. Then I hugged my pillow and went back to sleep.

My vision spins when I sit up. The walls are blue with moonlight, the air chilly from the open window. Clarence's next laugh is even more blaring. My anger needs no warm-up, eager to finally have a bag I won't feel so bad punching. I stand, sway, then exit the bedroom, prepared to beat him out the door with a broom. What has he said to Randy? What has Randy said to him?

As quickly as these questions drive me forward, they

make me halt. It is the best thing to listen to and the worst thing to overhear, the story of your own life. Didn't someone say that? I withdraw to the landing, rest my elbows on its banister, and listen.

"I don't think that's true," Randy is saying.

"Then what is it?"

"Luck."

"Luck?" Clarence groans. "Don't give me luck."

A glass moves across the counter. Lips smack.

"But there is luck," Randy says. "Luck in who you know, who your friends know. Luck in who comes to your show and writes about it."

"Sure. Luck just isn't the heavenly fulcrum everyone makes it out to be. It's not the thing that finally makes you. True vision rises. That's what I think."

A stretch of silence. I can practically see Randy's thinking face. I drop to the floor. My face and neck are warm, flush from the thrill and shame of eavesdropping.

"I'd bet there are more unknown visionaries than known ones," Randy says.

"But them being unknown now doesn't mean they're unknown forever. Think of Darger. Dickinson. Their visions rose. They never gave up on the work. That's what I mean. So maybe the luck component is whether you get to see your vision rise. In that way, you are lucky. I don't think you're famous because of that luck. You were always going to rise."

"Kind of you to say."

"I mean it."

Their glasses clink. I make a face so ugly my muscles hurt. A protest brews in my chest, one that threatens to call down to make known that Clarence said Randy's work wasn't for him. Then it occurs to me that Claude said that, not Clarence. I release my hold on the banister. Claude, the one who started over, who quit the salmon farm and was living a happy life, a simple life. Of course he didn't like Randy's work. He was a chimp in a chapel. A moron.

"What's next?" Clarence asks. "Anything in the pipeline?"

"I haven't picked up my camera in a long time. I can't even remember the last thing I photographed. There is something in my head, though. Not photography. I don't know, it's all concept right now. And the concept is thin as mist."

"Not photography?"

"Maybe some photography. I'm not sure. It would be an installation of sorts. Mixed media." A glass taps three times against the counter, most likely Randy, who fidgets when he talks about new work.

"Tell me more."

"There isn't much to say. It's thin, like I said. But I know how I want it to feel," he says. "I know how I want it to feel when you walk in. It will be a warehouse. You'll walk in and you'll feel it right away. This thing, this weightiness. I don't have a name for it. I know there will be sound—I've been doing these recordings—and I might find some way to bring this book into it." There is a ruffling of pages, followed by laughter from Clarence.

"I thought you said it was terrible."

"It is terrible." The pages ruffle again, like a bothered bird. "One of the worst books I've ever read. I don't know what my father liked about it. But if I erase parts away, I was thinking I might find something that makes sense. It's a collaboration in that way. Both parts are—the recordings and the book. That's how I want it to feel. A whole family affair."

He is speaking in the voice that takes over when he talks about his work for long enough to cross more fully into its realm than ours. His artist-is-present voice. Historically I've found this voice inspiring or cloying, depending on the context. Now I find it practically unbelievable. When did Randy find time to reconstruct his faculty of invention when most days he forgets how to dress himself? It seems unfair, unjust, even, that his griefscape should be only selectively blighted.

Clarence begins asking a round of questions about the installation, suggesting possible approaches, including performance art, which he does have experience in, just so Randy knows. My stomach feels like it's been filled with hot oil. How cheap, the prospect of using the recordings. How selfish to capitalize on his parents' deaths. When I close my eyes I can already see it—the installation, the accolades—and I want to torch it all. Of course it will be marvelous. The crowd will go wild; the critics will bay from their pulpits. An artist sui generis, they will say.

I blow a stream of air toward the vaulted ceiling. My imagination is never so active as when I'm imagining Randy's possible successes or my possible failures, and I feel sick with the spiraling grandeur. The oil in my stomach has spread evenly through me, making my fingers and toes feverish. How lucky that Randy will be able to make something beautiful from all this pain we've suffered. How very fortunate for him.

"I wonder what Sally and Fran will think about this new thing," Clarence says. "You're like Led Zeppelin to them."

"Led Zeppelin?" Randy laughs.

"Look around, friend. You're on every wall. It's cool. I

know your work got them through tough times. You were like medicine to Fran during her troubles."

"She's told me. It's funny, when other people say things like that, about my photos having saved them, I never believe it. With her, I do."

I press myself forward, hungry for any unhappiness other than my own. Randy's never mentioned misfortune in relation to Fran, whom I've long taken as indomitable.

"What makes her different?" Clarence asks.

"Fran sees the photos how I see the photos. I don't know how else to say it. The first time she sent me a letter, I felt like the luckiest man alive."

I make another face. Hours and hours I've spent discussing Randy's photos with him, and not once has he expressed a feeling of good fortune at my appraisal.

"It's okay to get emotional!" Clarence says. "It's a beautiful thing, being seen. Do you know what Fran told me? She said that during the worst of it, she sat in front of one of your pictures for hours every day. I think it was the one of the woman dancing. They moved it to the living room so she could look at it from the couch. She couldn't stand for very long."

"I didn't know that," Randy says. "About it being that picture."

"It's true. Hours, she said. That's vision. That's your vision."

The photo is of a woman spinning in a crowd, everything about her blurry except for her face, which has been captured in a moment of ecstatic abandon. People often describe the photo as joyous, a grand departure in Randy Rourke's catalog of melancholy. I think she looks terrified to be so free. And what of Fran—what did she see that was so right, so accurate?

"What do you say to another?" Clarence asks. "Nightcap for the nightcap?"

"I shouldn't. I'm already seeing stars. Jack's probably wondering where I am."

"Jack, Jack, Jack. You will tell him I'm sorry, won't you? I really didn't mean any harm. Sometimes I get caught up when Claude has me in his grip. You understand."

"Sure."

They go quiet. I imagine them whispering about how sensitive I am, how incapable of dealing with life, death, the in-between.

"Do you think luck would've changed things for him?" Clarence asks. "Because I don't sense his problem is with luck. I sense his problem is with perseverance."

Randy grunts his disagreement. "Jack doesn't have a problem with perseverance. The best thing Jack ever did for himself was to stop persevering. Perseverance almost killed him."

My cheek throbs where I have it pressed against the railing.

"I guess that's as good a reason to quit as any," Clarence says. "Although it sounds worse to me, if I'm honest. Not making art sounds like hell. I'd be a bag."

One of them moves the glasses to the sink.

"I don't think it would have mattered," Randy says. "Luck. I don't think luck would have mattered for Jack. Not luck or money or success. He was always going to be unhappy."

"You think so?"

"I do. I don't know if anything can give Jack what he needs. He'd sooner throw a tomato at his own production than feel satisfied with it."

"What do you think Jack needs?"

I can't hear Randy's answer. I hung there briefly, in the interstitial space separating injury and pain, but now the hurt has caught me. I roll onto my back. My lungs feel small as coin purses, impossible to inflate. I grab for my fury, my sense of righteousness. But there is nothing warm in me. Randy is right: I am destined for unhappiness. And what an awful way to live and thing to be known for. I clutch my stomach as if I've been punched—I have been—jerking up when I hear footsteps. But they are not coming to me.

"I thought they'd blocked it off," Randy says.

"The tunnel? No way. It's my favorite way home."

Their voices diminish as they go into the basement. Soon, all I can hear is the rattle of the blinds moving with the wind.

I don't know how I get to bed, except perhaps by fear of being found prone and pathetic on the landing. I do not move when Randy steps through the door, do not move when he brushes his teeth and pees, do not move when he climbs beneath the covers beside me. The scent of brandy breaks through the spearmint of our toothpaste. He places his palm against the center of my back. "Jack," he says, less as an address than a naming.

Jack, Jack, Jack. Tell him I'm sorry.

PROOF BY EXHAUSTION

The earthquake, I decide the next morning, will interrupt Fabio's brunch after Julian cleans up the water spill. I awoke with this knowledge, alongside a vengeful urge to push my opening scene forward. Forget Clarence, forget Randy, who breathes so heavily beside me, his exhales sour with alcohol. I glare at him every time he moves, relishing my anger like a midnight cigarette.

You know, Julian, Fabio says. *You're about as agreeable as my fleshlight.*

That's rude, Sue Ellen replies. *Fleshlights have backbone. Julian is an invertebrate.*

You own a fleshlight? Ray asks.

Of course I own a fleshlight. I'm the prince of modernity.

Julian moves as if to speak, then things begin to tremble.

It starts at their table, the cups and plates and cutlery clanking, then expands to the whole diner.

Is this what an earthquake feels like? Ray asks, retrieving his coffee mug and taking a sip. No one can answer, because the noise has drastically increased. People are screaming outside. The other diners begin wolfing down their meals. One woman shoves bacon into her bra.

Julian looks up as a piece of the ceiling comes loose and falls toward him—time will be slowed for this—and as soon as it lands on his head, the stage goes black.

Randy stirs. I scoot away from his searching arm.

When the stage lights return, Julian is on the floor, illuminated by a beam of sunlight coming through a hole in the wall. He is alone in the ruined diner. It is silent, or maybe music trickles through unseen speakers, bent and unrecognizable. He sits up and rubs his head. Once he has regained orientation, he picks up a napkin, reading aloud the message written upon it: *Seemed like a surface wound! See you soon! (We hope!)*

What next? Julian walking miles and miles through desolate cityscape. Where is he headed? To his friends, surely. That's part of Julian's problem, his inability to detach from these idiots who don't care for him. He will go on a quest to find them. Seeking revenge? Apology? No. He is simply doing what he has always done, which is turning to them like a plant to the sun.

Outside of the diner, birds flock en masse, their poop falling like snow. Julian finds a woman throwing clothes into a crevasse. *What happened?* he asks her.

I lost weight. None of this stuff fits anymore.

I meant everywhere. What happened everywhere?

She narrows her eyes. *What happened is what always*

happens. We suffer the tumultuous love of a shifting planet. Where have you been? You smell like ketchup.

I was having brunch with my friends.

Brunch—now there's something. Anything good?

Eggs.

The woman gags, leaning dangerously far over the edge. *I'm a vegan*, she says. *I don't partake in the diet of corpses.*

A noise of vulturous satisfaction rises out of me. Randy shifts again, this time securing his arm over my chest. "I'm getting up," I say.

Downstairs it is another gray morning, the fog pressed like a voyeur against the windows. With the outer world shrouded, the house feels lost in a cloud, the rooms lit with steely light. The kitchen floor is cold under my feet and the chair I settle in hard against my back.

Which way is Green Street? Julian asks the woman.

Five blocks that way. She points behind him with the sleeve of the jacket she's holding. *Except it isn't Green Street anymore. Nothing is anything anymore.*

This last line prompts an idea: time will have passed in a substantial way since the earthquake, and will continue to pass in a substantial way as Julian journeys to each friend. The thought excites, then stalls me. How much time should elapse between visits. One year? Ten?

With a banana in hand, I pass through the office, not sparing Ms. Rourke's ashes or Randy's tape recorder so much as a glance—history's most minor act of defiance. I do catch sight of the notebook, and feel certain that Fran must have drawn the faceless girl during her convalescence. How else to account for the tedious method, the page-by-page process that must have taken hours, then days?

I stall at the top of the stairs, holding the banana like a gun. Then I go down. Where yesterday there was only floor at the base of the storm cellar, today there is an open hatch, the handle to which I must have missed in my quick assessment. I approach as if the doors might come alive, snapping me in their wooden jaws. Air rises from the dark with a mineral stink.

I find the ladder's first rung with my outstretched foot. The wood is smooth, well worn; beneath it are six additional rungs that eventually drop me to stone floor. In the darkness, the air hurtles past me. The ground has the gloss of glazed ceramic when I ignite my phone's flashlight, the tunnel walls as round as a cored apple. I continue forward.

Once the ladder has shrunk to a matchstick behind me, I speak. The speech feels unreal, stripped of resonance, so I repeat myself: "I wasn't born for this." It is Fabio's line, lacking sorely in spirit coming from my mouth. I shout a few times, delightedly disturbed to have my voice so wholly swallowed, before turning off the flashlight. In the dark, I feel the instantaneous freedom of imperceivability. It is a gift to escape the world's gaze. I lean against the wall and lower myself to the ground. I feel primordial. Un-alive. Hyper-alive. Down here, there is no such thing as opening nights or expiring produce, dead batteries or sick parents. What's a play? What's a husband? My neck touches the wall and a magnetic chill courses through me. Who is Jack? Not I. I am a pocket of air.

After a minute, or ten, my nonexistence sours. I reignite the light and am happy to see my hands and feet, no matter that they look made of clay. I flex my toes and the tendons leap out. Beyond them, there are markings on the wall, penciled missives I bend forward to read.

Bring back the toothbrush, Ollie. My turn to feel your teeth.

The wall is covered in messages, plus the smudged residue of many more. One set of handwriting is faint and delicate, the other dark and bold. The two merge only in content, nearly all of which is fanatically horny: *Make me a beard with your muff, Marie. Left some unwasheds for you. Sniff up, you dirty hog. I die every time you spit.*

The raunchiness defuses my unease. I track my way up the wall in staggered leaps—*Won't you bring me more cunt-soaked fruit? Lick the floor, I came barefoot.*—before finding a note straight above: *Did you find me all the way up here, my little spigot?* The note makes me smile, then frown. The message is for Marie, except by having looked up myself I feel it is for me, too. Goosebumps parade down my arms. I hoist myself up.

Behind me, a single question fills the wall. *Where did you go?* Penned by Marie, the sentence must appear a hundred times. I imagine Oliver swept out to sea, knocked down by a heart attack, or, worse, simply losing interest. Then I imagine Randy, sitting with Ms. Rourke's urn in his lap not even two weeks ago, tracing a finger through her ashes as if tending to a Zen garden. Randy on the floor, Randy chewing on a watermelon rind. Where does he go?

I press forward, congested with our collective bad weather. When I finally reach Clarence's ladder, Sally and Fran's is a speck of light. The air snakes its way up my shirt and grips my ribs. These rungs are rougher than the others. I picture Sally and Frank sandpapering theirs while debating something ploddingly academic. The vision, meant to distract, brings an unexpected surge of affection for our hosts. Fran's troubles, Sally's voice on the phone when Ms. Rourke died, so spotlessly kind.

Hunched at the top of the ladder, I listen for movement overhead. I inch the hatch upward, then climb into the cellar, the upper doors of which are still closed. I ought to rush upstairs, clutch Clarence's shirt in my hands, and tell him that his is the sad life, not mine. He's the one who lives alone, who pretends to be someone else for a low-budget production no one will ever see, directed (I imagine) by a film school dropout. What kind of artistry is that?

I push through the next set of doors. A window well lights the basement. I am so poised to see someone that at first I think I've revealed myself to an entire room people. But I am looking at a crowd of garments. Clarence has strung up three clotheslines with outfits hanging from each. A tuxedo beside a pair of stained overalls, a flannel and jeans beside a sequined jumper. Characters he has played over the years. They are flattened and stiff, as if frozen by liquid nitrogen. One of the T-shirts is torn and bloody. One pair of shorts has peaches painted on its pockets.

Pacing thuds sound overhead. The first intact sentence I hear from Clarence is this: "His nickname was The Arm." The second and third, moments later: "I could have hit a dog or a family. I didn't care." And the fourth: "My father has been trying to apologize for years."

Except this fourth line should come before the other three. I know because I wrote them. The monologue, delivered by the main character in my third play, *Proof by Exhaustion*, is about her father's unrelenting efforts to apologize to her and her unrelenting efforts to refuse his apologies. He has filled her mailbox with letters, her telephone with voicemails, and her windowsill with pebbles. That he was able to get the pebbles to her fourth-floor window is a testament to his baseball years, where "The Arm" moniker was born. It is the pebbles she thinks might hit a dog or a family, because she pushes them off when they accumulate too highly. "I rained them down," Clarence says, getting her pride exactly right.

I lean my head on the lip of the cellar. If Clarence weren't approaching the part so reverently, I'd think he was reading it as a form of sadistic mockery. Each time he restarts, he is closer to character. I'd want him to be terrible if he were performing anyone else's work; with mine, his talent delights me. And the monologue, to my relief, is compelling. Funny and ridiculous, desperate and surprising. This is unexpected, as the appeal of my own writing rarely lasts longer than six months. Maybe it has aged through its repugnance like certain cheeses will, given a new life by refashioning its moldy edges into something you want to sink your teeth into.

Clarence has begun the monologue for the fifth time when my phone rings. The ringtone, a violin rendition of "Bohemian Rhapsody" chosen as a joke by Randy two years ago, is jarring even when you are expecting it. Today it almost throws me down the hole. It takes a frantic moment to turn it off. The silence that follows is cosmic.

For a moment, every breath is held, even the garments appearing frightened.

Then there is a step.

And another.

By the third, my instincts pull the cellar door closed. I land hard on the tunnel floor, the impact sending a jolt of pain from my ankles to my knees. My hobble becomes a jog. Then my jog becomes a hobble. I am afraid, and embarrassed to be afraid. Clarence will not hurt me if he finds me. At worst, he will ask if I am searching for my lost ambition.

I tell myself these things, and still am intermittently overcome with panic. I speed up, get embarrassed, slow again.

By the time I surface in Sally and Fran's basement, I am wild with my own gaslit adrenaline, collapsing in a fit of laughter. I kick the doors closed, then flatten myself out on the floor. The thought of Clarence battering against the hatch passes through my mind and leaves as easily. It feels too good to lie here, to regain my breath against cool carpet.

Eventually I settle down and retrieve my phone. After calling, my father texted a new photo of my mother, this time back home at their kitchen table. People used to ask me if *Proof by Exhaustion* was about him, if he was the persistent apologizer. My answer was no. Or, yes and no. If the play is about him, it is about anyone who I have ever wanted more from in my life, which is everyone. Plus, I don't think my father has ever apologized for anything. I consider a reply, then navigate elsewhere. I have two new woofs and one new message on Scruff. The woofs are from blank profiles. The message is from Mr. Steve, sent just an hour ago.

Jerked off to your pics this morning. LOL.

Beneath the message is a video of him masturbating. He strokes himself roughly, yet moans like a tiny animal. I rewind, holding the phone close to my face so I can better hear. My rising erection strains beneath my zipper, nearly painful. I rub it with my free hand, not thinking about Randy or the stories Abigail told us about Mr. Steve when I respond, but about how Mr. Steve's stubble would feel against my lower back.

Wow, wow, wow.

Haha. You like? Come over for a closer look.

I close the app and move my hand from my crotch to my sternum, where I clutch it in a fist. *That Jack is a cheat,* Ms. Rourke whispers in my ear. *A cheat, a creep, a phony. That Jack is the worst thing to ever happen to my son.*

Self-loathing puddles inside me, but then I hear Randy in my other ear, not talking to me but to Clarence—*Jack was always going to be unhappy*—and the feeling evaporates. With another vengeful impulse, I unzip my pants, fish my cock from my briefs, and watch it promptly die in my hand. I close my eyes, palpating myself, thinking of Mr. Steve, of Leila, of Polly and Paul and Randy between them. The effort goes nowhere, my naked crew lifeless. I let go and feel properly spent, an IV bag drained of its meaningful fluids.

This time, I don't pass by the desk when I return to the office. The baggie of ashes is meticulously smoothed down and looks harmless, though a shuffle would expose the bone shards within. I could write a message for Randy in the powder. *I'm okay, I love you, I had a good life, move on.* Instead, I pick up the recorder, which feels menacing in my hand. I almost drop it when I press the rewind button and the machine comes alive. The house is quiet when I listen for Randy. After letting the thing whir for a while, I press play.

"—scared of flying?" The speaker thins Randy's voice.

Fifteen seconds pass, the break filled with white noise. Randy's speech startles me when it returns, for it is so shapely, breaking through the ambient surface like a fin.

"Did you prefer the window seat, the aisle seat, or the middle seat?"

Another fifteen blank seconds.

"What was your longest flight?"

I sag. Surely he has asked something more interesting than this.

"What kind of drink did you order on the plane?"

"Did you get pretzels or peanuts?"

"Did you ever talk to the people you were seated beside?"

The pauses lengthen. I wonder if he began running low on travel questions, or else was gathering courage to ask something more substantive. What is dying like? Do I deserve better than what I've got? After a long break, he asks if she went on many road trips as a kid. I go to stop the tape, then hear a new noise. Two scrapes followed by a slightly longer one, like a trash can being dragged across a sidewalk. The static isn't interrupted again until Randy's voice comes back, asking how many hours she drove in a single day. I rewind. The scrapes hold a vocal quality. I listen for words. I listen for Ms. Rourke. And as soon as I realize what I'm doing, the prospect of her speaking to me makes me feel faint.

A door closes upstairs. I abandon the recorder, then move to the kitchen. Randy enters soon after, looking tousled by sleep. He picks up a banana, making me realize that mine got lost somewhere down below.

"I need to swim off this hangover," he says.

"Big night?"

"Your friend Clarence showed up."

"Friend." I laugh. "I thought I heard you all talking." I scan his face for shame, for any ounce of concern about what I may have heard. He is impassive, puffy with exhaustion.

"He was looking for you, I think. Looking for you but found me."

"Lucky duck."

Randy lets out his own tired laugh. "Right. Lucky duck."

He takes half of the banana into his mouth in one bite, chewing it with a queasy look on his face. The remainder gets tossed on the counter. "I feel waterlogged."

"What did you talk about?"

"Stupid things. Brandy. Art."

"Me?"

"You? Of course you. I'm always talking about you."

"Is that right?"

Randy, who seems primarily focused on standing straight, doesn't catch the edge in my voice. "Bananas are awful," he says. "Will you swim with me?"

I try to cling to my bitter leaves, but the question blows them from me. Again my eager tears—born not from sadness but from a desperate want to be happy—blinked quickly away.

"Of course I want to swim with you," I say, crossing the room.

"Don't squeeze too hard. I might barf."

But he's the one who holds me closer. I can smell the alcohol in his skin. This time I breathe him deeper, kissing the place where his shoulder curves into his neck.

"What's the story with the tunnel?" I ask. "I was just down there."

"I guess two cousins built these houses at the start of the twentieth century and had them connected. They were together. Romantically, I mean. The cousins."

"The cousins were fucking?"

"The cousins were fucking."

Marie and Oliver. I could take Randy down there to show him the messages. That would mean letting him go.

"Very Nabokovian," I say.

"It's probably made-up. You know Clarence has a flair for the dramatic."

"He told you?"

"Who else?"

Beneath the alcohol, or mixed within it, is Randy's core scent. I stick my nose against it, then draw the tip of my tongue over the same stretch of skin.

Randy's inhales are even deeper than mine. He sniffs down my neck and shoulder, then lifts my arm over my head, burying his face in my armpit. I push him against me with my free hand, hoping to encourage his tongue to come out for a taste. But after four deep breaths, he pulls away, puzzled. "You smell like sex."

"Sex?" I laugh, though Mr. Steve, Leila, Polly, and Paul are all twisting within me. "I wish. We haven't fucked all week."

"Did the tunnel fuck you, Jack?"

"Yes, Randy. All two hundred yards of it."

He teeters between his seriousness, or his faux seriousness, and what I imagine will be a big laugh. The wait is just long enough for me to wonder if he isn't kidding.

"That's good," he says, finally smiling. "You could afford some loosening up."

He gives my ass a full-palmed thwack. The sting is good, great, and not nearly enough.

"If you want me loosened up," I say, "you should do something about it."

"Maybe later. Right now I have a hangover to drown."

THE BONERS GRIMM

The trailhead is ten minutes south. Randy looks like he might retch the duration of the ride, but he successfully directs me to the unmarked parking lot, where only one other car—a minivan with a deep, rusted gouge running down its side—is parked.

"Dinosaur damage," Randy says. He walks over to the van and runs his finger along the scarred edge, bringing back grit.

"How long do you think they've been parked here?" I ask.

The car's exterior is covered in a film of dust. Along the base of the windshield, a heap of pinecones and nettles has settled.

"Who knows?" Randy wipes his finger on his leg. "They're probably camping. These aren't really woods you can get lost in."

As if to defy this claim, the trees above us start to sway, narrowing the gaps between their trunks. Whatever wind moves them doesn't reach where we are.

"I hope we don't run into them," I say.

"Who?" Randy has already turned away from me and toward the trail.

"The van owners."

He shakes his head without looking back. "You always think the world is out to get you."

"A casualty of my overinflated sense of self."

Randy doesn't laugh at this, making me feel embarrassed by my own accuracy.

I reach forward, grabbing his waistband and pulling him back toward me. "I thought we were walking together."

He slows, smiles. "We are walking together."

We keep our hands held as the path winds uphill, letting go when Randy runs face-first into a spiderweb. The spider, which races away after Randy flicks it to the ground, opens the door to the wildlife around us. Over the next half mile, I spot banana slugs, beetles, a pickled-looking newt, birds, a centipede, and a pair of squirrels locked in a staring match.

Randy and I keep our conversation low, speaking only to acknowledge the beauty of the forest. The canopy blocks the sun, leaving us in an emerald world that swells and drops in mossy grooves. Trees stand in such abundance that you would not be able to run a straight line for more than five feet without hitting one, their bottom halves shaggy with undergrowth.

"I feel like we're in a Brothers Grimm story," I say as we pass over a bridge. The bog beneath us is the first sign of the lake. In its water, a dozen frog eyes stare up at us. "They would be so horny for this place. The Boners Grimm, more like."

"What's our fairy tale?"

"The Photographer and the Failure."

Randy laughs, tugging at his shirt hem to air himself. "Come on."

"You don't remember it? Maybe you know it by a different translation. The Artist and the Ass. The Artiste and the Beast."

He scratches his head in imitation of effortful remembrance. "No bells."

We've stopped on the bridge and face one another.

"The Dream and the Disappointment? The Ingénue and the Idiot?"

"You're ridiculous."

The strings on our nylon shorts meet. Randy reaches down and twists them together.

"But am I wrong?"

It is an impossible question, the sort I used to make Randy try to answer all the time. Why doesn't the world see me the way I want to be seen? Still, I want him to disagree, to say it does, or it should. If not that, I want him to at least validate my poor lot in life by agreeing.

"It doesn't matter," he says. "We aren't in a fairy tale."

"You're right. We're in something much worse."

Randy leans forward and puts our cheeks together. "Not always."

Our stubble makes a scratching sound.

"Not always," I repeat.

His tongue feels cool as it enters my mouth. I ask for more of it by giving more of mine.

"Let's find the lake," I say, pulling away.

"The Cock and the Tease." Randy grins. "There's our fairy tale."

We reach the lake five minutes later. I'm relieved to see a sky free of branches and a wide expanse of water. Listening to it lap against the shore, I feel as if my ears have come unplugged, possibly for the first time in days. The cove is small, protected from the wind that ruffles the lake farther out. Apart from the stretch of sand we are on, there is no proper waterfront, the trees coming all the way to the edge before halting their advance.

"I'm surprised there aren't any boats out," I say.

"Maybe the water is poisoned."

Randy's shirt is heavy with sweat when he throws it at me. I watch him kick off his shoes and socks, then slide out of his swimsuit.

"One night with Paul and Polly and you're ready to join a nudist colony," I say.

He jerks as if bitten. "No," he says. "No, I'm not like them."

"I—"

"Sometimes you can see it, really see it—people who have been down low. I thought I saw it. But they're hollow. Those are hollow people." He flinches again, possibly at his own remark, then walks forward until his feet are in the water. "It's sick what they did," he continues, speaking faster now. "Already the dead get no rest. They're stuck running but they have no space to run. I can't believe I thought those two had been there."

He lifts his face toward the sky and throws it a hatchet of a laugh. Then he looks at me, and something in his expression sets off a primal instinct in my body, one that tells me to run.

"Jack," he says. "Did you want to have sex with those hollow people?"

My first attempt to speak fails, a mouthful of stringy air. "I thought you wanted to," I eventually manage. "I thought you might want to."

Randy's head jerks again, tugged by an invisible wire. I'm waiting for his eyes to take the turn that tells me he's been lost behind jealousy, the one that tells me to duck for cover or crawl toward him, begging. When his eyelids flutter, it takes a moment to realize he is trying to blink away tears. Whatever venom was just in him is lost.

"I'm sorry, Randy," I say, walking to him. "I didn't—"

"I did want to," he says. "I wanted to go to the bottom with them. With you, too." He wipes his face. "How could they do that?"

It takes a moment for him to return my hug. We stand, swaying slightly in the cold water. Then Randy pulls away, looking down at our waists.

"Are you getting hard right now?" he asks, his laugh full of disbelief. "You're the worst."

I pull him back. "That's residual. That's nothing."

He relents to my embrace. I will my erection to subside, but it is difficult when it is pressed against Randy's stomach, where the hair is matted with sweat, and when Randy's head is next to my head, still emitting heat that could be confused for rage. He is rageful, maybe. I am the worst, probably. A bird passes overhead, casting its uncertainty down on us.

When Randy sighs, I feel the breath roll down my back.

"How are you feeling?" I ask.

This time Randy laughs in earnest.

"What? What's funny?"

"I can't remember the last time you asked me that." He must see the look on my face, because he immediately says, "Don't spiral. You asked me. You can ask me again."

"Now?"

"Anytime."

"How are you feeling?"

"Hungover. Tired, and like I miss my mother, and like the world is chasing after me. Confused about my father's book. Upset with Paul and Polly. I really thought we were the same kind. I don't know. I was confused. I am confused."

"Are you mad at me?"

His jaw clenches twice, dimpling his cheek. "It's not always you, Jack," he says. "I love you, but it's not always you."

"Sorry."

"Don't say sorry. I'm tired of sorry." He pulls my shirt off of me.

"What should I say?"

"You're supposed to say, 'Let's go for a swim, old man. Isn't that the whole reason we came?'" He hoists me over his shoulder, his strength always a surprise.

We are waist deep when his legs give. We topple, plunging into the cold. The submersion is a shock, dark and frigid. Also, a revelation, soothing me of my irritating ego.

Randy looks refreshed when we meet at the surface, cleansed of his hangover, the sleep washed from his eyes. We swim deeper. The water is black, our limbs carrying us through it like pale fish. My breathing levels. My skin stops stinging. When we float on our backs, our exposed faces, stomachs, and toes make the whitest archipelagos.

I feel like we've gotten somewhere new when we return to the shore, lying in the sun with our thighs overlapped. I almost ask Randy how he is feeling, a half-joke to remind him that I've taken note, taken charge, that I won't let his feelings go unspotted any longer.

"The door to your room is the door to mine," I say instead. The phrase comes, with minor adaptation, from the ending of an Anne Sexton poem Randy showed me the night we moved in together. It's an expression we've kept in our shared box ever since.

For a moment I worry he has forgotten his line. Then, eyes closed against the bright light, he says what he is meant to say: "I remember."

We rest for another hour, eventually driven out by mosquitoes. Back in the parking lot, the van is gone, a single leaf sitting in its place. Someone has drawn a T-rex shitting on a pair of stick figures in the dirt on our rear windshield.

"They must have heard us," Randy says, reaching forward and writing, *DINOSAUR DAMAGE* across the top of the glass. Then he touches one of the stick figure's bulbous heads. "Imagine if you were this small," he says. "I'd put you in my pocket and never have to worry."

"Since when are you worrying about me?"

"I'm always worrying about you."

He keeps his finger on the car as he walks around to the passenger door, skin squeaking across the glass as he goes.

ALAS, ALAS, ALAS!

Randy spots the luggage by the back door before I do.

It is early evening when we return to the house, having spent the remainder of the afternoon wandering between shops in Old Town, and the bag blends into the house's shaded paneling. When Randy points to it from the car, I first think it is a balled-up creature. That would be better. Why had the air been so quiet behind Allen when he called? The house's rear-facing windows are empty. The chambers of my heart are clogged by a hundred faceless men. When was he here? Where is he now? Randy opens his door.

"What are you doing?"

"I'm going inside."

"Shouldn't we call someone?"

"Call who?"

"The airport? The police? He found us. He shouldn't have found us."

"Okay," he says. "Let me look around. You stay."

I regret agreeing as soon as he disappears around the southern side of the house. My eyes can't settle between the windows of the house and the dunes looming in the car mirrors. I envision Allen loping across the sand, or bludgeoning Randy to death. The visions are terrifying, exhilarating, itchy under my eyelids.

A minute passes, then two. I become aware of the ticking engine and welcome, willfully, its soothing effect. The calm opens up room for self-reprimand—am I really hiding in the car with the doors locked?—alongside fear's other odd counterpart: boredom. I pick at my nail. I yawn. Where is Randy? When I open my door, he emerges from the house's north side.

"Anything?" I call out.

"Nothing. Some footprints. Maybe ours."

I meet him at the porch steps. His short walk has left him windswept, his shirt askew.

"Do you recognize it?" I ask.

"It looks like every bag."

It does. Small enough to use as a carry-on, polyester, black. The only aberration is at the top, where someone has slid a rolled-up piece of paper through the handle.

"Do you think it's safe to open?"

"What do you think's in there?" Randy laughs. "A bomb?"

I stand behind him while he pulls the paper free. The unfurled letter is crowded with words, each pressed deeply enough to be more etch than scribble.

Dear Mr. & Mr. Randy Rourke. I spent so long imagining your faces. I sped the whole way here. Alas, the house is empty. Alas, the house is empty! Still, I'm certain I will feel it—the moment you are reunited with what you've lost. You will open the bag and I will be wherever I am, and then a warmth will come surging from the inside, and I will stand up and say, HALLELUJAH! There's nothing like it. I stood on the porch for a long time. I held out hope. I'm in the business of happy faces. Is there a luckier job? I did not start out this way. I started out a little rough-and-tumble. I stole from my sister. I was just a kid. We lived in the ugliest neighborhood and I was not in the business of happy faces. What I stole was a songbook. I hid it under my mattress and listened to my sister cry. It felt good. I did not believe I held much sway in the world. But then I took something my sister loved and I felt it. Sway. It was like a cherry. Except when I gave the songbook back I found something even better. My sister wrapped me in her arms and said I'd saved her life. Her life! Sometimes something feels good and its opposite feels even better. Hers was the first happy face I saw. I am lucky the world takes so much from people. I no longer have to do that myself. Lucky me, lucky you. Alas, the page is full! Alas, alas, alas!

Randy rerolls the paper. "I guess he wasn't lying."

"About what?"

"Being employee of the month."

I laugh, though the letter has made me feel deeply unwell.

"Do you think he stole your bag?" I ask.

"Who knows."

The living room is full of gray shadows that I vanquish with the overhead light. Something feels off, three inches from where it ought to be. Was the armchair at that angle? Did I leave my book in that position? I continue into the kitchen, where the sense of wrongness persists. Outside, a seagull is perched on the deck's railing, preening its feathers.

"Should we check the house?" I ask.

Randy doesn't answer. He lays the bag down in the hallway and unzips it. "Countdown to boom," he says, flipping open the top and revealing hundreds of packing peanuts, not unlike the ones in Abigail's boat, only more spherical.

"Be careful," I say.

Randy's hand is already deep in the peanuts. He freezes. "Jack."

"What?" Cold grips my neck. "What?"

"It has me."

"What has you?"

He starts thrashing around. I stagger back before realizing that Randy is laughing. "It has me, Jack!" he cries out.

"You're an ass."

"You were going to run away!" Randy is breathing hard, gleeful. "You were going to let me get eaten." He pulls his hand from the peanuts, bringing a smaller bag with it. He sits, finally sobered, undoes the new bag's buckles, then pulls a camera from inside. "I must have left this last time I was here."

"It's one of yours?"

"I guess. One of my throwaways."

"You guess?"

"It's been years. I have no idea what's on here." He sets the camera in his lap, then digs his hand through the packing peanuts. "That's it." He tilts the bag and spills the peanuts across the floor. "No severed head. No songbook. I wanted more."

"You're sure it's yours?"

"My name is here."

"Maybe you shouldn't touch that," I say, suddenly wanting to decontaminate the whole house. I'm about to suggest we spray everything down with Lysol, or leave the bag where the tide might pull it away, when my phone rings.

"He must have felt it," Randy says. "Allen must have felt the warm surge."

"Stop." I wrestle the phone from my pocket. "My dad."

"Say hi for me. I'm going to pee."

I take the call on the deck, leaning against the railing near where the seagull stood. The bird has gone, a white splotch of excrement sitting in its place like a rapture mark.

"Jack?" my father says. "Can you hear me?"

"I can hear you. Can you hear me? How's Mom?"

"Ask her yourself!"

"Hi, Jack." I'm surprised to hear her voice so clear and bright, as if her injury should have garbled her. "How's Oregon?"

"Oregon is fine. I want to know how you are. I've been worried."

"Not too worried, I hope. I've got a bright-green cast. Your father signed it."

"Save a spot for me."

"Are you coming?" She sounds concerned. "We have a busy fall."

"I'm not, but thanks for the proactive dismissal."

"We're finally cruising down the Danube!" my father says.

"Is that the ocean behind you?" my mother asks. "I can hear it."

It is a two-step method, perfected over decades: my father dodging and my mother redirecting. The surf isn't loud enough to reach their end of the line. I say yes anyway. My parents want to know if we've been eating blueberries from the bush, if we've driven up to Cannon Beach, where they've heard the views are sublime. They sound reluctant when they ask about Randy. With some spite I oblige their reticence, saying yes, yes, he's fine.

"Well, that's good," my mother says. "It's about time for fine."

I turn away from the house, the phone pressed hard against my ear. "He's suffering," I say, my voice low. "You can't rush suffering. He's doing what he can."

"No need to snap," my mother says. "I'm not saying anything you haven't said."

"And we just want you two to be happy!" my father adds. "You've always had a penchant for wallowing."

I rip a small piece of wood from the railing. "That isn't true," I say, trying to sound more measured than I feel. I do have a penchant for wallowing, but I'd rather refuse this claim than say what I'm actually thinking, which is that they don't really know me, and therefore have no grounds to speak to who I am. I flick the wood over the edge. "What's happening with your head, Mom? Is everything okay?"

"My head is fine," she says. "Except I've had the same dream three nights in a row. I'm just like me, except I'm the captain of a ship, and your father has no legs. I have to give a speech. I wake up right when I'm about to start. I wear a crown so large I use it as a necklace. And there's a pack of greyhounds. They carry me around and their barks sound like whistles."

"Wow."

"I know. So much to unpack. I think the ship is my childhood home."

"I must be the dogs," I say.

"The dogs?" She laughs. "Don't be silly, Jack. You're not there."

It is existential, the way I sink inward. "I should go," I say. "Randy says hi, by the way."

"Nice timing," my father says. "We just got to our restaurant."

"I'm glad you're okay."

"Italian," my mother says. "We're having Italian. I'll eat a meatball on your behalf."

A pang of loneliness sounds within me when we hang up. I am a struck bell, surprised not just by my sadness, but by my sudden longing for something other than what we have. To end our call on a meatball makes me feel that we, the three of us, hardly amount to anything at all. I close my eyes. Before me, vividly, is Randy's failed camping trip with his mother. I see them huddled by the fire. Her wedges, his slumping adolescence, the spangled stars above. I want to sit with them. I want to zipper the tent shut, open it again, drive north through the night with the heater blasting.

It is all enviable. Randy's love for his mother, Randy's grief for his mother. I enter the house eager to find him, to share with him these thoughts, which feel like minor revelations that might serve as adequate reasoning for my lesser parts. The kitchen is dark and quiet. I switch on the light and register what I may have seen earlier without quite realizing, the fundamental offness in the house: on the table is the banana I took with me to Clarence's. Its peel is split and darkly bruised, as if squeezed by an angry hand. Clarence must have brought it while we were gone. Seeing it fills my stomach with something like butterflies, if those butterflies were flapping for their lives.

"Randy?" His name, called out, readily disappears, as if the house has fallen into the tunnel, or absorbed its properties. I'm about to call out again, louder, when Randy replies, much closer than I expect.

"She's mine," he says.

I turn to the office, where he is crouched in the dark.

"What are you doing?" I ask, fumbling for a kitchen chair to lean against, my legs feeling distant from me.

"She's my mother," he says, his voice as narrow and cold as a frozen pipe.

For a confused moment I think he has somehow picked up on my thinking and is trying to pull his memories away from me.

"Why did you listen?" he says.

You're the one who listened, I almost say. The impossibility of my thinking catches up with itself even before Randy drops the tape recorder before him, the plastic clattering against the floor. His hunched shoulders hunch higher, erasing his neck and nearly reaching his earlobes.

"You weren't asking anything," I say. "I didn't think you were asking anything."

Randy crawls forward, closer to the threshold of the doorway. "I'm asking everything, Jack." He snatches the tape recorder up from the ground. "Everything."

"I wanted to know. I want to help you."

"I don't need help! I need to hear my mother say my name."

It seems like he might rush toward me when he leaps up, and so I prepare for impact, leaning against the kitchen table, the banana breaking beneath my outstretched hand.

"*Mine*," he says again. Then he slams the office door, closing himself within.

HOLD ME CLOSE, I'M TIRED OF DANCING

For several minutes, I sit at the table as if detuned, completely uncalibrated from my thinking. Each thought I have—what to do, what to think, what to feel—makes it no further than an inch before vanishing. I am not confused by the possibilities so much as scrubbed clean of all decision-making faculties. Even my body feels factory-reset, the skin fitted a size too small.

Then I lift the ceramic salt shaker and tip a cluster of granules across the table. The movement helps my thoughts lengthen into more sizeable segments, only for them to then tangle and overlap. I should go. I should stay. I should break into the office and sweep the dust pile of Randy up, help put him back together, or else tell him he's acting like a child, barricading himself away like this. I should apologize, or demand an apology from him. For what? He's sick, he's suffering, he's ruining our lives, or at least it feels that way some of the time. And what of my life? My stupid career, my stupid parents, my stupid stomach paunch. When is the last time Randy asked how I was doing?

The more the threads knot, the more anxious I become trying to parse them. My pulse beats in the roof of my mouth. My too-tight skin seems at risk of splitting, at the wrists in particular. I fidget, pour more salt, have a sudden craving for bread—the same craving I get when I realize I've had too much to drink too late in the night and want to save my body from the full extent of incoming pain. I should go upstairs and lie down. I should knock gently on the door. I should open the windows and release our unhappy ghosts.

Something thumps in the office.

"Randy?" His name comes out of my mouth reflexively, but it helps break my inertia. I approach the door and set my hands against it, half expecting the wood to be hot to the touch. Standing has dispatched my stress from my head to my stomach. I bend over to endure the cramping feeling, then lower myself all the way to the ground, laying my head on the floor. Maybe all the better if Randy pushes open the door and breaks my skull with it. Penance, guilt, lack of consciousness—three birds, one stone.

"I didn't know it was private," I say, speaking into the dark door gap. "Weren't we about to listen to it with Abigail?"

Another two thumps that tremble the floor, followed by a string of broken words, impossible to understand but not impossible to feel. I scoot closer to the door. As I smell for the unique tang of Randy's fury, my stomach starts to loosen. What strange comfort exists in that which is dreaded yet familiar? If I close my eyes, forget the house, forget some multitude of seasons passed, I can almost believe that we are back to a scene we've lived before, some night of wracked agony. And though they may not be our best selves, they are recognizable selves, which is more than I can say for who we have lately become.

"You weren't asking anything," I say, no longer a plea but a taunt. "There wasn't anything to hear, Randy. Nothing."

Something hits the door. My flinch leaves behind the flicker of a smile.

"Jesus, Randy. Calm down."

Typically these words are gasoline. I feel evil. Evil and excited, fearful and yearning. I ready for a collapsing of walls. Randy is silent. My skin hugs closer to my bones, then shivers like a sheet of aluminum when he speaks.

"What do you want?" His voice is no longer a frozen pipe but a cracked one. A moment ago I wanted to push him there, down wherever he is. Now I'm appalled to have done so.

"I want to be let in," I say. "You've been holding me so far out."

"What do you care?" He lets out a single, incredulous laugh. "You didn't like her. You couldn't be bothered to go to her funeral."

My hands extend away from me. They want to flee my body and find better hosts. Or they want to protect me, finding purchase on the wall and pushing me away from it.

"You told me not to come," I say.

"What?"

I try again, though it is hard to say defenseless things loudly.

"I told you not to come. So what?"

"I didn't know you needed me."

"My mother died! My mother died and her funeral was empty. My mother's funeral was empty, Jack. Do you hear what I'm saying? Where were you?"

"You know where I was."

"Say it."

I'm too far from the wall to push myself any farther.

"I was bowling."

"Bowling!" Some part of Randy smacks some other of Randy—hands on thighs, face on palm. "You were bowling and my mother was dead. Do you remember what happened when I called you? What I had to ask?"

"You asked me to step outside. The music was too loud."

"I asked you to step outside because all I could hear were breaking pins. I called you to tell you about my dead mother's empty funeral and you didn't think to step outside. It was just breaking pins and breaking pins and breaking pins. Why would I let you in?"

A foot stands on my chest and a foot stands on my stomach, the weight they're supporting much larger than any human's. To speak requires me to cough each word forcibly forward. "I'm lonely. It's lonely being on the outside."

The door opens, stopping short against my arm. I can't look at Randy, so I fix my eyes on the floorboards, where a skin of mold-like dust has gathered. If Randy stomps on me, this dirt will be the last thing I see. Rightfully so.

"You don't have to put on a show," he says. He stands directly above me, the view up his swimsuit black enough to suggest no body within.

"I'm not putting on a show," I say. "I'm telling you how I

feel. It's lonely without you. That's why I listened. I'm trying to find you."

Randy drops to his knees and grips my face between his hands. "I'm right here, Jack." He is shaking, and so my whole head shakes, too, caught between his palms. He doesn't look angry, staring at me upside down. He looks devastated. "I'm right here. What are you looking for?"

Wetness on my face. Randy's spit. No. My tears. I see it in his eyes—compassion, or at the least pity—even before he thumbs at my cheeks.

"I'm here, too. You keep going to other people and I'm right here. Sally and Fran. Abigail. I heard you talking to Clarence last night." My voice hitches, possibly telling me to stop speaking, a warning I fail to heed. "I heard you tell Clarence I'd never be happy. You said I could have all the luck in the world and still have been miserable."

What happens to Randy's face is something I've seen only rarely. It occurred most in the week after things with Leila fell apart, that disconcertingly still time before his jealousy ran free: his expression would succumb to a sudden and total confusion, a bewilderment that was terrible to witness. He looked genuinely uncertain about the quality of his life.

"It's not a big deal," I say. "I was just saying—"

"How are we possibly talking about you?"

Nothing comes in or goes out when I open my mouth.

"You weren't going to be happy, Jack." He lets go of my head, then stands. "You're the most miserable person I know."

A third invisible foot steps down, this time on my throat. My hands are heavy on the floor, impossible to lift, though I want to, to bring them to my windpipe to see if it's collapsed.

"I can't breathe," I say.

Randy steps backward. "Yes, you can."

All is still for the time it takes for me to suck in a thimbleful of air. Then a tremendous pounding fills the house. I've done it, I think, listening to the stampede of furious hooves. I've brought on something awful, a cataclysm that is here to finally blink us out.

"FBI!" Carolina's voice cuts through the knocking. "We've got the place surrounded!"

Randy leaves me, flipping on the hallway light on his way to the door. Somehow I roll over, stand, wipe my face and stumble after him, though by the time I reach him I wonder what instinct has told me to follow rather than retreat. I should be in bed. I should be in the tunnel, face down in the dark.

Shelby and Carolina stand on the porch as if for a photo shoot, backlit by headlights.

"Evening, boys," Carolina says. "We were worried. All the lights were off."

"But the car is here." Shelby puts her arm over Carolina's shoulder. "Parked car, dark house. What were we supposed to think?"

"Murder," Carolina says. "Murder-suicide. It's all the true crime we watch, but still."

They smile. Then, giving us a once-over, Shelby says, "You don't look very party ready. What's with the swimsuits and the cursed vibes?"

We stand motionless, silent. I can't speak, for I am still primarily on the floor, Randy's condemnation loud in my ears—*most miserable, most miserable, most miserable.*

"What party?" Randy asks. He sounds impossibly normal.

"*The* party," Carolina says. "The big bash. The night of grown adults stumbling around like oversized toddlers." She glances at Shelby. "I thought you said they left a voicemail?"

"They did. My aunt and uncle called this afternoon. You didn't get the message? Mr. Steve is having his monthly shit show. They thought you two would like to go. A further sampling of local culture. The worst of the worst."

Mr. Steve's name overrides my failing system. "I don't think that's in the cards for us tonight," I say. "We haven't showered or eaten. We fly out tomorrow."

"What does tomorrow have to do with today?" Carolina asks.

"Nothing," Shelby says. "Case closed."

My laugh is like a malfunctioning printer. The doorframe beneath my hand is slick, and it takes me a moment to realize it is because my palm is heavily sweating, along with the rest of me. I'm glad Randy isn't touching me for fear of what my damp back might reveal. *When are we going to get those legs over my shoulders? I dream about fucking men like you.*

"Dinner," I say again.

"Mr. Steve is barbecuing a billion hot dogs, I'm sure," Shelby says.

"I'm in." Randy bends down to pull on his sandals. "I won't speak for Jack. Maybe Jack needs some time alone. I could use a change of scenery."

"Come on, Jack." Shelby wields her keys like a shiv. "Are you ready to party rock?"

Another dying laugh. I can smell myself, stinking of sweat and lake water. My hand gripping the doorframe is skeletal with strain. "A moment, please?" I say, closing the door.

Randy stares straight ahead.

"You seriously want to go?" I ask. "We're still talking."

"We're not talking. I'm done with tonight, Jack." He says this to the door, his voice flat as paper. "And I'm not leaving Abigail at that party alone." He looks sick, imagining this. "Stay if you want. I don't care."

"Déjà vu," Shelby and Carolina say when he reopens the door.

"Déjà vu," Randy repeats.

And because all three look at me, I say it, too. Then we walk toward the headlights, the three of them confidently, me at a drag. Overhead, a bat cuts circles in the dark. I imagine it shitting on my forehead, marking me heathen, marking me heartless, marking me in desperate need of cosmic redemption.

Inside the van, Elton John's "Tiny Dancer" plays. Polly and Paul sing accompaniment, pliant with drink. My father misheard the lyrics to the chorus of this song for years. I focus on this, the past, to avoid thinking about the present we are in or the future we are heading toward.

Hold me close, he thought Elton sang, I'm tired of dancing.

MR. STEVE'S BLUE PERIOD

Randy and I cram ourselves into the van's backmost row, still digging for our seatbelts while Shelby veers through the moonlit dunes. That we are here, and with these people, so soon after we were there, miserable on the floor, makes the whole thing feel dreamlike, propelled by illogic.

"Welcome to the paddy wagon," Polly says, smiling drunkenly back at us. "We were so sorry to kick you two out last night. These two are driving as a big old IOU."

"It's an honor to protect and serve," Carolina says from the front passenger seat.

"I'd die for this country," Shelby adds.

"No dying." Polly lifts a Nalgene from her lap. "Not until you drop us off." She unscrews the lid, takes a swig, then offers the bottle to Randy. "Merlot for the monsieur?"

She and Paul watch happily as he begins to drink, then less happily when he doesn't stop.

"Save some for the rest of us, man!" Paul says. "That's good stuff."

Randy's lips are sopping blue when he passes the Nalgene to me. "Whoops." He burps with his mouth uncovered. "I guess I'm thirsty for a good time."

"Oh, I love that!" Polly cries. "Thirsty for a good time. Yes!"

"You haven't had any food," I say, touching Randy's arm, which he pulls away. "It's going to go right through you."

Randy grips Polly's headrest as Shelby careens around a curve. "I've got the death drive in me!" Shelby shouts. The wine sloshes, but just low enough to not spill over the lip.

"Who cares?" Randy says once the car levels.

"I'm trying to look out for your future hangover."

"A thousand thanks, Jack," he says. "I can look out for myself."

"Is that a buzzkill I hear?" Paul grabs the Nalgene from me before I have a sip. He begins to make a *Z* noise with his tongue, swatting imaginary bugs from around his head. "No killed buzzes! No killed buzzes! Let the man drink." He drinks himself, noises of pleasure escaping him as if from a nursing pup.

I lean back and cross my arms over my chest. The AC blasts straight on my face, flushing my sinuses with the sharp scent of coolant. Outside, the pale dunes seem to have multiplied and grown, surrounding us like a treacherous sea.

"Don't go sour," Polly says to me. "Tonight is about fun, remember? Drinking fun—was that what Randy said?" She looks briefly woozy, then steadies her face. "Tell me, did you two have fun last night? Any fun at all? I know things got a bit wonked."

"Jack did," Randy says. He looks even more petulant than I do, balled in the corner and spiky as an urchin. Polly doesn't seem to notice.

"That's good," she says. "We had plenty of fun. Right, Paul?"

"Plenty." His smile is delayed, yet full when it comes. "And more to come."

"Steve throws the best parties," Polly says. "Last Halloween, Paul and I dressed up as pigs in a blanket and woke up to the sunrise in the middle of the lake. Apparently we thought canoeing was a good idea. A one-eyed bird was sitting on one of the oars. It shouted a word at us, then flew away. Paul, do the word like the bird did. Do the bird's word."

Paul closes his eyes, then shouts, "Peace!" After a brief fumble, he grabs Polly's hand.

"How do you two know Mr. Steve?" Randy asks.

I expect my anxiety to erupt, hearing Mr. Steve's name in Randy's mouth. But my anxiety no longer seems to be with me. No sweaty limbs, no arrhythmic heart. It is out the window, on the road, or back at the house, sniffing around for me. Seeing what I lack helps me see what I have: an island in the backseat of the car, created by the others but claimed, now, by me. It is cold and rocky, treeless and desolate, home of the buzzkills and the bad husbands. But I don't care. If I am so abject, then let me act abjectly. I frame Mr. Steve in my mind's eye, sitting on his corduroy chair. Now I am the one he looks at adoringly.

"Everyone knows him," Polly says. "He's a Florence legend. One of the first people we met after moving to town. He's got a special way about him. How would you describe him, Paul? How would you describe Mr. Steve and his special way?"

"He's like a big tree."

Polly lets out a burst of laughter, then becomes serious. "He is like a big tree. Good call, Paul. What do you girls say? Is Steve a big tree?"

"A big tree on the verge of tipping over," Shelby says. "The man's a hazard."

"We haven't heard great things." Randy sounds snooty, his nose lifted despite already being high on his horse. I roll my eyes. He can keep his overdosed levels of goodness. I'll take Steve as he is, smoke-stained and wasted, urine spewing in all directions. He is the only good feeling in the car.

"Steve hasn't had it easy," Polly says. "Let's go easy on the guy."

Paul looks back at us. "Mr. Steve's sister—"

"Paul." Polly's voice slaps him quiet. "That's not our business to broadcast. Let's just say Steve's had several blue periods. So blue they were almost black. You'd never guess it. Well, apart from the occasional bad night where he breaks right open."

"Hard times don't justify bad behavior," Randy says. He looks my way, but I refuse to look back, to look anywhere other than Steve in the chair, though the vision is starting to fray.

"Geez," Polly says. "Give him a chance, would you?"

"Especially since you're attending his party." I'm surprised by the power of my voice, which all night has felt so powerless. And now I do look at Randy, who stares at me with true shock, as if I have abandoned him, abandoned Abigail, abandoned all that is right and just.

"Zing!" Paul says. "Jack's got a point. Let us be gracious guests to those who give us booze and backyards."

Randy turns from me as I have turned from him, a mirrored rejection. The car goes silent as we pass through the woods dividing the dunes from the 101, turn right, and merge. There are no other cars out. I'd like the company of traffic, if only for the reminder that the world is going on, always, in a thousand different directions. A stray dog runs along the road's shoulder. I'm glad to see the town motto disproven, at least once, by this mutt's existence. I crane my neck skyward. There are no people there, no shadows of people. I try to project Mr. Steve in his chair onto the darkness, but when I reach for the image it seems to have escaped my mind. It is a perfectly clear night, the stars hanging overhead like smashed glass.

Soon we exit left. Antiquated lampposts cast long shadows on another tableau of artifice—perfect lawns and shutters, impeccable coats of paint. We are in the neighborhood version of Bay Street, a suburban paradise, hellishly neat. Every yard has a sign about Proposition 11. The call to vote yes or no seems to alternate house to house.

"What's Prop 11?" I ask.

"The question of corporal punishment," Paul says. "Lashings, canings, cattle prods—you name it. Some people are arguing it should be offered as an alternative to jail time."

I reach for Randy, an old habit that assures us, with a touch, that whatever irrationality we've just confronted is not our irrationality; that it is beyond us, a thing to laugh at and scorn. My hand stops midway. Randy does not want it, and I don't want to give it. Plus, the question of corporal punishment isn't so irrational, particularly for someone who was just hoping to have his head caved in by a door.

"I'd rather be flogged than locked up," Polly says.

"Brand for me," Paul says. "I don't mind a little sizzle."

From the front seat, Carolina offers a bed of nails while Shelby opts for the jail cell. "Think of the reading time," she says. "Proust would stand no chance."

I don't hear them when they ask us what we would choose, not at first. I am distracted by my hand, failed in its mission and dead on the seat between us. That I reached for Randy makes me feel like I am not on an island after all, not cold to the wants of others. But to lose the island is to lose the only grounding I had. They have not yet found me—my guilt, anxiety, or self-loathing—but now that I am in open water, I am exposed to their searching mouths.

"That's a good one," Polly says in response to whatever Randy has just chosen, something I have failed to hear. "Jack? Pick your poison."

"I feel a little sick, actually."

"Jack would choose the stocks," Randy says. "Whatever would get him in front of the highest number of people."

The jab, plus the group's laughter, brings me straight back to my barren shore.

"Fuck off," I say, so humorlessly that the car falls silent. I look out the window, impressed by my own resolve. I'm the big tree, I think. And then, just as easily, I feel humiliated. "Okay, okay," I say, pushing out a laugh. "Let's talk about something else."

I see Polly catch Paul's eye, then Carolina catch Shelby's,

then Shelby, in the rearview, catch Randy's. "How's *Bruiser* treating you?" she asks him.

Everyone seems to breathe easier.

"*Bruiser* is treating me badly." Randy sounds defeated, admitting this. "It has more plot holes than plot. And, for a thriller, it has no real thrill."

"I'm a fan of plot holes," Carolina says. "No one deserves to know everything."

"Maybe that's why we aren't writing books, Caro," Shelby says. "We think the best stuff is in the void."

"I tried to write a novel once," Paul says. "I couldn't get past chapter two."

"Oh, Paul, I loved your novel." Polly rubs his neck. "Especially the first paragraph."

They are all trying to rekindle the flames I've put out, eagerly contributing sticks and sparks and puffs of oxygen. I feel badly, though I worry that any contribution by me will seem hostile, and so I lean away, turning again to the window, where a pair of deer are eating the flowers in a roadside memorial.

"Why *Bruiser* in the first place?" Shelby asks. "Even the cover seemed dumb."

"I thought I'd learn something about my dad. It was his favorite book."

"You did learn something." Carolina turns all the way around to face Randy. "Either your dad had terrible taste, or he also thought the best stuff was in the void. Maybe both."

We turn down a street preceded by a dead end sign. There are no streetlights, making it feel as if we are plunging into a pool of black liquid as we head downhill. My stomach seems to float freely around my other organs. I can't determine if it is anxiety or excitement that makes it sway so fully. Mr. Steve. My failure, my savior. Will Randy sense it, seeing us talk?

Shelby hits hard on the brakes before turning down a long gravel driveway that leads to a lawn full of parked cars. A cabin sulks beyond them, a one-story with a brick chimney and a disproportionately large front door. Unlike the other houses in the neighborhood, Mr. Steve's looks like it hasn't ever been painted, like its exterior would take any opportunity to splinter you. It is a villain's house, a ruin. I feel destined for it, doomed for it, an exterior befitting my interior. Beyond the cabin and down another slope is the lake. The moonlight is spread across its surface like spilled mercury.

"Don't forget to tip," Shelby says after parking.

Polly and Paul unclip their seatbelts in tandem.

"I hope Steve's grilling steak," Paul says.

Polly turns to us. "Last time we were here, we ate our weight in beef. Maybe food will do you some good. Huh, Jack?"

I conjure a smile, though I'm sure it looks closer to a sneer.

Carolina and Shelby waste no time leaving when we are out of the car. "Call when you're blasted!" Shelby shouts out her window, revving the engine and speeding away.

"Those two are going places," Paul says, full of pride.

We walk toward the house. Ahead, meaty smoke and the brook-like murmur of many voices talking at once. We move in a single file line: Polly at the front, Randy and Paul at the center, and me at the end. I'd hoped the fresh air would resettle my body, but now I'm certain that I left some crucial portion of it behind, back in the hallway.

As we maneuver around the side of the house, I glance through the windows, looking for Mr. Steve, Abigail, anyone. The house is empty apart from its furnishings, the party all gathered by the water. The interior scene is warm, dusted with loneliness. A large dining table, a rug with geometric patterning, a painting of a woman hanging linen on a clothesline.

I see the corduroy recliner when we pass by the third window. My severed body divides further, spotting it, and whatever numbness held me in the car is gone, leaving me like an exposed nerve, rocked by pleasure and pain. Now I am just two things: a head cleaved by guilt and a pulsating groin. When Randy asks if I'm coming, I see I've stopped. My smiling face surprises me. If it is awful, the division of self, it is also enlivening.

A footpath leads us to the lake. As we wind through the trees, the party gets louder, the scent of smoke stronger. I feel as if I might lift off the ground. That, or vomit. Vomit, then lift, then split apart like a firework.

"What's with the happy face?" Randy asks when I suddenly speed up, running into him.

My smile seems like it might never stop. "I have no idea," I say.

We round the final bend, which provides a straight shot to the beach. From nowhere, the name of Mr. Steve's sister comes to me. Patricia, Trish. What happened to her? A blue so blue as to be black. We've all seen that shade. It is the one that happens in the interstice between what we call *day* and what we call *night*. The color of purgatory.

HEARTSTOPPER

My mania is hungry for mania. I am giddy to see the untamed lawn, overgrown and free of the civilized trappings of the neighboring homes—docks, motorboats, croquet wickets—giddy to see tiki torches burning bright holes in the crowd; giddy to see the grill, from which a tremendous column of white smoke rises taller than the trees. I feel these things in my groin, for they come from the same stateless state. No codes, no scruples. Maybe I have also been feeling homesick, not for New York, not for the life Randy and I used to have, but for something more lawless. I imagine stripping off my clothes, cartwheeling, announcing to the crowd that I am the most miserable person, and isn't that liberating, to have abandoned the demand to be good?

Except the crowd fails me. They are the same people I

see at any gathering—slouched and gray streaked, modest in dress and nodding like bobbleheads—so far from the dancing demons Abigail's description of these parties summoned. That they are just people reminds me that I am just a person, and obliged, therefore, to act with some humanity. My groin cools until I can no longer feel it and my head hardens, perhaps to ward off any other flights of fancy by making a cinder block of itself. Re-grounded, I reach out and grab the back of Randy's shirt.

"What are you doing?" He glares back at me. "You almost pulled me over."

"I think we should go home. I really feel sick."

"You look fine."

"It's inside." I touch my throat. That's one place I feel it, my esophagus scorched by bile. Except it is not just there. My churning stomach is back, and my bruised chest. When I hear someone say Mr. Steve's name nearby, my blood swells my veins. If we weren't heading toward a table of drinks set up away from the grill, I might balloon out, showering the party in red.

Randy continues on. I focus on my breathing so that, if nothing else, I won't faint. But maybe I should faint. Blacked out from the night, I could wake up in Sally and Fran's bed with Randy holding a washcloth to my head.

"I'm making Heartstoppers," Paul says, looking down at the alcohol like a maestro.

"Do mine the way I like." Polly taps her nail against a vodka bottle. "It's cold tonight. Are you two cold?"

"I'm fine," Randy says. "I come from cold."

I hadn't noticed the temperature, distracted by internal weather. Having it named makes me realize it is quite cold, and that the cold is coming from all directions—breathing off the water and grass, descending from the sky. "I'm freezing," I say.

"This will help." Paul hands me a plastic cup that I sip eagerly, hoping to rid my mouth of its sourness. The drink tastes like a melted Slurpee with four shots mixed into it. I take a second sip, and a third, the carbonation tickling my jowls.

"This is terrible," Randy says after trying his.

Paul's laugh is a bellow. "Terribly delicious," he says.

"Or deliciously terrible," Polly adds.

They press their cups against ours. Hollow people, Randy called them, a claim that feels both ungenerous and right as they rub their noses together.

"Let's meet our host, shall we?" Polly says. "All I ask is for open minds. Capisce?" She lifts her eyebrows at Randy.

"My mind is always open," Randy says. "That's what gets me into trouble."

"I'd go easy on that Heartstopper, Jack," Paul says. "It's aptly named."

My drink is nearly gone, and seems to already be doing the trick. I smile at Paul, grateful for a lighter head and a stiller heart. "Thank you," I say. "Really."

Back at the end of the line, an odd stillness overtakes me as we cross the lawn. Perhaps it is the Heartstopper, or a moment of exact equilibrium between my lowest and highest parts, a break in the battle that provides an illusion, however fleeting, of peace. Perhaps it is the fact that the worst thing is happening—there is Steve, finally visible through the smoke, and here is Randy, heading straight toward him. Is it not better for the dreaded event to come, rather than to be forever stuck waiting for its arrival?

In my bubble, I am aware of the grass dampening my shoes, the gentle slosh of ice in my cocktail, and the chance that my guilt, brought to a head, will vaporize us all. Passing by a series of bland faces, I wonder if I ought to warn them. But that would require piercing my tranquility. I don't feel afraid, imagining the end; I feel relieved.

Ten feet from the grill, someone slams against me. I'm so jarred by the incursion, which delivers me back to the world so unceremoniously, that it takes a moment to recognize who it is.

"Claude," I say.

"Clarence," he corrects, putting a chummy arm around my neck. "I don't want to be Claude tonight. I don't want life to be so awful." He pauses, shaking his head. "Not awful. Boring. I'm trying to be more compassionate to old Claude. My mentor says the only way a character will really let you in is if you prove you think theirs is a life worth living."

At the grill, Polly and Paul stand beside Mr. Steve. He is taller than I expected, mightier. He smiles more readily than I would have guessed. Paul forces him to take a sip of his drink, laughing as he does, while Polly seems to be looking, like me, for Randy.

"—worse lives for sure," Clarence is saying. "God knows I've lived plenty of them. I think I have an aversion to peace. Claude is all about peace. When life isn't turbulent, I worry I've become a stone. I'd rather be a bomb than a stone. Know what I mean?"

The smoke envelops us, making us cough before swinging away. For a moment I imagine Randy has gone up with it, that he is the one who has been vaporized. But no. Beyond the grill, beyond the man juggling three hamburger buns and the woman clapping him on, is Abigail. She stands in the lake, not deep, the water only reaching her lower thighs, yet seeming impossibly far away. The only proof that her reality can interact with ours is that Randy has made the crossing. They stand together facing the deeper water.

Clarence catches on to my distraction. "A bit chilly for a swim, wouldn't you say? That girl out there once had my head over a plastic bottle."

"She thinks we've ruined the planet."

"You and me?"

"Our generation."

"Fair enough," Clarence says. "But isn't that the human way? People put people first. And really, people put *their* people first. Is that generational? I don't think so." He seems expectant for me to answer or disagree. "Do you think it's biological?"

"What?"

"Selfishness."

"I don't know."

"Don't undersell yourself, Jack. Don't play the fool. I read your play. You've thought about human nature much more than the average person."

"That doesn't mean I have anything to say."

Clarence pouts. "I didn't know Steve was holding a pity party. Where are the violins?" He glances around for the missing string quartet, then drops the charade. "Come on, man! You're better than that. You act like you can't go back. You can. You should. I loved the play. The play is good. Can I tell you my favorite part?"

It feels like a drug, being told the play is good. I don't hesitate to nod. If he asked me to get on my knees and beg,

I would. I'm sure Clarence can see the neediness in my eyes, can see, too, the way I'm already guessing what he might say.

"I loved that this woman who refuses to forgive her father, who seems to take great pride in rejecting his efforts at reconciliation, sends him money every month so he can afford rent. When I read that, every piece of her fell into place. It broke my heart, Jack. It broke my heart that she couldn't let go." He catches my eyes, and I wishfully think he might cry. "That's when the play became real to me. Does that make sense? That moment is when the whole thing became real. Yet you think you have nothing to say about human nature. Really?"

There's no fighting the smile from my face. Its insistence is like the one from before, only dopier, and less deranged. "That's nice of you to say."

"It's not nice. It's true. Say it with me, Jack. Say, 'I have something to say.'"

I do say it with him, only after making sure no one is listening. When I take another sip, I discover my Heartstopper is gone. Then my vision dilates. "I might be getting drunk."

"You should get drunk! And you should go back to the plays. You've got something. I knew it when we first met. That's why I was so down when you told me you'd given up."

A mulleted couple passes between us, and before their woodsy odor has faded I am telling Clarence all about my imaginary play. The plot comes out in a surprisingly shapely arc. I describe the opening scene, the four characters, the diner; I tell him the opening line. Clarence's enthusiasm goads mine. Yes, the note they leave Julian is funny! Yes, the encounter with the woman throwing away her clothes is absurd! Even when I reach the limits of my story, the unknown feels less unmade than undiscovered, a landscape awaiting a cartographer. I do have something to say. Maybe it is about time, about friendship, about passivity or power; maybe it is about forgiveness, about learning your worth, about the loneliness of the twenty-first century. Isn't everything about that now, in one way or another? Julian's voyage across ruinous decades will be a portrait of the times, for the times.

"What do you think?" I ask, nearly out of breath. "Do you think it has legs?"

"I loved every minute. I'm going to give you something, Jack." He pulls out his wallet. "It's my business card. Want me to run lines? Workshop ideas? Call me." He passes the card to me. Above his cell number and email address, it reads, *CLARENCE FREEMAN / METHOD ACTOR*. "I'm off to Fiji next month for a shoot. I've got international data."

Seeing *method actor* steals some thunder from the moment, but I assure myself that Clarence Freeman can't also be a character hiding some third man.

"Fiji," I say. "Who will you be there?"

"God knows."

"Don't you have the script?"

"Of course I have the script. But I can't know who I am until I am them."

My vision falters again. The flame of a nearby tiki torch expands, haloing Clarence.

"You never asked me what I thought," he says.

"About what?"

"The selfishness of humanity."

"I thought you said it was biological."

"No, I asked if *you* thought it was. I don't think it's biological."

"Then what do you think it is?"

He beckons me close with a finger. I lean toward him, then am practically leaning on him. "We're filthy capitalists!" he shouts.

I pull away, holding a hand to my ringing ear as he laughs.

"I'm kidding. Half-kidding. I don't think there's any one answer. We're filthy capitalists, filthy Americans, filthy offspring of Judeo-Christian values. And we're filthy animals. So maybe it is biology, in part." He shrugs. "We're just filthy, full stop. I don't mind. What say you, Jack? What say you to the filth of existence?"

"I say yes. Definitely yes."

"Jack says yes!" He holds his hands high. "Let's roll around in the mud later on, yeah? I'm setting up something special for you. First, I've gotta drain the yellow." He begins to walk away, then turns back. "I meant to ask you something. Did a gorilla break into your house?"

"A gorilla?"

"That's right. There was a gorilla in my basement this morning. Can you believe it? He left a banana and everything. Absolutely filthy." He holds my gaze, winks, then stumbles toward the bushes, leaving me at the center of the crowd.

My drunkenness absorbs the embarrassment of being caught trespassing and redirects the feeling. I am filthy, I am an ape, and I do have something to say.

Randy and Abigail are no longer in the lake, and Paul and Polly are no longer by the grill. Good riddance. The space between my crotch and navel is thrumming with warm electricity even before I spot Mr. Steve. He is standing alone in the smoky gloaming, holding an empty plate, and, spotting me, smiling.

HAPPY ENDING

"You found your way," Mr. Steve says. He goes as if to shake my hand, then smiles at himself, at the silliness of this gesture. "Clarence can be hard to escape."

I laugh. "He's all right. I'm glad to be here, though. Smells like heaven."

My hunger, long dormant, is wide awake, slavering over the steaming patties and bringing me to the edge of the grill. The force of it contributes to my feeling beastly, as if I might grab a burger from the flames, devour it, then shit on the grass.

"Let me make you one," Mr. Steve says. "Are you an everything man?"

"Everything but the pickle."

"What a shame." He throws a bun on the plate, flicks

it open, then sets two smashed patties on the lower half. "Pickles are my favorite part." He stares at me straight on, with a gaze so direct that it seems to suggest he'd rather be rid of the innuendo entirely.

I take a step away from the grill. "Warm," I say, gesturing toward the fire.

"Even in your little shorts?" He smirks, not at me but at the plate, where he is heaping caramelized onions, bacon, and bleu cheese onto my patties. My mouth remains viscous with saliva even after I swallow.

"Especially in my little shorts," I say.

Now I can see I've put Mr. Steve on his heels, that he is also having to swallow down some feeling within him. He hands me the burger and watches as I shovel it in my mouth. When ketchup drips down my chin, he stares hungrily there until I wipe the smear away; when I lick the grease from my fingers, his gaze lingers on my fingertips.

"Sorry to eat like a pig," I say, popping the final bite in my mouth.

"It's good," Mr. Steve says. "Means you like it."

The fire leaps through the grill grate. The fire leaps in our eyes. When I notice Mr. Steve's bulge, my arousal spikes—what I would do, and have done, to feel someone pressed against me in a public place—then withdraws, suddenly aware of our surroundings, and of Randy, who is still somewhere out of sight.

"Lots of dark houses," I say. "Is everyone here?"

Mr. Steve seems surprised by this shift, surveying the surrounding houses. "Most have gone off some place or other. The only ones still around are over there." He nods to a man and woman who appear to be cutting a lock of the woman's hair with scissors. "The Ravens."

"Are you friends?"

"They're here, aren't they?" His tone is surprisingly acerbic. I fold my plate for something to do while he removes the remaining patties from the heat, stacking them on a plate. "Sorry," he says. "I'm having a weird go of it lately. I don't know if we're friends, the Ravens and me. We're friends enough for them to come to my party. Friends enough for Tom Raven to sneak over every now and then for a stroke and toke."

"Really?"

He laughs. "Not really. But it sounds fun, doesn't it?"

Now I have to turn away, looking down to where my grease-stained plate has been reduced to a triangular wedge.

"I could see it getting lonely out here," I say. "Once everyone's gone."

The bacon comes off, heaped atop the patties. "It can be lonely with or without them. Sometimes it's worse to look across the lake and see a bunch of lights."

"Do you ever think about moving?"

"I think about moving. I think about getting a dog, a husband, a wife. I could learn piano. I could make a whistle and play a little song. I could read a goddamn book for once in my life." He bangs his spatula against the grill. "Or I could just keep talking to handsome men like you."

I pinch the plate wedge with one hand and my thigh with the other. Being talked to this way feels unbearably good, as if Mr. Steve were stroking my innermost spirit.

"I grew up in this house, you know." Mr. Steve closes

the grill. "Maybe that's part of the problem. I'm all crowded with history. Would you move if you were me?"

"I don't know what I would do."

"Are you ever lonely?"

"Of course."

"Even with your husband?"

"Definitely with my husband."

Another lance of shame for how eagerly this comes out of me. I don't want the conversation to end, or for Mr. Steve to have any reason to stop adoring me. The fresh spark in his eye beckons me away from my guilt

"Sorry if I sound like a sinkhole," he says. "Usually I kick sinkholes out of the party. Like I said, a weird go of it lately. But you're making me feel better." He sips his beer. I picture him urinating in the water near Abigail and Dallas, then push the image away. Or, really, I push Abigail and Dallas out of the image, and me into it, collapsed on my knees beneath him.

"Don't worry," I say. "I'm familiar with sinkholes."

I don't mean this as an innuendo, but Mr. Steve looks at me as if willing it to be. Again I become aware of the place we are standing. When I look around, no one seems bothered by our existence, let alone aware of it. In some ways, it feels as if the stillness from before has reabsorbed me, with Mr. Steve alongside. I look for Randy and Abigail and find nothing. Polly and Paul are dancing near a small speaker. Only now does the music reach my ears. They are both lost in the strange tango, eyes closed and bodies gyrating.

"If those two are reliable for one thing, it's dancing," Mr. Steve says. "They dance at my parties. They dance at town hall. I used to think they looked dumb, then realized

I was just jealous." He steps backward. "Can I show you something?"

I feel my mind reach for Randy, strain for him, even, except when it finds him all I see is him rejecting me, again and again. Randy shrugging off my hand, climbing over me on the stairs, telling me I should talk to someone else about my career frustrations. Randy looking at me, sometimes, as if my walking away would do nothing to him at all.

Mr. Steve looks at me like a trophy. I must nod, because he turns and I follow, back toward the bushes where Clarence went earlier. We weave between teetering bodies, sidestep ruptures of laughter and conversation. "Daylight savings is a goner." "I've always thought Godzilla was sort of sexy." "You can imagine what it feels like to lick anything. Try it. Look at my purse and imagine licking it." The last person we pass is a woman with dozens of rollers in her hair.

"Is my daughter here, Mr. Steve?" she asks. "I haven't seen my daughter in months."

He tells her that her daughter isn't here, but that there's plenty of food if she's hungry. The woman pulls a curler free, drops it, then stumbles toward the grill.

Soon we are divided from the party by a hedge of dense branches. Then we are crossing from the grass into the woods, where the sounds of people drop away. In their place is what first fronts as silence, then reveals itself to be an orchestra of subliminal noises: the creak of bark, the rub of leaves, the guarded adjustments of nocturnal life.

"Where are we going?" I sound excited, no longer worried about monitoring myself. It is colder here. I look for my breath when I exhale but see nothing in the dark.

Mr. Steve doesn't answer. He continues walking, footsteps

made light by the plush bed of pine needles, and I continue following, until we come to the base of a Douglas fir.

"This is the oldest tree in a five-mile radius," he says, slapping its side. He laughs when I tell him what Polly and Paul said about him being a tree. "Those two would see nectar in sap. I really do envy them, even if they're always making complete fools of themselves."

"They were teaching us about tantra last night."

"They've taught this whole town about tantra. I think that stuff is bullcrap, but I guess the proof is in the pudding. I've yet to see two people who smile more. And they've been good to me. They're not hoarders of a good time." He looks up at the branches, which provide a hundred twisted frames for the night. "This tree has seen a lot of me."

"Is that right?"

"Very right. My first cigarette and twisted ankle. My first blowjob."

Mr. Steve watches me laugh, amused. His gaze is reminiscent of Randy's when he is at his most wanting.

"Really?" I ask.

"Really." His hand moves over the furrows of bark. "The thing I remember most is the way the moon hit us. It made me feel beautiful. All my teenage shame fell away because we looked so beautiful." He steps toward me. "You look beautiful, too. Do you feel beautiful?"

Something snaps under my shifting weight. A branch, a pinecone, a bone. "I don't know." My mouth has dried out, leaving me with a paper tongue.

"It's okay." He touches my chin. "You are. Do you think I'm beautiful?"

A break in the canopy concentrates the moon upon us.

Mr. Steve is lit in silver and is beautiful, beyond beautiful. The stubble and the swell of his lips. The height and the smell of sweat breaking through minty deodorant. There is beauty, too, in the woods, the way they hold us from the world with their conspiring brambles. Beauty in the meeting of two people who stand together after confessing their loneliness, providing a possible answer to the problem posed. Maybe this is why I turned away from the man whose apartment I circled four times, or why Leila turned away from me: we did not see the share of loneliness needed to match our own.

Mr. Steve touches the place where the ketchup ran down my chin, my vacation stubble sandpapery under the pad of his finger. "He wouldn't kiss me," he says. "The boy I took here. He never kissed me."

"That's awful."

"Awfully cliché. I knew that even then. A year of blowjobs and not one kiss."

"But kissing is the best part," I say.

"But kissing is the best part."

His repetition secures something between us that clicks into place like a lock. When Mr. Steve leans toward me, I believe our pathway forward is inevitable, unbreakable. It doesn't matter if we're beyond escape on account of entrapment or enmeshment, if I am caught here or clinging. I am surrendered to the latch.

Or so it feels. A second after opening my mouth to meet his, my feet step backward once, twice, before hitting a tree root. Mr. Steve catches my arm to prevent me from tripping.

"I should go," I say. "I want to be good."

He drops my arm. Our severance is clean and painless,

like a perforated edge. Then I look at Mr. Steve's face and realize the pain has broken more like a wishbone, leaving him the unlucky victor. He makes no effort to conceal his hurt because he is caught too far out in it. Just when I think he might topple, he inhales sharply; the breath, full of hops and mighty enough to blow my hair back when he lets it go, provides him a foothold. He clears his throat twice before speaking. "That boy lives in Seattle now," he says. "He's got a husband and a kid. He got a happy ending." He smiles. "I didn't even care about the kissing, not back then. That's how beautiful the rest of it felt."

"It sounds beautiful."

"And now?"

"Now?"

"Do you think I'm still beautiful?"

I can tell the question hurts him to ask. When I tell him yes, he closes his eyes, not in comfort but in response to a different, albeit connected, pain.

"Nothing is like a tree," he says after a moment. "Not me or anyone. You could say a tree looked down on me. A tree looked down and didn't look away. That's all."

Again I think he might fall. I go toward him reflexively, hug him, and think, in a triumphant rush, that I do have it, the empathy instinct. Mr. Steve squeezes my chest to his. His face is under my chin and he is crying, I think. Then I feel his erection against my thigh and realize that I need to pull away, that something has been lost in translation, though the heft of him feels good, too, and possibly even innocent, so long as I don't reach down.

My name cuts through the air with the brutal authority of a tomahawk. I must know it is Randy who has thrown it, though I don't initially process it that way. Or I do process it that way, but as a simultaneous collapsing of time and space, as if it has all been brought together and bunched up, our life, bringing another Randy back. That's what it is. The Randy who said my name is not the Randy I have but the Randy I once had.

Seeing him confirms this. He stands some fifteen feet away, my black-eyed husband, forged out of shrapnel and jealousy. His mouth twitches. His fists clench. How often did I kiss the rosy imprints his fingernails left dug in his palms? How many buttons did I resew onto shirts he tore off himself? I should be scared, or at least concerned, for this is the person he's worked so assiduously to banish. What I feel is the undeniable elation of encountering an old friend.

"Randy," I say, virtually jubilant.

He stands with his knees bent and his chest pushed forward. Lake water drips down his naked calves. "What are you doing, Jack?" he asks. I've always thought that this voice, which lays so low, has a similar effect to a dog muzzle: a means of control that draws your entire focus to whatever potential violence is being so blatantly suppressed.

My voice, meanwhile, has an eager fringe. "Nothing," I say. "Nothing happened."

"It's true," Mr. Steve echoes. "Nothing happened."

"I don't want to hear you," Randy says. "There are kids here." He points backward. "There are kids here and you ruin their lives. So shut the fuck up."

I'm surprised by my sharpness when I tell Randy to relax. I feel protective of Mr. Steve, especially when I see that he does seem to have been crying, at least at some point.

"Fuck you, Jack. Fuck you." His eyes and voice are

murderous. He doesn't hold a bludgeoning object, but may as well. "You know what he did to Abigail's head and you're still out here. What are you doing out here, Jack? What are you doing, knowing what he did?"

"It felt good," I say before I can help myself. "You barely look at me, Randy."

"I don't look at anything, Jack!" The wail that issues forth from his mouth is a terrible sound. "I can't see. My own mirror is empty. Who wants that?"

"I didn't mean—"

"Be quiet. Please, god, be quiet. Your voice is going to kill me."

He grabs a nearby branch and tugs it toward him with startling force. Just when the wood begins to crack, he lets go. The branch swings through the air, releasing a flurry of leaves. Randy seems suddenly dumbstruck. Wide-eyed, frightened, stunned by regret.

"What do you do to me?" he asks. The question is so laden with sadness that I feel it pressing in on me from all sides. Whatever crazed joy I felt has been squeezed out by the pressure. My heart seems like it will be next. I almost trip when I step forward. "I promise—"

"I'm the one who thought you cheated," Randy says. "With Leila. My mother told me to give you another chance. How stupid is that?" He laughs. "She saved you. And not because of anything you did. She just knew what you meant to me." He chokes on another laugh. "Incredible. Look at you. I hope you have fun."

In a moment he has disappeared into the trees. I call out after him, though the words don't seem to make any noise. I look at Mr. Steve despairingly. Save me, I think, except he no longer looks like someone who can. He looks so evacuated from himself that I fear some dissociated self may be hovering like a hologram nearby.

"Sorry." It's the only word I have left, the only word I might ever have left. I say it twice more, then I run after Randy.

Twigs thwack against my arms and legs. Leaves slap the sides of my face. I believe I'm going back the way we came, but the forest does not thin. The trees seem to draw closer to one another, knitting themselves to prevent my passage.

It shouldn't surprise me when my head hits a branch. That's the sound I make. A noise of astonishment. *Oh.* The pain in my forehead is dull, then sharp. I realize I'm no longer standing when I feel moss tickling my ears. My fingers press into the earth and the ground gives easily, swallowing my hands. Then my vision fogs, and I'm transported back to the steamy porcelain of my childhood bathroom, where I used to write curse words in the mirror's condensation and wait for a scolding that never came. *Fuck. Shit. Bitch.* My forehead is intact when I touch it, not the crushed skull I expect. I consider my wet fingers, trying to distinguish blood from mud, and then it comes again, the pain, this time shutting my eyes.

HONORED GUEST

When I come to, something is licking my forehead. A jerk of my arms makes the thing scurry away, stepping on my hand with a clammy paw as it does. My eyes have defogged, though the world has slipped free from its ordinary machinations. The trees expand and contract above me like a living cage, the moon darts around the sky, and the creature huddles formless and growling near my hand. I blink at it repeatedly, waiting for its edges to become clear.

With slow, cautious movements, I lift myself to a sitting position. A burp brings a trickle of bile to my mouth that is sharp with the taste of the Heartstopper. I am drunk. Drunk and injured and alone. The creature flinches when I reach for my forehead, where I find sticky skin and a protruding bump. Another hard stare at the animal and it finally assembles.

"Hello," I say to the raccoon staring back at me.

The animal's next noise is less of a growl than a hiss, which devolves into something almost cute. I reach my hand out, excited when the raccoon sniffs my dirty fingers.

"You like my blood," I say.

The raccoon blinks back curiously. It doesn't seem interested in my empty palm. What compels me to get on my hands and knees and bow to the creature is beyond me.

"You can lick it," I say, practically begging, my head growing heavy with the redirected blood flow. The wait feels long, but could be any amount of time. Eventually the raccoon steps forward and begins to lap again at my wounded head. The derangement in my laugh makes the raccoon pause, but only briefly. The tongue feels good slipping across my forehead.

I abandon my prostration when the throbbing in my head turns malevolent.

"Thank you for staying with me," I say. The raccoon appears disappointed by my withdrawal and wanders away. Overhead, trees sag and leaves droop. A moth thuds against a trunk and cascades to the ground, twitching.

I hoist myself up with the same branch that knocked me over, closing my eyes to fight off another wave of nausea. Faced with higher altitude, I feel both clarified and opaque: clarified on what happened with Randy and Mr. Steve, which torches across my mind like a world-ending comet, and opaque on the matter of physics. I am standing, yet I feel pitched backward, as if on a steep incline. Falling seems inevitable when I step forward, except then I do step forward without going down. This minor miracle recurs again and again. Though I keep a hand stuck out before me, afraid of hitting another tree, I pass untouched through the woods. I float through the moonlit world, which recognizes it has struck me too hard, too often.

Eventually my hand meets someone's bony back. It is the woman with curlers, more of which have fallen from her hair. It feels I've gone years away from another human, and I almost cry out in relief. She appears equally happy to see me.

"Hey, guy!" Her smile is wide. "Have you seen my daughter? I don't want her to miss the show."

"I haven't, no."

I pull my hand back, realizing it is still resting on her. She and I stand among a scattered few. Most everyone else is gathered near the beach. The crowd looks multiplied many times over. Profuse, too, are the tiki torches, whose numbers and flames have undeniably grown, looking like a cornfield on fire. I scan the crowd for familiar faces. Nearly everyone is turned toward the water.

"My daughter is a pretty girl," the woman says. "Untraditional, sure. I think you'd like her. I think you two would hit it off. Have you seen her?"

"I don't think she's here." I try to step past the woman. She clings to my sleeve.

"Why won't you meet her? She's pretty, in her own way. You seem like a good man."

"I don't think I am a very good man."

The woman frowns. "You sound just like her. My daughter says she isn't pretty and I tell her she is. How many times do you have to tell someone something before they get it through their hard skulls?" Two more curlers pop out when she hits the side of her head, landing between my feet. "Please meet her if you find her. Okay?"

"Okay."

She pats me on the shoulder as I walk away. My shuffle is impeded by the many beer bottles underfoot, plus the constant threat of fire. I advance with a slow weave through the torches, my face sweating, until I reach the edge of the crowd. Standing there is Mr. Raven, assessing the pair of scissors in his hand.

"What's everyone doing down here?" I ask.

"Everyone's here for the big show. Or I suppose it's billed as a rather small show. Say, did something happen to your head?"

"I hit a tree. Am I bleeding?"

"Not that. Your hair's gone all wild and crazy. I'm giving out free cuts." He snips the scissors. "Twenty tonight, and counting."

"I'm okay. I need to find my husband."

"Looking like that?" He widens his eyes. "I need to find my wife. Everyone needs to find someone. No point trying to sort through this crowd before the show starts. These folks aren't afraid to throw elbows." He jabs me with his own elbow, then lets out a big laugh.

"Is that water?" I point to his drink. "I need water. I feel strange."

"Water this, water that. You might die tomorrow. Wouldn't you rather have Fireball?"

I don't reply, as a new voice has taken hold of the night, blaring forth from a loudspeaker.

"Florentines! Come closer, come closer. What's with the shyness? I get tested regularly!"

The crowd rumbles with laughter punctuated by a few catcalling whistles. I try to see through their bobbing heads, standing high on my toes as the speaker continues.

"We have a special performance for you tonight. It is a rare and beautiful thing to enter into the creative act in such a nascent stage. Who here would've liked to see the making of Eden? Think of the gardening! Raise your hand if you would've liked to see that."

The people lift their hands high, their bodies mirroring and merging for a moment with the tiki flames. When they drop their arms, I spot Clarence, grinning behind the loudspeaker.

"Don't move," Mr. Raven says, his voice close to my ear.

Reflex pulls me away. Mr. Raven accidentally yanks the lock of my hair he was holding. In his other hand, the scissors shine.

"Your head looks terrible!" he says. "Your head looks all messed up. What you need is some shaping. Your husband will thank me."

I pull away from him and make my way along the crowd's outer edge in search of a better vantage point. Clarence continues, louder than before.

"You may find this production rough. You may find it drafty. An old house in the dead of winter, you'll think. Splintery and cold. Good! We call it a rough draft for a reason, folks. Tonight is about seeds. Saplings. Newborn babes trying their best to greet the bright light of day. Can I hear some noise for newborn babes greeting the bright light of day?"

The crowd's cheer is thunderous. Someone behind me

taps me to move, I'm standing on their foot, and I see that many more people have filled in the lawn. I am no longer at the fringe of the audience but near to its center. Finding Randy here seems impossible. But as soon as I think this, it dawns on me that Randy isn't here at all. I sense this with the certainty that comes from long-term love, the kind of rarified knowledge that lets me know when Randy is hungry, thirsty, needing time to see friends or take a day trip on his own. This type of knowing is not divine, is actually built by dailiness, but often feels divine.

Randy is next door, with Abigail, trying to reach his mother.

I fight my way outward with new drive. People move grudgingly if at all, their bodies stiff as cattle on a meat rack. The farther I go the more agitated they grow: shushing me, then telling me to piss off, then swatting. At one point I collide with an elderly woman who is wearing a *VOTE YES ON PROP 11!* shirt. She holds a switch in her hand and manages to lash my back twice as I pass her by. "Bad boy!" she cries after me. "I'm trying to enjoy my show!"

The taunts and shoves distract me from Clarence's monologue, and only when I'm near the crowd's edge do I pick back up on what he's saying. I'm finally able to see him clearly, a rise in the landscape positioning me higher. Clarence sits in a camping chair on a small platform beside three others, all of whom have loudspeakers in their laps.

"I'm just one piece of this raw matter," he says. "Before we start I'd like to extend thanks to my costars, Benny, Bonnie, and Drake, and to the imagination from which our stems sprout. If you're out there, Jack, make yourself known." He scans the audience with squinted eyes, giving up at the end of his third pass. "I wish I knew where he's gone off to, folks. He can be very shy, but his is a mind to behold. He's writing from the badlands. He's growing crops in the middle of Death Valley. This is our effort to show him that it's worth it, all that hard work. Creativity at the brink of extinction. To Jack I say: Keep going. You are our honored guest."

The crowd lifts their cups. A hundred Heartstoppers, a thousand. If am touched, the feeling is lost behind bewilderment. Again I inspect my forehead. No crack, no fracture, but some fresh blood, potentially. I put my finger in my mouth, tasting for copper and finding dirt. I spit it out. The four actors inhale and exhale in tandem, guided by the one at the end, a blond woman with glossy hair. The crowd quiets, pressed close and leaning forward. They are a field of flowers bent by an eastward wind. They are bowing for me.

The man beside Clarence speaks first. "I wasn't born for this," he says into his loudspeaker. He stares at his empty lap. Except the lap is not empty. The plate holding his too-runny birthday egg is there. The actor looks there with such conviction that everyone else must see it, too. He is my Fabio, and as he continues his rant, I know he is perfect. They all are. Fabio, Sue Ellen, Ray, and Julian. I'm not surprised to see that Clarence has cast himself as Julian, because Clarence understands that Julian is the production's soul. When he pretends to clean up the water spill, he embodies deference in a way that makes my lip twitch, then lift, then smile.

THE BEST THINGS IN LIFE AREN'T THINGS

The play is not bad. The audience laughs when I want them to laugh, the actors deliver their lines with aplomb. Where are their stage directions? What paperless script are they working from? I only told Clarence so much, yet they hit my vision beat for beat. The characters, my characters, grow larger, more complex and human than how I conceived them on the page. This is how it should be. Everything is how it should be.

And yet I find myself shrinking away as the scenes progress. It's true that describing the play to Clarence earlier in the night riled my enthusiasm. Now I find an empty vault where the golden dream stood. I could return, could write a play about someone passing through time, and that play could be good, could be great, could win an award or be written about favorably by my favorite critic, could get me profiled in the same venues where Randy is so often profiled. And even if all of that happened, it would not be enough. Some of that did happen, and it was not enough. "You're killing yourself, Jack," Randy once said to me. I was on the ground. I was trying to start something new. "You shouldn't kill yourself for art."

I wished then that Randy wasn't an artist, especially not a famous artist, especially not a famous artist who had been granted the miracle of a healthy relationship to his art, because then I could sustain the myth that suffering and art were always co-constitutive. Except Randy was all of these things, and his relationship to art has always been healthy. I didn't give up that night on the floor, didn't give up until a year later, when Beatrice cringed, though I think I understood then that he was right. I was killing myself for art.

Watching the play advance, I see this again, more absolutely. Good or bad, the play is a whirlpool that would drown me if I let it. Julian is talking to the woman who throws clothes in the crevasse, a fifth actor whose back is to me. They have reached the outer limits of my imagination. They stand, or sit, where the creation goes dark. I'm no longer watching to see how I have done. I'm watching to see what happens beyond my invention. Everything has been so smooth that it's impossible to imagine them stopping. But then the woman says, "Nothing is anything anymore," and the scene halts. The actors freeze in their chairs and, after a prolonged silence, Clarence looks helplessly out at the audience.

"Throw us a bone, Jackie boy." He speaks in an exaggerated stage whisper. "We're at the end of our rope."

My head throbs in a new way, beckoned to come forward and create. I feel sure that it would happen, that if I thought the story onward I would see the actors follow me, their actions siphoned directly from my mind. I step back. One audience member boos, then a few others. "Where's Julian going!" someone shouts. "Why is Fabio such a goddamn bastard!" someone else yells. The booing spreads.

"I told you this play was raw!" Clarence cries. "Raw and nascent!"

Dozens of thrown cups clatter against the makeshift stage. A few tiki torches are yanked from the earth and held threateningly in the sky. Then, from the top of the lawn, Mr. Steve lets out a shrieking whistle.

"No riots," he calls down. "You know the rules. I've opened a fresh keg. Let's clap for the effort and drink, drink, drink."

From here I can't tell if he is still sad. From here I can't tell if Clarence is upset by the premature curtain call. From here I can't see Polly and Paul, though I hope they are dancing together somewhere in the dark. I leave the party. The crowd's lackluster applause carries me like a laugh track across the property line, through the small thicket of trees north of the lawn. It is nice to leave humanity behind without being lost to it completely, and nicer still to step onto the manicured grass of the neighboring house. The grass is thick, the same crabgrass that the houses in my parents' neighborhood have, and still wet from a recent watering.

Until I reach the deck, the house appears fully dark. Once there, a faint glow emits from one of the windows. Randy and Abigail sit on the living room floor with a lit flashlight on the ground between them. Bedsheets cover the room's furniture. Postcard-sized picture frames cover the wall, their size making it impossible to see what images they hold. Beside the flashlight is the tape recorder. Beside the tape recorder, the bag of ash.

I've always loved separating from Randy at parties for the moment when we find each other again, always a lighting up between us, no matter if it's been minutes or hours. Through the window, I feel the same surge of love, the desire to tell him all that's happened since we parted ways. But what has happened, and why? It all returns—Randy's wails, Randy's accusations, and Randy's question: *What do you do to me?*

The deck creaks beneath me. Abigail snaps her head up, narrows her eyes, then points. Randy follows her finger. When our eyes meet, I look for any trace of the usual light. His gaze is flat, then troubled, like a cup of water made to tremble by a passerby. He doesn't look angry. If anything, he looks scared. When I wave, they don't wave back, speaking to one another instead. Eventually a conclusion is reached. Abigail rubs Randy's arm before beckoning me in.

"Jack," she says after I've closed the door behind me. "You reek of dead meat and poor decisions. Didn't I tell you to beware the beanstalk?"

"Sorry."

"Me too. Welcome to the Johnston residence. Make yourself at home, except not really. You've got to sit on the floor and you can't touch anything. Dallas used to want to touch everything, but Dallas was just a kid. Do you have any self-control?"

"Some, I hope." I sit beside Randy, wanting to touch his leg but not allowing myself to. "I found you," I say.

"You found me."

"Did you meet my parents?" Abigail asks. "They would have talked to you about JFK's assassination. JFK or the boom in cryptocurrency."

"I don't think so."

"For the best. It seems you've had a bad night of your own making. Your hair looks like crap."

I fight the want to defend myself, to seek pity for my injury, to be praised for my decision to leave my play and Mr. Steve behind. "I know."

"What was that?" Abigail puts a hand behind her ear.

"I know," I say, louder this time. "I know I look like crap."

She doesn't cut her smile short this time. "Good. Randy, how are you feeling? Are you ready to get back to it?"

Randy nods like a little boy, meek and eager. His features, like Abigail's, are heavily shadowed with the flashlight's diverted beam.

"You missed the song," he says. "Dallas's song." The statement sounds pointed. Exhaustion keeps its tip from being too sharp. "It was the most extraordinary thing."

"You heard it?"

"Of course he heard it," Abigail says. "Dallas is the reason we're here. I told you this. I told you he sang to me." She looks to her left. Across from me, completing the circle, is one of her recyclable sculptures. Five googly eyes look out at me, and a pink tape recorder is duct-taped to one of its appendages. A small red light indicates that the recorder is on. Listening. This makes my head throb again, or maybe my head hasn't stopped throbbing.

"Hi, Dallas," I say.

Abigail rolls her eyes. "Dallas isn't here tonight. We only listened to his song. The dead don't make room for the dead, and tonight's slot is reserved, obviously."

We all look down at the bag of ash. It is unzipped and stretched wide. I'm sure I smell it, her, Ms. Rourke. The last time I saw her, toward the start of her illness, Randy and I were at the house in Ohio. I was surprised by the number of novelty signs with hallmark sayings she had hung since our last visit. *THE BEST THINGS IN LIFE AREN'T THINGS. LIFE IS NOT MEASURED BY THE NUMBER OF BREATHS YOU TAKE, BUT BY THE NUMBER OF MOMENTS THAT TAKE YOUR BREATH AWAY.* When she asked me to help tidy the house, I took it as a peace offering, an invitation to make myself valuable. I vacuumed and dusted with verve while Randy drove her to various appointments. During my cleaning I found a jar of Randy's baby teeth sitting on the mantel. My impulse was toward ridicule—I even took a photo to send to Martina—except then I found myself overcome with emotion. I deleted the photo and cleaned the jar. It touched me that she'd held on to the teeth for all these years. Later, sitting with me in the kitchen while Randy searched for lightbulbs in the basement, she ran her finger across the windowsill. "I'm leaving my son with someone who can't even dust," she grieved.

Abigail picks up Randy's recorder. "Should we get started?"

"Are you sure you want me here?" I ask Randy. "I can wait outside."

"Do you want to be here?"

"I do."

"Actually?"

"Yes."

"Then stay."

Abigail nods decisively. "Let's get going. I've got about a million aluminum cans to pick up after this. I'm assuming you two will help me."

She must have rewound, because when she presses play, Randy is not asking about airplanes or road trips. He is asking about board games and hopscotch. In each gap, he and Abigail bend forward, working to decipher within the noise some sonic trace of Ms. Rourke. I consider telling them what I heard, wondering if Randy might forgive me sooner if I'm the one to welcome Ms. Rourke into the room. But even I know it is the wrong impulse.

It is lulling, the alternating questions and silences. We must listen to fifty inquiries before Randy starts asking about travel. My breathing shallows and I lean in, eager to see if I hear the scraping sound again.

"Did you go on many road trips when you were young?"

I brace, realizing that I've been bracing for Ms. Rourke's return ever since she left. She comes through the tape recorder or the chimney, the bathroom mirror or the front door. She is here to avenge her empty funeral. She is here to convince Randy he's married a complete and total dud. My head feels like it could split open. Here, I think, she's coming from my cracked skull. Abigail's eyes go wide. The first scrape has come, then the second and third. Abigail lifts the recorder up between the three of us. We both look at Randy. He is slack, poised for nothing.

"What?" Abigail pauses the recorder, angry to have her excitement burst so quickly.

"That's Jack."

Abigail doesn't seem ready to believe this. "Really?"

"Just watch."

She presses play. On the recording, Randy starts his next question, then stops, because my voice has broken cleanly through, singing "Jingle Bell Rock." Hearing the words clarifies the earlier sounds. The scraping was my own atonal humming. Abigail pauses the tape after I'm heard calling out Randy's name.

"Damnit, Jack," she says. "I'm impressed you picked him out so quickly."

"I'd know him anywhere."

He must have stopped recording after I called out. When it picks up again his voice is different, more gravelly, suggesting late night or early day. "Did you ever speed?" he asks. "Did you ever get a ticket? Did you ever get lost in a place you knew well?"

ONLY BETTER

Randy does not look at me when we help Abigail clean Mr. Steve's desecrated lawn, which is void of most everyone when we return. No Ravens, no Mr. Steve, no Clarence. He does not look at me on our careening drive back, Carolina and Shelby screaming along to Joy Division while Polly and Paul fondle each other in the backseat. He does not look at me, or laugh, when we get inside and I tell him we look like Einstein and Warhol, only better. Our shoes are off, our steps heavy. I stand in his orbit while he drinks three cups of water, then inspects the camera Allen delivered. "No film," he says to himself, popping the cartridge open. "Nothing." Upstairs, we undress, keeping the bathroom unlit while we brush our teeth. The compounded absence of reflection and absence of acknowledgment make me wonder if I've finally vanished from the world. I can't recall any of the night's goodbyes. I can't recall getting in bed, either, yet that's where I am, the sheets cool and billowing above us. "You're hurt," Randy says, allowing his finger to touch down on my wound. "*You're* hurt," I say. His eyes stay on my face for even less time than his hand. When he nods toward the ceiling, his dejection makes the whole room ache. I put my palm against his chest and knead, trying to picture some warped geography within. "Not there," Randy says. I trail down his stomach, touch my finger to his navel, where on a brighter day I once fit a whole quarter. "I don't know where anything is," he says. I touch his trembling eyelids and his sun-cracked lips. "I'll find it," I say. "Okay." I pull back the covers, lighting the dark with his skin. Minutes pass, hours. I'm at his back, his neck, his heart. "Okay," he says again and again, an incantation with no resolve. Okay, okay, okay.

ACKNOWLEDGMENTS

An adequate acknowledgments section is nearly as daunting a task as an adequate novel. Granting myself preemptive grace for necessary imperfections, I would like to thank:

Alicia Kroell, for being such a perceptive, kind, and generous editor, with a seemingly effortless eye for matters big and small, and for telling me when my characters were putting their hands into one another's pants too often. This book was made much, much better by your guidance.

Kent Wolf, agent extraordinaire, for his fearlessness, pep talks, sharp editorial eye, and encouragement to let the weird get weirder. I'm so glad you took a chance on this book.

Sheldon Costa, my literary soulmate and forever first reader, who has made a lonely passion much less so, whose work (and work ethic) has been endlessly inspiring, and whose opinion I value as much as my own. I will shelve all the books you write beside mine.

The entire Catapult team: Alyson Forbes, Kendall Storey, Elizabeth Pankova, Rachel Fershleiser, Ashley Kiedrowski, Lily Philpott, Skye Tarshis, Megan Fishmann, Lena Moses-Schmitt, Katie Mantele, Nicole Caputo, Wah-Ming Chang, Olenka Burgess, and tracy danes. Also, to Jaya Miceli for the excellent cover and Megha Jain for the excellent proofreading.

My writing teachers, who span many years, genres, and geographies: Liz Stedem, Susan Meyers, Nick White, Lee Martin, Elissa Washuta, Kathy Fagan, Michelle Herman, and Marcus Jackson.

Anyone who has ever workshopped my writing, and especially my peers at Ohio State University, who accepted the offbeat horniness of my stories with reasonably open hearts, and whose work continues to fill me with admiration.

Anyone who has ever participated in one of my classes, for allowing me to geek out over line breaks and the uncanny, for being such smart and generous readers and writers, and for reminding me, every Saturday, of how life-affirming it can be to gather for the love of literature.

My bookstore coworkers, and booksellers in general, for being the undersung heroes of the literary world, graciously doing what an algorithm (or its creator) could only ever dream of.

The institutions and organizations that have supported me, in particular Seattle University, Ohio State University, Lambda Literary, Lighthouse Writers Workshop, and Tin House.

Ocean Vuong, Marie-Helene Bertino, Amina Cain, and Gabe Habash, for being early readers of this novel, for the immense generosity of their time, and for their own work, which has meant so much to mine. It is an honor to have your words backing this novel.

The additional writers and artists who influenced this book, some of whom are directly named within the text, and many more of whom are not. Abigail's line "Human refuse keeps me awake at night" is a rephrase of David Wojnarowicz's "History keeps me awake at night." When Jack struggles to remember who spoke of the mutual excitement and agony of overhearing the story of your own life, he is thinking of Mary Ruefle and her piece "Deconstruction."

My friends, who are a bedrock of my joy, for the laughter, the riffing, the conversations both weighty and weightless, and the proof that—yes!—I have a welcome place in the world. Imagining my life without you all makes me want to evaporate on the spot.

Isa, for showing me, daily, what it means to love and care for someone meaningfully, for reading my moods as if they were handwritten, and for letting me revel in proper romance for the first time in my life. I had to imagine certain intimacies and emotions while writing this novel, and am glad to now know, firsthand, that they're even sweeter than I supposed. Te amo.

My family, who have never cast doubt on my choosing to pursue a creative life, who have only occasionally expressed concern over the things I write about, and who have given me enough material to fill several more novels. You all have graced me with your humor, curiosity, kindness, and love. My appreciation is well beyond words.

And for Grammy and Grandad, who built a beautiful life, a beautiful community, and a beautiful house in Florence, where I will always feel most at home. I wish I had thanked you all more during your lives, but am glad to have my gratitude forever printed here.

Thank you, thank you, thank you.

© Martha Tesema

SCOTT BROKER is a queer writer, bookseller, and teacher based in Los Angeles. His work has appeared in *New England Review*, *Guernica*, *Fence*, *Ecotone*, and *The Idaho Review*, among other publications, and he has received fellowships from Tin House and Lambda Literary.